Room
for You

DATE DUE

ALSO BY BETH EHEMANN

Room for More

Room for Just a Little Bit More

Room *for* You

BETH EHEMANN

CRANBERRY INN SERIES, VOLUME I

Montlake
Romance

Published by Montlake Romance, Seattle

www.apub.com

Amazon, the Amazon logo, and Montlake Romance are trademarks of Amazon.com, Inc., or its affiliates.

ISBN-13: 9781477828458
ISBN-10: 1477828451

Cover design by Shasti O'Leary-Soudant / SOS CREATIVE LLC

Library of Congress Control Number: 2014957338

Printed in the United States of America

This book is dedicated to Gam, the first person to show me it's totally normal to stay up half the night reading. I love you.

1

KACIE

"Mooooooooooooom, Piper is bothering meeeeeeeeee!"

I rolled my eyes and looked up from my textbook. Lucy was sitting at the kitchen island scowling at Piper, who was poking her with a fork.

"Good morning, girls!" my mom called out cheerfully as she came into the kitchen, pausing to plant a kiss on top of each of their heads. "How about later we make bead necklaces together?"

"Yay!" they chimed in unison, all traces of the brewing fight evaporating.

Mom looked over at me and winked, then looked down and nodded toward my book. "Getting a lot of studying done?"

"Not so much. I can't seem to focus today. I wonder *why*," I replied sarcastically, sticking my tongue out at the girls. They giggled, making silly faces back at me.

I had a year of nursing school left and hoped to graduate the following spring. When Zach and I lived in Minneapolis, I worked overnights at the hospital—the front desk in the emergency room, to be exact. From the moment I started working there, I fell in love with the chaotic, high-paced environment. I would sit and daydream, watching the nurses, completely envious of their jobs. I wanted that so badly. As soon as we moved in with my mom and I saved up enough money, I enrolled in nursing school.

"So, what's on the agenda for today?" I asked, pouring myself a second cup of coffee.

"Have you watched the news yet?" Mom pulled her brows together, hooding her dark emerald eyes. She started twirling her already curly hair, something she did only when she was worried.

"No."

She glanced toward the girls, then back at me, leaning in close to make it difficult for two nosy five-year-olds to hear.

"Well, they're talking about the rainstorm of the century coming our way tomorrow morning. Torrential downpours, flooding, possible power outages."

Fabulous; summer has barely started and already a huge rainstorm.

"So, I'm heading into town to stock up on some things. I want to make sure we have enough for the week, just in case. You know how it gets out this way when it rains a lot, especially this close to Snake River." She grabbed her purse and keys off the kitchen counter and turned back to me. "Do you need anything while I'm out?"

"Nope, I think we're good, thanks," I answered, thankful that I stocked up on coloring books and crayons last month.

"Gigi!" Lucy called, causing my mom to halt in the doorway and turn around.

"Yes, honey?

Lucy bit her lip, looking nervously at my mom, snapping out of it only when Piper nudged her side.

"Can you get us popsicles?" Lucy asked sheepishly.

"Red ones!" Piper blurted out on the tail of Lucy's question.

"Maybe. I'll see what I can find. You girls behave for your mom, please. I'll be back in a few hours." She turned back to me one more time.

"Kacie, some of the guests might decide to check out early and be on their way before the rain starts. Can you help me out with that today?"

"Sure, but it will cost you extra," I teased her.

She winked and returned my smile before disappearing into the hallway.

My mom's generosity was beyond measure. Four years ago, when a tornado in the form of a piece of paper on my kitchen counter picked up my entire world, spinning it out of control, she didn't think twice about taking in the three of us. Once the dust settled, I packed up the few possessions I cared about and numbly drove the hour home to Pine City, where my mom owned and ran an inn. Not only did she not charge us anything to live with her, she also gave me a small salary, and lots of freedom, to cook for the guests.

"All right, girls, let's clean up your breakfast, please. You guys can come up front with me and help hold down the fort while Gigi's gone."

A couple of hours later, the girls and I curled up on the couch in the front room and said bye to the last couple to leave.

"Bye, Dr. Richardson, Mrs. Richardson! Drive safe," I called out, waving.

"Bye, Kacie dear, we'll be thinking about you guys. Stay safe in this storm." Mrs. Richardson waved back. "See you in a few weeks."

"How are my three favorite girls?" Alexa bellowed as she came through the front door of the inn. Piper and Lucy hopped off the couch and ran over to hug my best friend.

Alexa had been my best friend since the eighth grade. I had just moved here with my mom after my parents divorced. I was the new kid and also pretty shy. Add that together and you don't exactly head straight to the "cool kids" lunch table. Alexa was definitely a permanent fixture with the in crowd. She was beautiful, even for an eighth grader.

She had stick-straight, jet-black hair that she wore very long, all the way down to her waist. The boys practically drooled when she walked by, even the high school boys.

She sat at the table behind me in science class with a couple of jocks. One day, the guys were bored and decided to pass their time by harassing me. I think it was the fifth spitball I felt bounce off the back of my head when I heard Alexa pipe up.

"Jesus, guys, do you think you'll ever grow up?" she scolded them.

I was thankful to her for saying something but didn't turn around to acknowledge her.

"Relax, Alexa, we're just goofing around," one of them snorted back.

"Well, if you're going to continue to act like immature assholes, I'm moving."

I heard papers rustling, a book slammed, and finally her chair scraped across the science lab floor.

I was dying to turn around and watch what was happening, but I didn't dare. Not to mention, I was incredibly bummed that the girl who got them to stop was now switching seats. I just about jumped out of my skin when her large science book crashed onto the open table space next to me. I looked up just in time to catch the rest of her papers from sliding off the other side of the table.

"Hi, new girl, what's your name?" she asked, smiling sweetly at me as she sat down. She oozed confidence, and I was instantly envious of that about her.

"Kacie. Kacie Jensen," I replied, trying my hardest not to sound like a scared little mouse.

"I'm Alexa Campbell. Those two jerk-offs back there are Mark and Joey. Apparently they have yet to learn that the way to get a girl to notice you is to be nice to her, not pick on her as though we're still in second grade."

She glanced back at them and gave an overexaggerated fake smile, batting her eyelashes. I finally felt confident enough to turn around and take a peek. Two giant football jerseys sat there with their shoulders hanging, looking down like scolded toddlers.

From that day on, Alexa and I were best friends. At first, I was pretty sure she was using me to cheat off of, but we were inseparable and everyone knew it. I wasn't as openly self-confident as she was, but I was getting more comfortable in my own skin. I even ended up being pretty good friends with Mark and Joey. When Zach left and I moved home with the girls, Alexa told me they offered to find him and beat him up for me. The homecoming queen, Lauren Kolar, was also part of our group. She was innocent and always saw the good in everyone, pretty much the exact opposite of badass Alexa. The three of us evened each other out and were together constantly until Lauren moved away shortly after I had the girls. We were still close but got to see each other only when she came home to visit her parents.

"You guys ready for all this rain tomorrow?" Alexa handed the girls each a sucker.

"Eh, I'll believe it when I see it," I said, waving her off nonchalantly. "These weather people never know what the heck they're talking about."

"I don't know, last I heard they were calling for over ten inches of rain just in the next twenty-four hours." Her dark cobalt eyes were big and serious.

I sighed. "This is one of those times when living in the Land of Ten Thousand Lakes isn't so wonderful. Nor is it great living on one, not with this much rain coming. We'll be lucky if the gazebo doesn't float away."

"No shit." She quickly looked down at Lucy and Piper and then back up at me and grimaced. "Sorry."

I rolled my eyes at her. "Girls, ignore Auntie Alexa and her potty mouth."

"Mommy, you say that word sometimes too!" Lucy said with a big grin.

"Okay, let's not talk about that right now." I laughed and turned to Alexa. "So are you closing the shop tomorrow?"

Alexa owned a cute little flower shop in town called the Twisted Petal. She had an amazing eye for detail and was magnificent at the designs she created. People called from all over the county to place orders with her.

"Yeah, but hopefully just for tomorrow. Wedding season is just around the corner and I have a million things to do to get ready. But no work for tomorrow!"

She locked arms with Lucy and Piper and danced around the foyer. "Oh, wait." She stopped suddenly. "I did bring a bouquet for your mom, though." She went over by the front door and took a beautiful bouquet of roses, tulips, and lilies out of its paper cone.

"Suck-up." I shoulder bumped her, taking the flowers. "I'll give them to her when she gets back."

"Oh, I just saw her. She was in the garage talking to Fred. Something about sandbags."

Fred was our maintenance man, who lived in the apartment above the garage. He helped my mom with most of the outside chores and various repairs around the property. He'd been there as long as we had. He and my mom worked well together, and I was ecstatic when the girls unofficially adopted him as their surrogate grandpa.

"They're probably freaking out over nothing. I'm still hoping those crazy weather forecasters are wrong and we won't get as much as they think," I said, crossing my fingers in the air.

"Pssh, you keep thinking those positive thoughts. I, on the other hand, am heading out to get some gas for the generator, grabbing a case of beer for Derek, and heading indoors. Bye, girlies!" she yelled on her way out the door.

"Bye, Auntie Alexa!" they called out after her.

I left the girls munching on their suckers in the living room, while I went to the kitchen to put the flowers in water. I loved the kitchen in the inn. It was not only huge, but also warm and inviting. My mom made a point of telling guests to please make themselves at home, so she left the kitchen open at all times. The cabinets were full of mismatched antique dishes and every small appliance imaginable. She also kept the larger-than-normal pantry stocked with all sorts of snacks and kitchen staples for people to use as they pleased. There were shelves in the pantry lined with mason jars full of fruits and vegetables that she had preserved.

I had just finished putting the flowers in a vase when the back door flew open, and Mom came in, along with a huge gust of cold air.

"Whew! It's already getting windy out there," she said, trying to close the back door with an armful of groceries.

I set the vase on the island and hurried over to take the bags from her.

"Fabulous," I answered sarcastically.

She glanced at the flowers on the island. "Those are beautiful!"

"Yeah, Alexa brought those for you. She actually just left. She said she saw you in the garage."

"Oh, right," she said. "Fred and I were debating whether to put sandbags down by the shore or not. Did all the guests leave? Any problems?"

"Everything was fine. The Richardsons said they'd be back in a few weeks."

"Good. What about Alexa? Did she close up for the week?"

"Not sure, at least for tomorrow. She stopped by to bring you those and get the girls sugared up for me. She had to go and get a few things for Derek, then she's heading in for the next couple of days."

Derek was Alexa's husband. They'd been together since freshman year in high school and got married right after graduation. Everyone assumed she must have been pregnant, but they were just really in love and excited to start their life together. They had been married almost six years and still hadn't talked about having kids. She told me once that whenever she heard her biological clock start ticking, she spent a day with Piper and Lucy and hit the snooze button for another year.

"Alexa and Derek are a cute couple, aren't they?" my mom tried to ask innocently, though I knew where she was headed. I sighed, immediately wishing I hadn't said Derek's name. "Yes, Mom, they're adorable. Don't start."

"What? I'm not starting anything, I was simply making an observation," she said, matter-of-fact.

"Mm-hmm."

"Okay, fine, I was starting. I just think you would be so much happier if you found someone too." She started rambling as fast as she could. "I just want to see you happy. You deserve—"

"Stop," I interrupted her. "What makes you think I'm unhappy?"

"I didn't mean unhappy. You're only twenty-four years old, Kacie. You've been single for four years now. It's about time you get back out there. What about the Richardsons' son, Cameron?" She grinned and wiggled her eyebrows up and down at me.

"Mom, first of all, I have no interest in Cameron. Second of all, I've been on dates. None of them were what I was looking for . . . I need the right guy, the perfect guy, a *stable* guy. I need to give up on guys who are good kissers and use my brain this time. I've dated the immature, irresponsible loser before. Look where it got me."

"It got you two beautiful children, that's where," she said defensively, as she continued putting groceries in the cabinet.

"Of course they're wonderful, Mom, but I wish we had a real family. Raising two five-year-old girls alone isn't easy," I replied, rubbing my temples and quietly wishing away the impending headache.

"*Alone?*" she accused, whipping around to face me.

I knew I was in trouble.

"You're *hardly* alone, Kassandra!"

Uh-oh. She called me Kassandra; she never did that.

"I didn't mean that the way it sounded, Mom. You are extremely helpful. I just meant that I wish I had a traditional family. You know, two parents . . . ," I said quietly, tracing the raised glass decoration on the vase with my finger, trying not to make eye contact with my mom.

"Well, it's time you got out there, Kacie, for real. Zach left, and he's not coming back."

My mouth dropped open as my eyes shot up to meet hers. We didn't talk about him.

Ever. Just the mention of his name made me sick to my stomach.

She continued, her voice softer this time. "You need to move on and live your life."

I stood frozen to the ground, my stomach heavy with emotion-filled rocks. Did she think I didn't know that he was gone? I lived it; every single day, I lived it. I figured she, of all people, would understand the pain of someone walking out on you. Tears stung my eyes.

"Um, I'm gonna go lay down. I don't feel so good. Can you keep an eye on the girls for me?" I spat out, hurrying to leave the kitchen before she could answer.

"Kacie, please don't go!" she called out after me, but I didn't turn back. I was already halfway down the hall leading to our apartment, and right then all I wanted was to be alone. I heard her call my name one more time as I threw myself down on my bed and cried a deep, therapeutic cry into my pillow before falling asleep.

2

BRODY

After tossing my duffel bag on the floorboard of my black Ford F-250 Super Duty pickup truck, I stepped back so my black lab, Diesel, could hop up on the passenger seat. I turned to face my mom, who was standing behind me with her arms crossed over her chest, tapping her foot nervously. I couldn't help but grin at her.

"Mom, I'll be fine," I told her for what felt like the millionth time that morning.

"It's a long drive, Brody, and the weather is going to get *really* bad. Can't you leave your truck here for a couple of days and take a quick flight home?" Her eyes pleaded with me not to drive back to Minneapolis today.

"First of all, it's a three-hour drive, not that long. Second, if the weather is that bad, I wouldn't get a flight out today anyway. And third, I have a ton of shi—" I stopped myself as she raised her eyebrow at me. "Stuff to do at home. I'll be fine. And before you ask again—no, I won't leave my truck here." I walked over and picked her up off the ground in a bear hug.

"Please call me every five minutes," she mumbled into my shoulder, the worry evident in her voice.

"No problem. I won't be able to see through the downpours anyway, so taking my eyes off the road to keep calling you shouldn't be a problem."

She squirmed out of my arms. As soon as her feet hit the ground, she punched my arm as hard as she could.

"Not funny, Brody Michael."

It's amazing how even at twenty-seven years old, when your mom says your middle name, it reduces you to feeling like an eleven-year-old kid who just broke the living room window with a baseball. Or in my case, a hockey puck.

Bending my knees, I lowered myself to her level and put my hands on her shoulders, looking her straight in the eyes.

"I. Will. Be. Fine. Please stop worrying."

"When you have kids one day, Brody, you'll get it. They may grow up and leave your house, but they never leave your heart. You never stop worrying." She sighed, narrowing her eyes at me. "And when your son is Brody Murphy, you tend to worry more than most."

"Ha! Thanks for the confidence, Mom. Seriously, though, I'm good. The meteorologists were saying this morning we might not get as much rain as they were originally thinking anyway."

"Yeah, well, the meteorologists are idiots. It's already started south of here, and a lot of it." She wrapped her arms around herself, and her hair practically turned gray right in front of me.

"I'll just drive really fast through it. No problem. The longer I stand here, the longer it's going to take me to get home." I winked at her and hopped up into my truck as she returned a death stare. I'd already said good-bye to the whole family inside, but somehow I had known she'd follow me out, begging me one last time to stay, and I loved her for it. The engine roared to life as I started my truck and quickly pulled out of the driveway before she decided to throw herself on the hood. I rolled my window down and gave her one last wave on my way down the street.

"Okay, a big cup of coffee and we're good to go," I said out loud to myself as I pulled into the Dunkin' Donuts. I reached over to the radio and flipped it to the AM station to get a weather update. Mom would never know, but I was a little nervous. They were calling for one of the worst strings of storms we'd seen in a long time, and I really did want to beat it home. I had meant to leave a couple of hours ago, but she insisted on feeding me first, and who was I to turn down my mom's biscuits and gravy and bacon? The clock read 11:30.

Shit, I gotta get moving.

About an hour and a half later, I was tempted to call home and tell her what every mom wants to hear from her child.

You were right.

The roads were a slick mess and the rain was coming down so hard I could barely see through my windshield. I drove by car after car pulled off to the side of the highway, cars spun out in ditches, cars lined up at every exit. All of the motel signs I passed had their "No Vacancy" lights on. It was coming down hard and fast. My eyes were strained from focusing so hard, but I kept telling myself to just get through this bad patch, and then I could pull over and take a little coffee break. And a bathroom break, thanks to that large coffee and Big Gulp I'd had.

Up ahead of me was a small silver Civic, half off the road. I looked in the window as I passed and there was a woman sitting in the driver's seat with her hands covering her face, looking completely freaked out. I pulled over to the side and reversed my truck until I was just in front of her car. I threw on my baseball hat and hopped out of my truck.

As I made my way back to her car, she got out and met me halfway.

"Thank you so much for stopping," she called over the rain in a shaky voice. As I got closer I realized she was closer to my grandma's age than my mom's.

"No problem. Looks like your front end is stuck in the mud, huh?"

"Yeah, I slid off the road and now I can't get out."

"Let's see if we can get you out of here and on your way. I have chains in my truck to pull you out. I'll be right back."

About twenty minutes later, I waved good-bye to her and climbed back into my truck with a fresh blueberry pie. Turns out, the sweet old lady was out in this weather delivering pies to her church so they would have them for their bake sale this weekend. She tried to give me money after I pulled her car out. I said absolutely not, so she insisted that I at least take a pie. How could I tell her no? I pulled out my phone and took a picture of the pie and sent it to my mom with a text that said:

At least if I skid off the road and no one can find me, I won't be hungry tonight.

She should love that text. I laughed to myself as I put my phone back in the center compartment of my truck. It chirped a minute later, and before I even opened the phone, I was pretty sure I was in trouble.

DO NOT make me come and find you. Eyes on the road, Mister.

I swear she would still ground me if she could. She was right, though; the roads were getting worse by the minute and I needed to pay attention. Four very slow and torturous miles later, I decided if I was going to continue, I needed a gas station and a bathroom, fast. After a quick pit stop, I pulled out of the gas station with a full gas tank and a fresh cup of coffee in hand. I turned back toward the highway and continued through the stoplight that I had just come from.

That's when panic hit me. There were no other stoplights anywhere around.

"You've gotta be fucking kidding me!" I yelled out loud, startling a sleeping Diesel on the passenger seat. Out of all the damn exits I passed, I picked the only one without a returning entrance back onto the highway. I angrily pulled a U-turn and sulked back into the gas station, then left as fast as I could with my tail between my legs.

A few minutes later, we were back on track, I hoped. "Okay, Diesel, that dude said the road should be coming up here on our right, but honestly, I have no idea where the hell we are. If you ever let me leave the house again without grabbing my GPS, you'll sleep on the porch for a week." Diesel cocked his head to the side and lifted one ear at me. I reached over and patted the top of his head.

Suddenly, I slammed on my brakes and jerked my truck to the right, almost missing the road we needed to get back to the highway. Thunder crashed so loud it shook my truck, and lightning lit up the gloomy sky. My truck splashed and pounded its way through deep puddles on the country road. I was never so thankful for my truck's lift than at that very moment. An orange blinking light up ahead caught my attention. As I got closer to the wooden bridge, my hands gripped the steering wheel tight in frustration. I took a deep breath and counted to ten as I watched the blinking light on the orange sawhorse in front of me. The sawhorse had been stenciled with the words "Bridge Closed" and had yellow caution tape all over it.

"Well, buddy, that damn blueberry pie joke might just turn around and bite us in the ass, huh?"

Once again, I turned the truck around and started back where I came from. On my right, I noticed another dirt road that looked like it led farther into the middle of nowhere.

"Eh, what the hell. Why not?" I said out loud as I turned the wheel and followed it. At this point, I was so lost I didn't really care where I ended up. I drove a couple hundred yards in thick mud and sighed as I pulled up to a house. This wasn't a road after all; it was a fucking driveway. Go figure.

"So, do we knock and ask for directions or just turn around and go at it on our own?" Diesel got up, stretching his front legs out as far as he could, and leaned over and licked my face. I pulled back and play-fully pushed him away. "You're right, we don't need help, damn it."

I put the truck in reverse, turning to look out my back window, and heard the unmistakable sound of tires spinning. My chest tightened as I pushed the gas pedal again. My entire truck shook as the tires spun round and round, digging deeper into the mud.

"No, no, no, *no!*" I slammed my fist down hard on my steering wheel. My chest heaved in anger as I scanned the property for any sign of a vehicle that might be able to pull me out.

Nothing.

Squeezing my phone, I had to fight the urge to throw it as I looked down and saw the battery light slowly fade. Dead. I laid the side of my head down on my steering wheel and stared at Diesel, who was wagging his tail with his tongue hanging out, happy as can be. The ridiculousness of my situation overcame me, and I started laughing deliriously until there were tears in my eyes.

"Okay, you hang here and be a good watch dog. Make sure no one drives off, and I'll go check it out." Diesel yawned and laid his head on the center console as I hopped down from my truck and made my way through the muck toward the front door.

A wooden sign hanging next to the front door read "Cranberry Inn." I had no idea what town I was in or if I was even still in fucking Minnesota, but surprisingly, this might not have been the worst decision after all. Hopefully we could hang here for the night and head home tomorrow morning. A deafening clap of thunder rattled my chest as I reached up and knocked on the door.

3

KACIE

"Ow!" I rubbed the spot on my forehead now sore from being poked over and over by a tiny finger.

"Mom! Mom! Wake up! Look at all the rain!" Lucy and Piper jumped up and down on my bed like it was Christmas morning. I wished I shared their enthusiasm. I was cocooned in my warm quilt, dreaming about palm trees, sandy beaches, and fruity drinks with little umbrellas in them. I had no desire to get out of bed and face the day, the rain, or my mom. However, duty called, and my girls were asking for breakfast. I sat up in bed, pulled on my slippers and robe, and glanced over at my two angels looking out my bedroom window, giggling about all the rain.

"Come on, you two, I'm starving."

While I got busy making monkey bread, the girls' favorite treat, Fred kept the girls preoccupied playing Candy Land in the family room. Mom's eyes were glued to the TV, not wanting to miss the latest storm update. A fire was blazing in the fireplace, and other than the house being empty of guests, it felt like a normal day.

I was standing at the counter, mixing melted butter and cinnamon in a bowl, when my mom came up next to me and rested her head on my shoulder.

"I love you, you know that, right?" she asked.

"I do. I love you too, Mom."

I leaned over and kissed her cheek, knowing that was her way of apologizing for last night. We didn't argue often, and I couldn't remember any other time when she'd made me cry. It wasn't really her who'd made me cry, though; it was more the painful memories of my relationship with Zach and doubt that I'd ever find the perfect man for me and the girls.

Suddenly there was a loud knock at the door. We all looked at each other, wondering who would be out in this weather. Before Mom could even make a move toward the door . . . another loud knock. She hurried out of the kitchen, with Fred right behind her. The girls and I hung back. I heard talking, and a few minutes later, Mom reappeared in the kitchen with a beautiful redhead who looked to be in her early forties and a little girl who I guessed was about the same age as Piper and Lucy.

"Kacie, this is Catherine. Catherine, this is my daughter, Kacie. Those are her girls, Piper and Lucy," she said, turning toward the girls, who were already by her side, anxious to meet their new friend.

I wiped my hands on a dish towel and went over to shake hands with her.

"Hi, Catherine. Nice to meet you." I smiled warmly.

"Nice to meet you too, Kacie. This is my daughter, Jenna." She wrapped her arm around the shy little girl who was hiding behind her. "Sorry to barge in on you guys like this. I drove as far as I could, but the roads are getting worse by the minute, and the bridge at the end of the road is closed. I didn't know what else to do."

Her voice cracked as she held back tears.

"Oh, it's no problem." My mom rushed over and put her arm around

Catherine's shoulders. "All of our guests left early, so there's plenty of room. Besides, Piper and Lucy will be thrilled to have someone else to play with."

With that, Piper and Lucy took Jenna's hand and pulled her over to join in their Candy Land game.

There were three more knocks at the door that day, everyone saying the same thing. The roads were too bad to continue and they were desperate for a place to stay. Henry and Melissa, a sweet older couple, were first. Next was a spunky, cute college-aged girl named Ashley, who I thought I could get along with for the next couple of days, and last came a set of middle-aged sisters named Pat and Sue who were on their way to an antique show in Wisconsin.

Mom was thrilled as she went into full-on hostess mode. She was in her glory when the inn was full. She lived for it. The house was full of chatter all afternoon: people comparing their encounters of stuck cars and flooded roads.

It was late afternoon, and I was just taking a huge batch of my fabulous chili off the stove for dinner when I heard another knock at the door. Mom was out on the back deck grabbing more wood for the fire. With the noise level in the house, I wasn't surprised Fred didn't hear it, so I wiped my hands on my shirt and headed up front.

I opened the door and my breath caught—I wasn't sure if it was because of the ear-shattering thunderclap that came into the house with the swing of the door, or the man standing on the porch. The tall, wet figure stood in a black North Face hoodie and a baseball cap. His hands were shoved in his jeans pockets. The wind was whipping around him and his cheeks were bright red, but he looked up at me from under long, thick lashes and smiled a big, sexy smile. I swear the corners of his perfect teeth sparkled, like they do in the movies.

I stepped back, motioning for him to come in. Once he was in the door, my mouth went dry. He was big, much bigger than he'd looked when he was on the porch. I guessed he was almost a foot taller than my short five-foot-two-inch stature. He pulled his hat off, revealing dark chocolate-brown hair that was a wet mess of short, loose curls. He smiled that movie star smile again. This time I noticed the two big dimples, one on either side of his mouth.

My heart was pounding so loud I was sure it was about to jump out of my chest and land on the foyer floor at his feet.

"Whew! It's brutal out there." He shook the excess water off his jacket and ran his hands back and forth through his hair, messing it up in the most adorable way.

"Hi, I'm Brody Murphy." He extended his hand for me to shake.

"Hi, I'm . . ." My mind went blank. When I paused, he raised a curious eyebrow and smirked at me. Holy crap, I was going to pass out.

Pull yourself together, Kacie.

"Kacie. Kacie Jensen."

The minute his giant hand enveloped mine, I felt my entire body wake from hibernation. His warm, strong hand acted as an accelerant that set all the cells and nerves in my entire body on fire. I felt like an idiot when I realized that we were done shaking hands, but I hadn't bothered to pull mine away yet. Quickly, I snatched it back and wrapped my arms around myself instinctively.

"I took a wrong turn and thought I was on a road. Hard to see it was a driveway. Anyway, my truck is stuck in the mud out there. Any chance I could grab a room for the night?"

My shoulders sank, along with my heart.

"Uh-oh." He read the disappointment on my face. "Do you not have any rooms available?"

"No, they're all taken," I answered in a quiet, almost inaudible tone.

"Oh." He took a deep breath and forced it back out. "No biggie; I'll figure out a way to get my truck out and keep going. I'm sure there's something up the road a little more."

"Stay right here." I turned to go find my mom, but she was already coming around the corner from the kitchen.

"Hi there!" my mom said in her typical warm, welcoming tone.

"Hi, I'm Brody Murphy." He offered his hand again.

"Hi, Brody, I'm Sophia Jensen."

"You have a really nice place here," he said, flashing his gorgeous smile at my mom.

If there was a direct line to my mother's heart, it was complimenting her inn. This place was her other baby.

"I was actually just coming to get you. I know we're full, but it's awful out there. We can't send him back out in this weather, Mom," I blurted out, sounding more desperate than I meant to.

"Of course not, dear." She smiled curiously at me before turning her attention back to Brody.

"I don't have any rooms available, Brody, but I do have a pretty comfortable couch in the family room. It's not private at all, but it's much warmer than your vehicle. We would love to have you stay with us."

"Uh, one problem. I have a dog too. He's super-friendly and completely housebroken, but he'd probably be pretty mad at me if I told him he had to sleep in the truck. Any chance he could sleep on the floor in a laundry room maybe?"

"Absolutely not!" Mom said. "No laundry room for him, he can curl up by the fire."

"Are you sure? I don't want to put you out."

He was talking to my mom, but looking at me, causing my heart to race.

"Nonsense. You are staying here, and so is your dog. That's final. Come on in and take your wet jacket off and warm up for a few minutes before getting your dog. You're going to catch pneumonia."

She put her arm around him and led him toward the back of the house while I followed behind. "You're just in time, actually. My beau-tiful, *single* daughter just made a huge batch of her delicious chili."

Mom looked back at me and winked. My face flushed as I rolled my eyes, just in time to look up and catch Brody turning around, smirking at me. Suddenly, crawling into the couch cushions and hiding for the next couple of days sounded like a wonderful idea.

4

BRODY

"Room for one more?" Sophia called out as we entered the kitchen.

I immediately felt comfortable in her big, warm house.

She made her way around the room, introducing me to everyone. We finally got to three little girls, who were staring at me wide-eyed like I was an alien.

"This little one right here is Jenna, Catherine's daughter. And those two sweet little things are Lucy and Piper, Kacie's twins."

My mouth fell open slightly before I could reel the shock back in. I was blown away that Kacie, the cute girl with the messy, copper-colored ponytail, wearing the white, chili-stained T-shirt, was a mom. And not just a mom of one, but two. Kacie noticed the surprised look on my face, and her eyes turned sad and darted toward the floor in embarrassment. I suddenly felt like a giant douche.

"Here, Brody, come sit by me." Ashley started tugging my arm toward the large farmhouse-style table that separated the kitchen from the family room. She was in her early twenties and cute enough, but girls like her who were constantly trying to get my attention were like a tiny sheep in a huge herd.

"Okay, one sec," I replied before turning to Kacie. "Is there somewhere I can plug my phone in for a bit?"

"Sure." A tiny smile crossed her face as she pointed to an open outlet on the tile backsplash. "Right there."

"Thanks," I said, unable to look away from her gaze.

Once again Ashley tugged my arm. I followed over to the table and sat down next to her, but I couldn't peel my eyes off of Kacie.

I don't know what I was expecting when I knocked on the door to this inn—maybe a little old cat lady or a family of cannibals in the woods? Whatever it was, it definitely wasn't *her*. A pint-size little cutie whose sparkling green eyes nearly knocked me on my ass.

Every movement she made around the kitchen was hypnotizing, even the way she crinkled her nose when she focused on cutting the corn bread into perfect little squares. She walked over to the large pot on the stove, lifted the wooden spoon to her lips, and tasted the chili. I almost lost my shit right there at the table, but I couldn't look away. I didn't even care if anyone was watching me watch her. This was the most torturous accidental seduction I'd ever been a part of, and I was enjoying every second of it.

"So, Brody, we've all spent the afternoon getting to know each other. How about you? Where are you from?" Henry asked from the family room behind me. I jumped at the sound of my name, turning in my chair to face him.

"I grew up about two hours north of here, but now I live in Minneapolis."

"Ooooh, I love Minneapolis," Ashley cooed as she leaned in close, resting her hand on my knee.

"What do you do there?" Henry continued.

Crap. No one here seemed to know who I was, and I wanted to keep it that way. Being anonymous was a nice change. The sooner I was out of here and on my way home, the better. I quickly looked over at Kacie, who seemed to be just as interested in my answer as everyone else. The minute our eyes connected, she quickly turned back around to the counter.

"Uh . . . I'm in sales," I responded.

Really, Brody? That's the best you could come up with?

"Interesting. What do you sell?"

"Sports equipment," I answered confidently, hoping it sounded convincing but also boring enough that he wouldn't ask anything else. I wasn't a very good liar. Before he could ask anything else, I turned my attention to Fred.

"So, Fred, how long have you lived here?"

"Oh, about ten years now. I worked for the previous owner, and when they sold the place to Sophia, she asked me to stay on, and I was happy to." He looked over at Sophia and winked. Sophia smiled back as she finished setting down the plates.

"Brody, you look very familiar. Have you done any acting?" Henry looked right at me; his eyes squinted as he studied my face.

Ashley sat up straight and gasped. "Do you know any movie stars?"

I laughed uncomfortably, wishing someone would stop this impromptu interview before I said something stupid.

"Nope, never done any acting." Looking at Ashley, I added, "And sorry, no movie stars."

She stuck her bottom lip out dramatically and made an annoying little pout noise. I looked over at Kacie, who also noticed Ashley's childish behavior and rolled her eyes.

As if Kacie read my mind, she started putting bowls down on the table and called out, "Okay, everyone, dinner is served."

"Excuse me, Mommy," Lucy said, trying to squeeze in between Kacie and the table.

"Pay the toll." Kacie bent down and puckered her full, beautiful lips. Lucy giggled and kissed her mom back.

That interaction was the purest, most intriguing thing I'd ever seen.

Dinner was finishing up and people were sitting around talking about the weather when I pushed my chair back and stood up. "I hope you all don't mind if I excuse myself for a few minutes. I want to run out and check on Diesel real quick."

"Diesel?" Sophia looked at me, puzzled.

"My dog, he's in my truck."

She gasped as she pulled her hands up and clapped the sides of her face.

"Oh my gosh! I forgot all about him. That poor thing. Go get him, bring him in so we can feed him something."

"Thanks, I'll just be a few minutes."

I unplugged my phone, pulled my boots on, and trudged back out to my truck. Diesel was waiting for me when I got there, standing on the driver's seat with his tail wagging a hundred miles per hour. I pulled the truck door open and pushed him over to the passenger seat so I could get out of the pouring rain.

"Hey, buddy! Were you lonely out here?"

He panted and licked my face over and over.

"Okay, okay. Chill out, I gotta make a couple calls."

I grabbed my cell phone and dialed my mom's number.

"Are you home?" She answered the phone.

"Uh, hello to you too." I laughed.

"Sorry, hello. Are you home?"

"No, Mom. I'm not home, but I figured I'd better check in before you sent out a search party." I paused so she could laugh . . . nothing. I continued. "In a series of completely shitty events, which I'll explain later, my truck is stuck in the mud. I just had the *best* chili ever at a little inn where I'm spending the night."

Again, silence on the other end of the line.

"Mom?"

"I told you. Didn't I tell you to wait and go home tomorrow? Why don't you ever listen to me?"

"Mom," I sighed, "you were right, I was wrong. I don't want to argue, I just wanted you to know where I was. The bridge to get back to the highway is flooded, should be open tomorrow, so I'll be home then. I'll keep you posted, okay?"

More silence.

"Okay?"

This time, Mom sighed. "Yes, Brody. Fine. This place you're staying, is it decent?"

"Well, there are cleavers hanging on the walls and soft screams coming from the door with a padlock on it. Other than that, it's great."

Another sigh on the other end of the line.

"Brody, you are going to make me gray prematurely. Your sister doesn't give me problems. Why must you torture me?"

I laughed loudly into the phone. "I love you, Mom. I'll call you tomorrow."

"I love you too, Brody."

I hung up with her and looked over at Diesel. "Are women always like that, D? She worries constantly." He cocked his head to the side and eyed me curiously. "One more call and we'll go inside and find you some food."

Before I could dial the phone, my text alert noise chirped. It was from my mom . . .

Could you please text me the address of this "inn" . . . just in case I never hear from you again?

I laughed out loud and shook my head as I dialed my best friend and agent, Andy.

"Shaw."

"Why do you insist on answering the phone like a jackass?" I teased.

"Ah, there's my missing star."

"Missing?"

"I haven't talked to you in days. Where have you been?"

"I told you last week I was going home for a few days."

"Ah, that's right. Sorry, I don't pay attention when you call. I usually wait for the tabloids to let me know where you are. Or the police." He laughed, clearly proud of himself.

Andy had been my best friend since second grade. I was throwing rocks at cars driving past the playground at recess and I coerced him into joining me so that if I got caught, I didn't go down alone. We'd been friends ever since. He'd kept my ass out of trouble all through college, so it seemed only natural that he would just continue keeping tabs on me as an adult and become my agent. He was more like a brother than a friend; we'd been through every step of life together, and I'd take a bullet for the man. There weren't many people I trusted like him.

"You're hilarious, my suburbanite minivan-driving friend," I shot back at him jokingly.

"First of all, it's an SUV. Secondly, I don't drive that; my wife does, asshole. Listen, what are you doing tonight? I haven't left the office to head home yet. Wanna grab a beer?"

"I'd love to, man, but I'm still . . . somewhere north. It's a long story, but the rain fucked up my trip back home. I'm stuck at some inn until tomorrow when hopefully they open this damn bridge again. Why the hell are you working so late anyway? Need a new coat of fresh, white paint on the picket fence?" It was my turn to laugh at my own joke.

"You're a funny, funny man, Brody Murphy, but no. Someone needs to keep an eye on your contracts and deal with all the drama you bring. Try not to burn down this inn you're staying at, huh?"

"Got it, Boss. Talk to you soon."

I hung up the phone and looked over at Diesel. "Ready for some food, my man?"

5

KACIE

After dinner, Mom bathed the girls for me while I cleaned up the kitchen. The guests succumbed to their food comas and retired to their rooms for the night, everyone except Ashley. She was sitting on the couch with Fred, who was watching the news closely. She looked bored out of her mind, picking at her fake fingernails and yawning. I was sure she was waiting around for Brody, who mentioned going to take a shower.

"How's it looking?" One simple sentence in Brody's husky, baritone voice as he entered the room sent shivers through my entire body.

Ashley perked up from her intense session of hair twirling and beamed at Brody. She really was quite pretty, and it pissed me off. She'd look great on Brody's arm, I thought, letting out a heavy sigh.

"Not good, not good at all," Fred answered, running his hands through his salt-and-pepper hair and getting up from the couch. "Okay, you crazy kids, I'm off to bed. Gotta get up early and make sure the inn didn't float away."

Out the back door he went, making his way to his cozy apartment above the garage. I had been in it quite a few times. It smelled of cigars and was full of hot rod memorabilia. It was a comfortable place that fit Fred perfectly. I loved having him there.

"Wanna watch a movie, when she's done?" I heard Ashley whisper not so quietly to Brody. I was instantly annoyed that I felt like a nuisance in my own home as I started rinsing the dishes and loading them into the dishwasher faster. The last thing I wanted to see was the two of them all snuggled up on the couch, watching TV together.

"We'll see. I'm pretty tired after today." Brody smiled politely at her.

I looked up and saw her make that awful pouty face again. Someone should really tell her how unattractive she looked when she did that.

"Awww, come on. I'm not sleepy yet," she whined like a child.

"Sorry, Ashley. My girlfriend probably wouldn't be too happy with me spending the evening shacked up on the couch with a stranger either." He patted her on the shoulder and walked over, rifling through his duffel bag.

Girlfriend? He has a girlfriend? Bummer.

I wasn't really shocked, though. He seemed charming and charismatic, with the most infectious smile I had ever seen, not to mention hot as hell. I was immediately drawn to him; it's no surprise that others were as well.

"Mom, will you read us a bedtime story?" Lucy came into the kitchen, snapping me out of my thoughts. She was wearing her favorite Strawberry Shortcake pajamas and had an armful of books.

"I want *Pinkalicious*," pleaded Piper, following right behind her.

"Sure, I just have to finish the kitchen real quick," I answered, rinsing out the big chili pot.

"No! I want *If You Give a Moose a Muffin*," whined Lucy.

Piper squeezed her little hands into fists and tensed her arms down at her sides, ready for an argument, but I stepped in.

"Okay, I'll finish this later. How about we read both?" I tossed my sponge into the sink and turned to the girls, desperate to defuse the potential argument in front of Ashley and Brody.

I heard Ashley giggle from the couch, and I had to fight the urge to snatch the book out of Piper's hand and whip it at Ashley's forehead like a Frisbee.

"Yay!" Lucy and Piper both cheered as we turned down the hall toward their bedroom.

About an hour later, I woke up in Lucy's bed with the girls snuggled up on either side of me, sound asleep. Their favorite book, *Pinkalicious*, was open and lying on my chest. We were all so warm and toasty, I was tempted to pull the blanket up and go to sleep right there with them. Remembering the mess I'd left in the kitchen, I forced myself out of her bed, tucking them in on my way out.

I walked to the end of the hall, turned toward the kitchen, and stopped in my tracks. Not only was the dishwasher running, but the counters were clear, the table had been wiped down, and all the leftovers had been put away. Alexa's flowers were sitting perfectly in the center of the island. I looked around, and the only person left downstairs was Brody, who was sitting on the living room couch watching SportsCenter.

"Wow! It looks great in here," I called out. "Do I have you to thank for this?"

"Hey!" he said, getting up from the couch and coming over into the kitchen. "Yeah, I thought I would help out. It's the least I could do, ya know, as a thank-you for letting me stay here." He leaned his hip against the edge of the island and folded his muscular arms across his chest, giving me a sincere smile.

God, those dimples might be the death of me. They were like two little secret weapons perfectly placed on his cheeks, ready to strike at any moment and bring you to your knees.

"Well, thank you for this," I said, waving toward the kitchen. "I was sure I'd be elbow deep in chili grease until midnight."

"No problem. It also gave me an excuse to blow off Ashley." He laughed, his eyes wide.

"She was laying it on pretty thick, huh?"

"Ugh," he groaned. "She was obnoxious. She's as intelligent as this countertop, and her laugh was really starting to get on my nerves."

"Did she back off once you told her about your girlfriend?" I tried to be coy when I asked, when really I wanted to know every disgusting detail about his relationship. How long had they been together? Were they serious? Was he going to marry her? Then I wanted her phone number so I could tastelessly call her and ask her what this sexy creature was like in bed.

"Yeah, she pouted . . . *again* and went up to bed." A mischievous grin crossed his face. "But . . . I don't have a girlfriend."

My heart leaped into my throat.

"What? But . . . I thought I heard . . ."

"I just told her that so she'd leave me alone." He chuckled like he was pretty proud of himself.

"Oh, well, your secret is safe with me." I zipped my lip shut and smiled at him nervously. For some reason, I felt safer when I thought he had a girlfriend. Since Zach and I had split, I had been so careful and precise about what type of man I was willing to allow myself to get close to. I wasn't about to throw that all away on one charming stranger with a smile that could melt glass.

"I was looking at the pictures your mom has out. There are lots of you and the girls. Are you an only child?" He walked over to the fridge, grabbed the orange juice, and set it on the island.

"Yep, just me."

"I also noticed that there wasn't a guy in any of the pictures with you and the girls, and your mom mentioned you were single. Where's the girls' dad?" He poured juice into two glasses and slid one toward me.

I raised the glass to my lips slowly in a desperate attempt to stall answering his questions. I never talked about Zach with my best friend, let alone someone I had known for a handful of hours.

"Uh . . . he's gone." My plan was to use the vaguest answers I possibly could.

"Hmm." He looked down at his glass for a minute, contemplating his next question. "Was he ever around? Does he know the girls? Does he see them?"

My eyes widened as I took a deep breath, overwhelmed with the avalanche of personal questions he was dumping on me all at once.

He must have noticed the hesitation on my face and put his hands up in front of him. "Whoa, I'm so sorry. That was really pushy of me."

I looked down and smiled shyly, picking at an imaginary spot on the counter.

When I didn't respond, he continued, "Listen, I really am sorry. I don't normally turn into Dr. Phil when talking to a pretty girl. I guess I was just trying to find something to talk about so that you wouldn't turn around and go back down that hall to bed. Let's talk about something else." He looked around the room, scrambling for something new to talk about. "So, how about this weather?"

I looked back up at him, and my stone heart cracked just a little bit at his adorable awkwardness as he tried to backpedal. I felt bad for being so standoffish and wondered if maybe talking to someone who I didn't have to see again would make me feel better. I took a deep breath and decided to go for it, hoping talking about my past, just a little, would feel therapeutic, not painful.

"No, he doesn't see them. He left right before their first birthday. I haven't seen him since. I don't even know where he is," I blurted out, one sentence right after the other.

"Wow, he left *you*?" He looked at me incredulously, shaking his head. "What an idiot."

His comment embarrassed me slightly, but also made my heart soar. It had been a long time since a man had complimented me, and never someone as good-looking as Brody. I didn't have time to respond before he continued his inquiry into my past.

"So, that was like four years ago, right? Have you dated since?"

I quickly thought about yawning or faking a sudden headache and going off to bed, but what I did next surprised even me. For once, I didn't feel like running. Talking to Brody and looking into his sincere green eyes was comfortable, like I had been friends with him for years.

"I've dated a little here and there, nothing serious. I'm pretty picky about who I go out with."

"Picky? How come?"

"My life isn't just about me anymore. I'm dragging two innocent little girls along on this ride, so I definitely have a pretty solid idea of what I want in a partner."

"Partner. Hmm, that sounds so . . . official. We'll get back to that—right now, though, I'm dying to know these qualities you're looking for."

He pulled the stool out, sat down, and leaned in closer, anxious to hear what I was going to say next.

I pulled out the other stool and followed suit.

"Well . . . he has to be responsible, stable, grounded . . ."

Brody's face was unreadable, as though he couldn't compute what I had just said.

"What?" I asked him defensively.

He didn't answer, he just dropped his head into his arms and pretended to snore, loudly.

I reached over and smacked his arm. "Knock it off!"

His head snapped back up, and he looked bewildered. "Why the hell would you want that guy? He sounds like a total buzzkill."

"He's not a buzzkill, he's responsible. A good role model for the girls."

"No way! The girls are five. They have you to be their good role model. They want someone who will stomp around in the mud with them and let them stay up late and eat junk food when you're not home. They need someone fun. Sounds like you do too."

"I have fun!" I blurted out.

"Calm down, Killer, I wasn't being mean. I think all the qualities you want in a guy are . . . nice. I just think you also need someone who will show you how fun life can be. Ya know, make it exciting too. Don't you want that?"

I shrugged. "I don't know. That's not really a priority to me. I just need someone who is willing to take on the dad role and not bail when it gets tough."

Saying that sentence out loud made a huge lump form in my throat.

"Your own happiness isn't a priority?" Brody looked at me with wide, shocked eyes. "Wow. That's incredible. How will your girls ever be happy if you aren't?"

"I don't know. I never really thought about that," I said quietly.

"Well, how about this . . . how about you let me come back up here in a week and show you a good time? Show you how fun life can be?" His eyes danced with an excitement that made me want to get up off the stool and twirl around with them.

6

BRODY

I woke up to the smell of bacon assaulting my nose, and my stomach responded with a loud growl.

"Is he dead?" a tiny voice whispered.

I cracked my eye open just a bit to see Lucy and Piper sitting on the fireplace bench staring at me.

"No, he's not. He just moved," Lucy whispered to Piper.

"His nose holes are opening and closing," Piper responded, making a gross face.

Unable to hold it together, I laughed out loud at Piper's comment.

"Girls, get over here!" Kacie whispered sternly. "Did you wake him?"

Lucy cupped her hands around her mouth and turned to face her mom. "We were making sure he wasn't dead," she not so quietly whispered back.

I laughed again as they scurried back to the kitchen. Rolling onto my stomach, I propped myself up on my elbows to face Kacie.

"I'm so sorry. Go back to sleep. I'll make them hush," she apologized.

She looked even cuter than she had last night, if that was possible. She had on little black pants that said "Pink" across the back and made her ass look phenomenal, and a Minnesota Twins T-shirt.

She's a sports fan too? This girl just gets better and better.

"It's okay, really. What time is it?" I rubbed my eyes and looked around for my cell phone.

"Seven thirty. I'm making breakfast. You hungry?" she asked, wiping her hands on a dish towel.

"Starving."

"Wanna help me cut up some fruit?" she asked shyly, biting her lip.

Can I eat it off of you after we cut it?

"Sure, I'll be right there. Just gimme a minute to wake up."

That was a lie. I didn't need to wake up. I was wide awake, but if I stood up right now I would most likely embarrass both of us.

"Okay, everyone else should be down soon. I'd better get cooking." She smiled again and turned back to whatever she was mixing on the counter.

I lay there for a minute, wishing the others weren't coming down. I couldn't pinpoint what it was exactly, but I liked being around her, especially alone. We'd had a blast talking late last night. She had no idea who I was but seemed to be into me. I wanted to explore that a little more.

I got up and folded up the blankets Kacie had given me the night before and piled them on the floor next to the fireplace.

"Good morning, everyone!" Ashley chirped loudly as she bounced into the kitchen.

"Morning, Ashley," I heard Kacie greet back.

"Hey, handsome," she cooed annoyingly when she came into the family room.

I studied her face as she got closer. Who wore that much makeup this early in the morning? She looked like she got smacked in the face by a drunk rainbow.

"Good morning," I said back politely.

She walked behind me, running her hand up my arm and over my shoulder. "Maybe today we can watch that movie?"

"Uh, maybe," I replied, trying to be polite.

I was used to girls throwing themselves at me and handing me phone numbers, even the occasional hotel room key, but I never followed up. It wasn't my style, and Ashley certainly wasn't the one changing that for me. Out of the corner of my eye, I caught Kacie watching us, cracking a grin when Ashley made the movie suggestion again. Kacie knew I'd lied to Ashley about having a girlfriend the night before, and she was thoroughly enjoying my squirming. Ashley turned around to look out the back door of the family room, and I shot Kacie a playful glare and shook my head. She threw her head back and laughed silently.

"How's the weather looking?" Fred said as he came into the family room.

"Mornin', Fred. Not sure, I haven't turned the TV on yet," I replied, shaking his hand.

"Well, let's check it out." Fred grabbed the remote and flipped on the morning news.

"Yes, Bob, raining cats and dogs is an understatement, and it doesn't look like it's stopping anytime soon. Folks, if you had plans today, you'd better cancel them. We are expecting more rain, and lots of it. In some areas it's coming down at the rate of one inch per hour. Massive flooding all over the county and power outages galore—"

Fred clicked the TV off in the middle of the weatherman's report and dropped the remote on the couch, his head falling back in exasperation. He looked over toward Sophia and my eyes followed. Poor Sophia. I knew that look anywhere—my mom made it too. She was panicked, clutching her necklace, staring back at Fred. He got up off the couch and walked over to her, putting his arm around her shoulders.

"It's okay, don't worry. The sandbags are keeping the lake at bay, and you bought that backup generator for a reason. It's business as usual around here." She looked over and smiled at him, her face more relaxed.

I walked into the kitchen, up behind Kacie, who was on her tiptoes trying to reach something in the fridge.

"Need help?"

"Ah!" she yelled, spinning around. Her back slammed against the refrigerator shelves.

"Whoa! Sorry, didn't mean to scare you. Are you okay?"

"Yeah, I'm fine. Sorry. My mind was somewhere else."

"I hope wherever it was, it was having fun." I winked at her playfully. "What can I help you with?"

"Knowing *my* brain, it was reorganizing a closet and sorting dirty laundry into color-coordinated piles." She grinned up at me. "Um . . . wanna cut up some strawberries?"

"Yep, I'm all over it." I grabbed the cutting board and pint of strawberries and got to work.

"Kacie, did Fred tell you about the shower in our unit?" Sophia asked her.

"The shower?" Kacie pulled her brows in close and looked at her mom, confused.

"Nothing major. I think it's just a broken cartridge, but no water comes out, so no one can use it until it's fixed. I'll get to it this afternoon," Fred said, walking over to pour himself a cup of coffee.

"Oh, no biggie. If I smell today, it's Fred's fault," Kacie teased, nudging him with her elbow as he walked by.

I discreetly stared at Kacie as she continued the small talk with her mom and Fred. I had found myself doing that a lot over the last eighteen hours, but I couldn't help it. She was mesmerizing, every little thing about her, from her bright green eyes to her cute little nose that crinkled just a little bit every time she smiled. When we were talking last night, I was trying hard to concentrate on what she was saying, but I kept drifting off, getting lost in her features. Twenty-four hours ago, I hadn't known this girl existed. Now I wanted to know every single detail about her, all the way down to her shoe size.

"Mmmmm, I love strawberries. So sweet and juicy." Ashley winked at me as she reached over and grabbed a berry, popping it into her mouth.

I smiled politely, finding it hard to hide my annoyance with her any longer. Though this detour to the Cranberry Inn wasn't planned, it had been surprisingly awesome so far, except for Ashley. She was a thorn in my side that I wished I could remove. I didn't have a lot of time left here, and she was not the one I wanted to spend it with.

Just then, Kacie wiggled in between Ashley and me with catlike prowess and set down a cast-iron skillet full of gooey, delicious-looking cinnamon rolls on the island. She took the cutting board from me, brushing the strawberries into a bowl. Her eyes sparkled when she looked at me out of the corner of her eye, and I knew what she was doing.

She was saving me from Ashley, among other things.

7

KACIE

A few hours after breakfast, I was holed up in my bedroom, listening to the rain bounce off the roof and avoiding reality. I needed a break . . . from the house, from the girls, from Brody. Not that Brody being at the house was a bad thing, but his presence was awakening a part of my brain that had been dormant for a long time, and that was exhausting. My life the last four years had been simple, and I liked that. I needed it. Our life with the inn was so chaotic that I craved as much routine as possible in our day-to-day lives. I woke up every day knowing what was going to happen and did my best to keep us organized and on schedule. Needless to say, the storm threw me off balance, especially with Brody showing up. I hadn't planned on dating anyone until after I was done with nursing school, but now I was questioning things. Was there room in my life for someone now?

Grabbing my cell phone, I decided to text Alexa to distract myself.

Hey! How are you guys doing over there?

It was less than thirty seconds before my phone beeped in return.

Pooks! We're okay. Power is out. I'm bored. Derek keeps trying
to have sex. It's annoying. How are you all doing?

I laughed at her ridiculous nickname for me. I had called her
Pookie Bear once in high school after a marathon wine cooler session, and she had shortened it and called me Pooks ever since. I made
the decision right then not to tell her about Brody. First, she wouldn't
understand my hesitation in opening myself up for an opportunity,
then she would call my mom and they would be picking out my wedding dress together. Alexa wanted me to get married almost as badly
as my mom did.

We're okay. Several surprise guests who were stuck. Power keeps
flickering on and off, other than that, nothing too exciting. I'll
text you tomorrow. Hopefully this rain lets up and we can meet
for lunch later in the week?

Obviously, once high school ended and I had the girls, life had
changed dramatically. I couldn't always drop everything and run out
and do what I wanted like most of my other friends. Sometimes I was
jealous of Alexa and her freedom to do whatever she wanted, whenever
she wanted. My mom insisted I still have a life outside of the inn, so she
agreed to babysit the girls once a week for a day out with Alexa. When
I first moved back, we would go out to clubs or bars on the weekends,
but I was a lightweight and was always yawning by ten o'clock. Eventually we switched the outings to lunch dates, or I would just grab takeout
and hang out at her flower shop.

Yes, for sure! Okay, Derek is sticking his hand down my pants yet
again, gotta go break it off. Stay dry. Love ya!

I put my phone down and looked outside at the pouring rain. Maybe
Alexa and my mom were right—I was too closed off from the possibility
of love again. Was I even really in love with Zach the last time? Ugh, just

saying his name to myself made my stomach turn. I couldn't think about this right now; my brain was as cloudy as the sky out my window. I went to find the girls and persuade them to play a game with me.

The house was silent. No one was in the living room or the kitchen. I walked through the hallway to the front room and found my mom sitting on the couch, looking out the window, smiling.

"Where is everyone?"

"Oh, they're all milling around here somewhere."

"Where are Piper and Lucy?"

"Brody was taking Diesel out to go potty and they asked if they could go with . . ." She smiled at me and nodded her head toward the window.

I walked over and looked out and my heart stuttered to a halt. Lucy and Piper were on the driveway with Brody, jumping in and out of rain puddles. I looked at my mom, who was all teary-eyed watching them have fun.

"You're such a sap," I said, sticking my tongue out at her on my way through the front door.

I stepped discreetly out onto the large country-style covered porch and hugged myself because of the chill in the air. My arms were cold, but my heart was warm watching the girls. Their soaking-wet hair was glued to their faces, but I didn't think I had ever seen them smile that big. They giggled wildly as the three of them held hands, jumping in and out of every puddle they could find.

"This one, Brody, do this one!" Lucy squealed.

"This one? Okay, Twinkies . . . get ready!" Brody stepped back a few feet and pumped his arms, gaining momentum before he jumped as high as I'd ever seen a grown man jump. He landed right in the center of a huge puddle. They shrieked and shielded their faces from the wave of water crashing over them.

"You guys are going to catch pneumonia!" I called out to them, not really wanting them to stop. I was having too much fun watching.

They looked over at me and whooped again when Brody jumped high and landed in the same puddle.

"Mom! Come jump with us!" Piper called out, marching around in a circle.

"No way, I'm just fine up here watching you. You have fun."

"Come on, Mom, pleeeeease!" Lucy begged.

"Yeah, come on, *Mom*," Brody teased, motioning me with his fingers. "Get out here."

"No thanks, you guys look like a bunch of wet dogs." I looked over at Diesel, who was curled up at the end of the porch watching them. He cocked his head and looked at me. "No offense, Diesel."

"Wet dogs? We look like wet dogs?" Brody exclaimed. "What do you think of that, girls?"

"Booooo!" they yelled in unison, still puddle jumping.

"I have an idea," Brody said, pulling the girls into a huddle. He put his arms around their shoulders and talked quietly.

"Okay, ready . . . one . . . two . . ."

"Three!" the girls yelled out together as Brody took off in a sprint straight for me. I held my hands up in front of me, backing up toward the house.

"No, no, no! What are you—?" Before I could finish the sentence, Brody picked me up and carried me out onto the driveway. I instinctively wrapped my hands around his neck, enjoying the feel of his strong shoulders under my arms. Before I had time to get comfortable, we were standing over a puddle and he was grinning devilishly at me.

"No way, don't you dare," I warned him.

"What do you think, Twinkies? She called us wet dogs. What should we do with her?"

"Pud-dles! Pud-dles!" they chanted in unison.

Little traitors.

With the girls cheering him on, Brody marched around the driveway in circles, splashing my butt in drops of cold water. The girls laughed louder and harder with each puddle. I forgot how cold I was when I looked at their sweet little faces and how much fun they were having.

"Jump! Jump!" Lucy jumped up and down, clapping.

Brody looked right into my eyes, our faces only inches apart. My heart was beating so hard I was wondering if he could feel it too. I hadn't wanted to kiss someone that bad in a really long time. If the girls hadn't been right there, I might have made the first move.

"You wouldn't do that to me." I narrowed my eyes, looking straight into his.

"Wouldn't I?" He raised an eyebrow in defiance and with that, up in the air we both went. His feet slammed to the ground two seconds before a huge rush of cold water covered my whole backside. I squealed and arched my back, almost falling out of Brody's grasp.

"Oh no you don't," he said, squeezing me tighter. "I'm gonna teach you to relax and have fun if it kills me." He jumped again, slamming his feet harder this time. Water covered my back and flew all the way up over my head. I blinked several times before my vision was clear enough to see Brody lick the water off his lips and flash that killer smile again. I threw my head back and laughed just as hard as the girls, quite relaxed in Brody's sturdy arms.

After another hour of playing in the rain with Brody and the girls, I was chilled to the bone and desperate for a hot shower. I grabbed my stuff out of our bathroom and headed to the guest wing of the house. Passing the first bathroom, I slipped quietly into the second and dropped my stuff on the small table in the corner.

"Oh, Kacie . . . you do look like a wet dog," I said, staring at myself in the mirror. I sighed, pulling off my T-shirt, which was completely plastered to my body, and cursed out loud at my decision to change into jeans after breakfast. Trying to pull them off was like trying to pull a sumo wrestler through a child's inner tube. I kicked and struggled until they were off and in a heap with the other wet clothes on the bathroom floor.

I stood, examining myself one more time in front of the mirror, wearing only my bra and panties. "A wet dog who needs to hit the gym, no less."

Just then, the bathroom door flew open and Piper came flying in. "Sorry, Mom, gotta pee!" She rushed by me, pulling her pants down as she ran.

"Piper!" I called out. "You have to learn to knock. You can't just barge in on people." I turned to shut the bathroom door and stopped dead in my tracks. Brody was standing in the hallway, carrying a bath towel, staring right at me.

"Uh . . . sorry," he said, covering his eyes like a toddler playing peek-a-boo while I jumped behind the bathroom door. "I was about to knock when she ran past and opened the door. I'm so sorry."

"It's okay. Um . . . I think the bathroom down the hall is . . . available." I was glad he was still covering his face because I was certain mine was twelve different shades of red.

"Okay, thanks. Sorry," he mumbled through his hands and turned to walk down the hall, bumping into a table my mom had full of picture frames, knocking almost all of them over.

"Shit!" he hissed as he bent over and picked up the frames, trying to put them back the way they were, but they kept falling over, taking new ones with them like dominoes.

Closing the door gently, I grinned to myself as I heard him continue to struggle with the frames. I lectured Piper on the importance of knocking before you barged through a door. She got dressed and scampered off as I closed the door behind her, locking it securely.

Embarrassed as I'd ever been in my whole life, I wanted to climb into the shower and let the scalding hot water wash away the last ten minutes of my life.

8

BRODY

"Well, that could have gone better." I sat on the closed toilet lid and held my head in my hands, wondering what the hell had just happened. I had raised my hand to knock on the door, and before I knew it, Piper flew by me, flung the door open, and suddenly I was staring at Kacie in her bra and underwear.

It was a total accident . . . or a blessing. A beautiful, messy-headed gift from God, wrapped in a package of sexy curves and sparkling green eyes, topped with a black lace bow just waiting for me to unwrap it. Jesus, she looked good. Simple, but just enough to drive me batshit crazy. *Every time I look at her for the rest of the day, I'll think of her standing there in her black skivvies, shocked as hell when she saw me.*

Just reliving that moment was too much.

I stood up, turned the shower on, and stepped in, leaving it on cold for a few minutes.

The rest of the afternoon, things were awkward with Kacie, and it was killing me. She avoided looking at me and left the room when

I entered it. She obviously didn't want to be around me. I wanted to talk to her and apologize again so we could go back to normal, but I couldn't get her alone. I had a hemorrhoid named Ashley following me around everywhere I went.

Fred kept me up-to-date on the latest weather reports.

"Looks like they're going to reopen that bridge tomorrow at five a.m., assuming the rain slows down overnight like they're saying it will."

I'd learned that Fred spent his evenings up in his apartment watching old cop shows and listening to his police scanner, which I assumed was how he had the insider info on the bridge closures.

"Really? Well, that's good. I'll work on getting my truck out before dark, then tomorrow I'll be on my way, bright and early."

Fred looked over at me and nodded slowly. He seemed a little bummed to hear I'd be leaving.

"I was thinking, maybe later in the summer, I could come back and you can show me what kind of fish we can pull out of that lake back there?"

"That sounds great, Brody. You just come back here anytime you want. Maybe next time you can rent a room and ditch that old couch." He reached across the island to shake my hand.

"Fred, did we just have a moment?" I teased him, grabbing his hand and giving it a firm shake back.

Fred laughed loudly. "I guess we did."

I missed dinner, instead spending the next three hours cramming branches under the tires of my truck to get it unstuck. I came inside and everything was pretty quiet. The kitchen was cleaned up except for a plate of food covered with plastic wrap on the island. I walked over and was thrilled that the note on top had my name on it. I didn't know Kacie's handwriting, but I was pretty sure she left this out for me. If pot roast and red potatoes were her idea of a peace offering, I was going to marry that girl tomorrow. I sat down and dived right in.

"Hey."

I looked up from my plate to see Kacie standing in the corner of the kitchen, nervously playing with her silver necklace. She probably thought I was staring at her boobs—she would have been right about that too. I cleared my throat.

"Hey. Uh . . . thanks for this. It's delicious, beyond delicious," I replied, hoping I didn't have gravy all over my face.

She smiled shyly and walked over to the refrigerator, grabbing the gallon of milk.

"No problem. Did you get your truck out?" she asked as she poured me a tall glass.

"Yeah, thankfully. I really didn't want to have to wait for a tow truck. Who knows how long that would have taken!"

"Fred said you're leaving tomorrow."

"Yeah, I'd like to try and go early, before Ashley grabs a hold of my leg and tries to go with me."

Kacie chuckled, but not a sincere laugh like I'd heard over the last couple of days.

"Listen," I continued, "I was hoping to talk to you before I left, but you seemed like you didn't want to talk to me all afternoon so I didn't push it. About today, in the bathroom—"

"Don't," Kacie cut me off. "Really, it's fine. I know it wasn't your fault." She bit her lip and started playing with her necklace again.

"I know it's not my fault, but I still feel bad about it. You seem so . . . uncomfortable around me now, and that's not how I want to leave things. I told Fred I might come back again soon, to fish with him. It'd be nice if you didn't hate me."

She rolled her eyes. "I don't hate you, I was just embarrassed. It's been . . . a long time . . . since anyone has, you know, seen me like that. I wasn't exactly prepared." She stared off into the family room, avoiding eye contact.

"Listen, what can I do to make things go back to the way they were this morning?"

"Nothing, really. It's fine. I'm gonna head to bed, I'm beat. Maybe I'll see you in the morning?" She gave me a polite smile that didn't quite reach her eyes and turned down the hall toward her apartment. I knew with that smile she wasn't done. She didn't want me to leave like this either. My mind reeled with what I could say or do in that ten feet she had left to walk to make her stay out here and get things back to normal.

Lightbulb moment!

"Kacie!" I called out in a loud whisper. By the time she turned around, I had pulled my T-shirt off and dropped my jeans down around my ankles, standing there in nothing but my boxer briefs.

"Oh my God! What are you doing?" She giggled and covered her eyes the way I had earlier.

"I thought it was only fair. I've seen you, now you've seen me, and we can go back to normal."

She peeked through her fingers at me, closing them quickly when she realized I was in no rush to get dressed again. She continued chuckling and said in a muffled tone, "Put your clothes back on, you lunatic."

What the hell was I doing? This might be the dumbest thing I'd ever done, and I'd done a lot of stupid things. I was standing in front of this girl I was unusually attracted to in nothing but my boxer briefs, talking myself out of getting hard right there in front of her. Every time she grinned at me or looked south, I had to think of nonsexual things in my head.

Remote control. Pepper spray. Winter jackets. Golf clubs.

"I will . . . *if* you promise to hang out here with me for a little while. If you continue down that hall, I'm going to follow you, just like this."

"Even *you* are not bold enough to do that." She was challenging me.

I never back down from a challenge.

49

"Actually, it's pretty hot in this house, don't ya think? Maybe I'd be more comfortable with these off?" I wiggled my eyebrows at her and started playing with the elastic band of my boxers.

Her eyes followed my hands as her mouth fell open. She threw her hands up over her face again and turned around, facing the hallway but not moving forward.

"Okay, okay. I'll stay, just pull your pants up."

9

KACIE

I lost all control of my body and let my head fall back on Brody's shoulder as he softly kissed his way down the side of my neck. His fingers lightly raked up and down my arms, covering them in goose bumps as I let out a soft moan.

"I've been wanting to do this for two days," he murmured against the base of my neck. "And now that I've finally touched you, I'm not going to be able to stop."

His words were intoxicating and my body was already drunk with lust. My breasts felt heavy, my nipples poking against the constricting cotton fabric of my bra. He continued kissing my neck as he slipped one hand inside my bra, teasing and kneading my swollen, needy breast. When his fingers clamped gently around my nipple, I let out a hiss and reached around behind me, feeling his excitement through his jeans.

"You keep making noises like that, this isn't going to last very long," he growled as he spun me around to face him. I grabbed at his jeans button and fumbled to get it open.

His eyes were on fire, egging me on with their blaze. "Slow down, Kacie."

"Kacie! Kacie!" I heard my mom calling. Lifting my head off my pillow, I cracked one eye open and looked over at my mom, standing in my bedroom doorway.

"It's past ten o'clock. You never sleep this late. Are you sick?"

I glanced over at the clock on my nightstand, and sure enough, it read 10:07.

"No, Mom, I'm not sick, just tired. Are the girls still asleep?" I asked.

"No, I got them up and dressed and fed them so you could sleep a little longer. This isn't like you."

"I'm okay, Mom. I'll be out in a minute, okay?" I said in a groggy haze, desperate for her to leave quickly so I could fall back asleep and pick up where Brody and I left off.

"Sure, honey, take your time. I just wanted to check and make sure you weren't sick." She smiled and closed the door gently behind her.

I buried my face in my pillow the way it had been when she woke me and pinched my eyes shut tight, determined to get back to sleep fast and have Brody's hands exploring my body again.

I lay there for about ten minutes, then gave up, flopping over onto my back in frustration and staring up at the ceiling. That was the most action I had seen in years, and I wasn't even conscious for it.

I looked over at the clock again . . . 10:19. Coffee was going to be my best friend today, but I guess that's what happens when you stay awake until three in the morning, talking. How could I not want to stay up late and chat with him after seeing him standing there with that charming, boyish grin on his face and his jeans around his ankles? His broad shoulders and chiseled body made it next to impossible not to stare. He was irresistible and he knew it.

I wasn't sorry, though. We'd had a great night with even better conversation.

We spent hours snacking on Twizzlers and talking about everything . . . books, movies, our families. I didn't have much to contribute to that part of the conversation. While my little family was happy, we weren't going to be on a poster for the typical American family anytime soon. I was an only child. My parents divorced when I was ten, and I hadn't seen my dad since, end of story. Brody's family sounded like the exact opposite of mine. His parents were happily married for over thirty years, he had one sister, and he still went home to visit often, when he wasn't traveling for his sales job. We talked about his job briefly, though he seemed pretty bored with it and changed the subject whenever I brought it up.

It was sweet that family was so important to him. I loved the way his face lit up when he talked about his mom and his sister. He had all the qualities I was looking for, and his sexiness factor was off the charts. I started thinking that maybe I should tap into my inner Alexa and go for it for once. Constantly playing it safe seemed only to be prepping me to be the crazy old cat lady with an extensive collection of NASCAR kitchen plates.

I decided right then to throw caution to the wind and make an effort with Brody. I jumped out of bed with a sudden burst of excitement for the day and hurried for the shower, thankful Fred had fixed it last night so there would be no repeats of yesterday.

Though if it would lead to Brody in his undies again, it might be worth it.

Twenty minutes later, I threw on my favorite jeans and some makeup—which was in itself a rarity these days—and composed myself before I headed out to the kitchen.

Deep breaths, Kacie, deep breaths.

"Mommy!!!" Lucy threw herself into my arms and wrapped herself around my neck.

"Hey, kiddo. Have you been good for Gigi?"

Piper bounced over and I pulled her in close to me too.

"Yes, we helped her make breakfast. I was in charge of pouring." Lucy beamed at me.

"I was in charge of mixing!" Piper squealed.

I kissed both of them and they went back to making paper flowers at the island.

My mom turned from the stove with a plate of pancakes for me. "Here, I saved you some—" She stopped and looked at me funny.

"What?" I said defensively.

"Nothing, you just don't usually wear makeup. You look very pretty." She walked over and set the plate down on the island and kissed my cheek.

I was overcome with a sudden shyness. "Thanks, just thought I'd try something new."

She nodded with a small smirk, like she knew exactly what I was doing. I was just thankful she didn't make a big deal out of it and embarrass me more.

"So, where's everyone else?" I tried to sound nonchalant.

"Fred's out back cleaning up sticks and other garbage that washed up from the lake. Everyone else left early this morning when we got news that the bridge was open."

"*Everyone* else is gone?" I blurted out in a panic. My stomach dropped through the wood floor. No way would he have left and not said anything, right? Last night, we were so comfortable talking to each other—neither of us wanted to go to bed. I thought for sure he'd stay and have breakfast before he left.

"Yep, everyone else is gone. Why?"

"No reason," I said back, disappointed.

Mom looked at me suspiciously as she walked over to the island.

"There is something for you on the fireplace bench, though, from Brody. What's going on with that?"

My eyes got wide and I nodded toward the girls, who appeared to be elbow deep in colorful flower petals and glue, but there was no doubt in my mind that their ears were open and listening. "There's nothing going on with that. He was a nice guy, that's all."

She pressed her lips together and narrowed her eyes at me. "Okay, if you say so."

I sat at the island, watching Lucy and Piper cut little hearts and flowers out of construction paper, wondering how long I should sit and wait before I could sprint into the family room and see what Brody left for me. While Mom had her back turned at the stove, I tried to sneak a peek over at the fireplace and saw what appeared to be some kind of a red hoodie folded up with a note on it. I was straining my neck so hard to get a better look I almost fell off the stool.

"Why don't you just go over and see what it is?" Mom said, amused.

I whipped back around and stared at my mom like a kid who just got caught with her hand in the candy jar.

"I knew you liked him. Mothers know these things. Go on." She winked and shooed me away with her hand.

I decided not to argue with her. Instead I rolled my eyes and hopped down from the stool, reminding myself that if I didn't want my mother sending out wedding invitations tomorrow, I needed to act like this was no big deal. As I got closer to the fireplace I saw that it was, in fact, a shirt of some sort. Before I picked it up, I grabbed the note and unfolded it impatiently.

Kacie,
Two days wasn't long enough. Please call me.

Brody

My eyes fixated on the phone number on the bottom of the note, the phone number that I could dial and hear Brody's voice within ten seconds if I wanted to. Just the thought of hearing his voice again sent a jolt of excitement through my body. I set the note aside and picked up the shirt curiously. It was a red jersey with a hunter-green circle in the middle that was surrounding a scene of evergreens and a sunset. Two thick green stripes, one on each sleeve, bordered two thin white stripes. Confusion flooded my brain . . . why did he leave this for me? It made no sense.

I flipped the jersey around to inspect the back and it hit me like a ton of bricks. At the top of the jersey, white block letters read MURPHY with the number thirty below it. Murphy? That was Brody's last name. I turned the jersey around again, still having no clue what exactly this was. In the thick green circle on the front, it said MINNESOTA WILD. What the hell was that?

The French doors leading to the back deck swung open and Fred came in, wiping his dirty hands on his jeans. He used his knee to gently close the door.

"Hey, Fred! What is this?" I asked, turning the front to face him.

"Minnesota Wild jersey."

I shrugged my shoulders and shook my head, bewildered.

"Hockey. Minnesota's professional hockey team. I hear they're really good."

My mouth fell open as the knot in my stomach grew bigger. Brody was a hockey player? No way. Why would he lie to me? It's not like he didn't have several opportunities. We chatted for hours. I was at a total loss and a little bit sad. If this was true, the chances of anything happening between us just washed away like sticks under the old bridge.

I put the note in my pocket, rolled up the jersey, and walked into the kitchen.

"Hockey player, huh?" My mom eyed me skeptically.

My mind was still back in the family room processing what I'd just learned. It hadn't caught up to my body enough to form a coherent sentence.

"Guess so," I said flatly. I looked at the girls, wondering if I'd ever be able to give them the one thing that should have been inherently natural, a father. I looked over at my mom, who hadn't taken her eyes off me. "Hey, can you keep an eye on them for a minute? I . . . have something to do."

"Of course, honey."

I got to my room and flopped down on my bed, stretching to reach my laptop. Thanks to the melded combination of Google and our fishbowl world, it was possible to find out just about anything. I took a deep breath and impatiently typed out B-R-O-D-Y M-U-R-P-H-Y in the search bar.

I stared wide-eyed at the screen, waiting impatiently.

YOUR SEARCH YIELDED 3,270,000 RESULTS.

Three *million* results? Holy shit! I scrolled down, quietly chanting to myself *please-no-naked-pictures, please-no-naked-pictures.* A head shot of Brody appeared at the top of the page that made my pulse race. His dark chocolate hair was a mess of loose curls that complemented his playful smile and shimmering green eyes. He was unwittingly seducing me and every other girl looking at his picture, probably a few guys too. Under his picture were action shots of him blocking goals, high-fiving his team-mates, and sparring with a guy from another team. The rest of the page was filled with personal stats, team stats, and articles with headlines.

MURPHY'S GLOVE STOPS BRUINS IN THEIR TRACKS

BRODY "THE WALL" MURPHY'S STELLAR
PERFORMANCE IN OVERTIME AIDS WILD IN
VICTORY

"The Wall"? I snickered out loud to myself. What a nickname. I continued skimming the page but came to a screeching halt when one headline jumped out at me.

BRODY MURPHY ARRESTED IN CHICAGO

Oh God. For the millionth time that day, my stomach dropped. I clicked on the article and started absorbing the words as fast as my brain would allow. Halfway through the article, I chuckled, shaking my head at the computer like it was an old gossipy friend.

He got arrested for *that*?

10

BRODY

It took me ninety-seven minutes to get home from the Cranberry Inn, and I spent at least ninety of those minutes thinking about Kacie. The other seven were spent pulling in and out of various rest stops so my psycho dog with a bladder the size of a thimble didn't pee in my truck.

I was up until three o'clock in the morning talking to Kacie, and despite my utter exhaustion, being with her all night was so worth it. Every time I thought about cutting the conversation short and heading to bed, a strand of her hair would break free from her ponytail and frame her face perfectly . . . or she'd flash that cute little dimple on her left cheek, and suddenly I didn't give a shit about sleep anymore. That's why God invented coffee anyway.

My cell phone alarm went off three hours after we finally turned in, and I packed up quietly and left. There was no real reason for me to leave so early. I had no exciting plans, but I wanted to sneak out before I saw Ashley again, and more importantly, I didn't want to see Kacie's face when she realized I'd lied to her about playing hockey.

The lie had started out innocently. I just hadn't felt like sitting at the dinner table answering all the typical questions that came along with being a professional athlete. Then when I talked to Kacie that night about her ex and what she was looking for now, I couldn't bring myself to tell her. I didn't want her making a snap judgment about me or my life, hoping that she'd get to know me before she blew me off . . . but I wanted to make sure that she found out about it from me, so I'd left my favorite jersey there for her.

My cell phone went off as I pulled into the parking garage of my condo building. For a quick second, I hoped it was Kacie already, but when I looked at my phone the screen said BOSSMAN.

"What's up, buddy?" I tried sounding as awake as possible after three hours of sleep.

"Whoa! You sound like shit!" Andy teased.

"Good morning to you too. What are you doing up so early?"

"Early? Most normal people are already at work by now, not crawling in from the night before, which is exactly what it sounds like you're doing. I'm already on my third cup of coffee, my friend."

"Not exactly. I'm just getting home from up north." I yawned.

"I thought you were getting home yesterday."

"That was my hope, but the weather didn't cooperate." *Thank God it didn't*, I thought.

"That sucks. Well, you wanna fill me in tonight over a beer or what?"

"Yeah, sounds good. Meet at the Bumper at six?" I asked.

"Perfect. If you're lucky, I'll let you buy me dinner too." He laughed as he hung up.

The Bumper was our favorite place to go. It was a hole-in-the-wall bar about four blocks from my condo, with grumpy waitresses and stale peanuts, but they made great burgers, the beer was ice-cold, and no one bugged me there.

Diesel and I slowly made our way upstairs to my condo. I tossed my keys on the kitchen counter while he headed straight for his oversize dog bed by the fireplace. I collapsed on the couch, debating whether to get up and head to the gym for a couple of hours or sleep the day away right where I landed. The more I thought about bicep curls, the more comfortable my couch got, and I let sleep take over.

A wet nose grazed my forehead, but I swatted it away. My eyelids felt like they were glued shut, refusing to budge, and I was in no rush to force them open. I lay there listening to the sounds of the city rushing by my window, when my phone vibrated from the kitchen counter.

"What do you think, Diesel? You think that's a text from her?" Diesel yawned and walked back to his bed, unimpressed. "Yeah, you're right, she probably hates me." I sighed, sitting up and resting my elbows on my knees. I took my time getting off the couch. I was in no rush to read a nasty message calling me a liar or see a picture of my jersey cut up in pieces on her bedroom floor. The idea of my jersey being on her floor was definitely exciting, but more in a trail-like fashion with her panties right next to it.

I made my way to the kitchen and grabbed my phone, both relieved and disappointed to see it was a text from Andy.

Let's make it 5:00. I'm starving. Shaw.

I couldn't help myself, I texted back . . .

You just want to see me sooner. I love you too, you sexy beast.

I was groggy as hell and needed to wake up. "All right, D, we have just enough time for a quick jog before I gotta get in the shower."

Diesel raised his brows and glared at me from his dog bed, not budging.

"Come on, lazy ass!" I shouted as I grabbed his leash from the hook by the fridge. The metallic clanging of the chain excited Diesel, and he jumped off his bed and bounced over to me. I bent down, secured the leash to his collar, and out the door we went.

It was early June and the air was still crisp and comfortable, perfect jogging weather. I walked a few blocks from my condo to Lake Calhoun, popped my earbuds in, and Diesel and I took off. The lake was crowded today . . . people jogging, out on the lake in paddleboats, picnicking. I ran past two teenagers sitting on a bench swapping more spit than a couple of porn stars. I just shook my head. To my right, a couple lay on a plaid blanket reading books and chomping on grapes. She looked around quickly and held her book up in front of them, pulling him in close.

Come on, Brody, focus.

Up ahead I noticed an older couple holding each other cheek-to-cheek near the lake shoreline, looking out at the water. As I got closer I tried to see what they were looking at, and I realized they weren't looking at anything: the water was clear.

They were slow dancing . . . with no music.

I came to a stop and shook my head in frustration. I felt . . . off, disconnected. I needed to get my shit together and get this run in. I blasted Korn on my iPod and started again, trying to shut the rest of the world out and focus on my pace. A girl ran toward me, giving me a megawatt smile as she passed. She was a cute brunette with green eyes, but they were nothing compared to Kacie's. They didn't have the same sparkle, the same life in them; they did nothing for me.

"Screw this, Diesel. I'm not feeling it today."

A scalding hot shower made me feel remotely better after that disappointing run. Despite Andy working right near my condo, I didn't get to see him often and was looking forward to shooting the shit with him over a beer, or five.

When I got to the bar, he was already sitting at our normal table in the corner. As I got to the table, he flashed me a big smile and stood to shake my hand.

"What's up, brother?" I pulled him in for a bear hug.

"Wow, you showered for me? Trying to get lucky?" He laughed, pushing one of the beers he'd already ordered toward me.

I lifted the beer to my lips and took several big gulps. "Something like that," I answered, looking around for Jan, our usual waitress. "I'm starving, let's order."

"Yeah, I can't stay out late tonight; I have to eat and run. Blaire is making dinner." He grimaced.

Blaire was superficial, materialistic, a megabitch, and unfortunately . . . my best friend's wife. She and Andy had met in college and married shortly after I signed my first big contract with the Wild. A little too convenient, if you asked me.

They lived about thirty minutes outside of the city in the biggest house in their town. She drove the most expensive luxury car they could find and had a whole slew of people employed at their house. One time at a charity dinner, someone asked her what she did for a living, and she said she didn't work outside of the home, but she was a "house manager." I choked on my drink and she shot eye daggers at me. She hasn't liked me since, not that she was a big fan of mine before that.

"Making dinner? I thought you wanted a burger," I said, finishing off my first beer.

"Uh, yes. She's trying to be more domestic, so she's cooking duck tonight. Needless to say I don't want to go to bed starving, so I'm going to eat a big dinner now and then make her dinner magically disappear. At least pretending I like her cooking will get me laid tonight."

I tried to shake the thought out of my head of anyone being forced to suffer through fucking that woman. I didn't know how he'd survived this long without that black widow killing him already.

"So this weekend, what happened?" Andy asked, after we ordered burgers, onion rings, and another round of beer.

"The weather happened. It was one crappy misfortune after another. Next thing I knew, my truck was axle deep in mud in the driveway of this inn up north. Thankfully, they were welcoming and let me stay for a couple days."

"An inn? Sounds like a total snoozefest. Was it all old retired people, or what?"

"No, actually. There were quite a few people there." I grinned.

Andy leaned forward and stared right into my eyes, raising a curious eyebrow. "Uh-oh, what's her name?"

"What are you talking about?" I shot back at him, looking around the bar to avoid eye contact.

He shook his head, his face beaming with pride like he'd just figured out some big secret. "No way, Brody. I know you better than anyone on this planet. Don't bullshit me. I've seen that look before. What's. Her. Name."

I looked around to make sure no one was within earshot. I had no chance of getting this girl to talk to me again if her name was in some tabloid tomorrow morning. "Kacie. Kacie Jensen. Now can we drop it, please?"

Andy sighed and rubbed his face with his hands. "Please tell me you were careful. Am I going to have a paternity suit to deal with right after Christmas? It would really ruin my winter."

"No, asshole. I didn't sleep with her. That's not what it was about. It was—" I stopped talking when Jan walked up with our food. After she set all the plates down and patted my arm, I dug right in to eating, avoiding Andy's curious eye.

"So, are we done talking about this?" Andy proceeded carefully.

"There's nothing to talk about, Andy. I met this girl and she's the most intriguing woman I've ever laid eyes on. I only spent two days with her, but it wasn't nearly enough time." I ran my hands through my hair in frustration. "And so far, she hasn't called me. I don't know if she ever will. I may never see her again, but I want to." I pushed my plate away and looked up at Andy, who furrowed his brow, deep in thought.

"Oh, and . . . she has two kids. Be right back, gotta piss."

Andy groaned and dropped his head in his hands, rubbing his eyes with his palms as I pushed away from the table. That poor man, I didn't pay him nearly enough.

11

KACIE

It had been three days since Brody left, and given the information I had learned about him, I was trying to ignore the embers burning in my belly and get my life back to normal. Mom had been grilling me nonstop about the situation, and I needed a break from the house, so I was taking the girls and spending the day with them at the zoo.

In the car, we told knock-knock jokes and belted out Taylor Swift songs at the top of our lungs. Once we got there, we grabbed a map and started checking off as many animals as we could before taking a break on a bench with some Dippin' Dots.

"Are you guys having fun?" I asked.

They both nodded excitedly with ice cream dripping down their chins.

HA! Who says I can't be spontaneous and fun?

I felt vindicated, like I was winning an imaginary contest against my subconscious.

"What should we do next?"

"Dolphin show!" Lucy shouted out.

"Yeah, then the train ride!" Piper blurted right after her.

I looked at the time on my phone. "Well, if we're gonna do all that, we better get moving." We tossed our ice cream cups into the garbage and headed for the dolphin show.

By the time Chloe the dolphin jumped through the fourth ring, my cell phone had gone off twice. I had two texts, one from my mom and one from Alexa.

MOM: There are flowers at the house for you . . .

ALEXA: Running behind on orders, but we need to chat. Wanna hang with me at the shop tonight?

The black-and-white words of Alexa's text blurred together as my mind ran circles around the text from my mom. Who would have sent me flowers? The one person who came to mind was as disappointing as it was exciting. I didn't want to think about it, so I closed my phone and put it away, deciding to concentrate the rest of the afternoon on nothing but the sweet smiles on my girls' faces. We filled the afternoon with balloon animals, train rides, and so much cotton candy I thought we were gonna burst.

A couple of hours later, we piled our exhausted bodies into my Jeep and made our way home.

"Mom, did you see that huge pile of zebra poop on the ground?" Piper held her arms about two feet apart, as Lucy giggled next to her.

The girls continued their poop discussion and argued over which animal would make the best mommy until they exhausted themselves and fell asleep in the backseat. When we got home, Mom came out and helped me carry them in. With Piper in my arms, I tiptoed through the kitchen, thankful my mom was walking in front of me and couldn't see my face when I passed the huge bouquet of beautiful pink and purple gladiolus on the island. I cringed when I saw that the card had the logo from the Twisted Petal on it. Alexa only had one employee, a teenage kid who made deliveries for her, so there was no question in my mind that she took this order and would be grilling me like a hamburger later.

I tucked the girls cozily in their beds and walked to my room to get ready to head to Alexa's shop. As much as I wanted to sprint into the kitchen and read the card, I wanted to get out of my mom's crosshairs more. She followed me to my room, her eyes focused on me, reading every awkward movement I was making around my bedroom.

She finally broke the silence. "So, what's the deal with the flowers?"

I turned to face her, expecting her to be judgmental.

"I have no idea, Mom. I haven't even looked at the envelope yet. I don't really want to."

Her eyes softened as she walked over and sat on my bed, patting the open space next to her. I went over and sat down.

"You like him, Kacie." I searched her eyes as she continued, curious where this conversation was headed. "I can tell. Why the hesitation?" She reached up and played with a strand of hair trailing down my back.

I immediately relaxed and rested my head on her shoulder. A mother's touch is so powerful; it makes you feel like the bad is actually tolerable.

"Mom, he's a hockey player, a *professional* hockey player. That type of lifestyle doesn't fit into ours."

"That's pretty presumptuous of you. You've spent two days with him. What can you possibly know about his lifestyle?"

I had no answer for her; she was right.

"Go to Alexa's. Talk to her. You need some girl talk, not advice from an old lady." She patted my knee and stood up, heading for my bedroom door.

"You're not an old lady. You're a pretty cool mom, and one of my best friends." I walked up behind her, wrapped my arms around her shoulders, and hugged. Her hand reached up and squeezed mine back.

"Thanks, Kacie; now go read that card. Maybe give Brody a shot—he had a cute rear end." She winked at me and closed my bedroom door.

I grabbed the card on my way out of the house a few minutes later. No way was I going to read it with my mom staring at me . . . but once I got to my car, I tore the envelope apart. It was a standard sage-green card from Alexa's shop, and the inside read . . .

It's been 3 days, you're killing me.
#30

My brain went into a fuzzy euphoric state. I couldn't believe he was still thinking about me. I was sure that once he went home and got back to his life of—whatever hockey players did—he'd forget I even existed. This wasn't fair, to me or to him; I definitely needed to text him and tell him thanks for the flowers but that we weren't possible. Just the thought of sending that text deflated me, but I was very good at compartmentalizing my thoughts, so I put that one away to deal with later. Right now I had sweet-and-sour chicken on the brain as I stopped at Chang's Kitchen and picked up takeout for Alexa and me.

The bell clanged as I walked through the bright red door of the Twisted Petal, which had closed an hour before, but Alexa hadn't locked up yet. I turned back and spun the silver latch to the left, jumping out of my skin when I heard Alexa bellow, "Three days since what? When did you meet Brody Murphy, and why the hell is he sending you flowers?"

I paused and leaned my forehead against her shop door, not ready for her onslaught of questions. When I turned to face her she was standing by the counter, her jet-black hair pulled up into a messy bun, hands on her hips, tapping her foot impatiently.

"I'll tell you all about it. Can we just eat first? I'm starving."

"You didn't know who he was?" Alexa exclaimed, rice flying out of her mouth and all over me.

"Keep your dinner to yourself, drama queen. No, I didn't know. How could I know? I watch baseball, not hockey."

"I thought everyone in the state of Minnesota knew who he was. I almost dropped the phone when he said his name, then I thought it was a postpubescent teenage boy pranking the shop, then he gave a credit card number and said they were for Kacie Jensen at the Cranberry Inn. I almost dropped the phone again."

A twinge of jealousy sprouted in my stomach and grew taller as Alexa told me about the rest of her conversation with Brody. I would have given anything to hear his voice again.

"Did he kiss you?" Her eyes sparkled, desperate for juicy details.

"Nope, nada."

"Kacie, you have this guy crazy enough to send you flowers and you haven't even kissed him yet?"

"It wasn't like that, *he* wasn't like that. He was really sweet." I sighed. "But God, I felt it, Lex. Every time our bodies accidentally touched—when he brushed past me and his hand rested on the small of my back, and when he smiled at me from across the dinner table—it was there. This ridiculous pull, this tension. It was totally there."

Alexa was frozen, her eyes the size of half-dollars and her fork suspended in midair halfway to her mouth. "Kacie, I haven't heard you talk about a guy like *that* in a long time . . . since Zach. You can't just let this go."

"Our lifestyles don't exactly match up. It would never work, and I'm not putting myself out there to get hurt again." I grabbed a piece of broccoli and popped it in my mouth.

"Do you know the last time Derek got me flowers? Let's see . . ." She looked up at the sky and tapped her chin. "Oh yes, I remember. I was seventeen, wearing braces, and the flowers were on a band on my wrist. And if I remember correctly, we capped off the night by doing it in the backseat of his parents' car."

"That's not fair, you *own* a flower shop. Should he call *you* to place your own order?"

"My point is, why shoot this down before it's even had a chance to get off the ground?"

"Alexa! He was arrested for swimming naked in Buckingham Fountain in Chicago, for Christ's sake! You think that's a good role model?"

Alexa threw her head back and laughed. "I remember reading about that. Boy, I would love to see that security camera footage. That man is scorching hot, and I'm assuming his southern hemisphere is pretty heavily populated, if you know what I mean," she said, wiggling her eyebrows up and down.

I picked up a fortune cookie and threw it at her. "You're not helping."

"Why do you need a good role model anyway? You're a grown woman," she teased, cracking the fortune cookie open.

"You know what I mean, Lex. I've got the girls to think about too. Anyone who comes into my life comes into theirs. I have to make good decisions."

"And I get that, but you're not dead, Kacie. You're young, you're hot, and you have a lot of life left. Those girls are going to grow up and move out one day. Then what? No one is saying you have to marry him, but lighten the fuck up. Have some fun." She paused, looking down. Her face swept back up, looking at me impassively, and she chuckled. "Here, I think this belongs to you." She reached over and handed me the small strip of paper from the fortune cookie.

IF YOU NEVER GIVE UP ON LOVE, IT WILL NEVER
GIVE UP ON YOU.

12

BRODY

Hey, Brody, it's Kacie. Thank you so much for the jersey and the flowers, especially the flowers. They are beautiful. It was very thoughtful of you. :)

I stared down at my phone, my mind a blank slate. Six days ago I met her, four days ago I left her my favorite jersey, yesterday I sent her flowers, today she was finally answering me, and now the noodles of my brain didn't want to connect enough to form a coherent sentence. I felt like an awkward fifteen-year-old kid trying hard not to fuck it up.

Smiley face. She put a smiley face—I might have a shot. I would have felt better about my odds if it were one of those winky faces, but I'd take what I could get.

Here goes nothing . . .

You're welcome, I'm glad you like them. Maybe next time I give you flowers, I can deliver them in person when I'm picking you up for dinner?

My heart pounded in my chest. I had never asked a girl out via text before, and it definitely wasn't my preferred method, but at this point, I'd take what I could get from her. It was forty-five minutes before my phone beeped again. Okay, it was really only two, but it felt like forty-five.

K: About that . . . it would be fun to have dinner, I'm just really busy right now with school and the girls.

Bullshit.

So, you don't eat during the school year? Thank God it's summer.

K: Of course I eat, I'm just kinda too busy right now for dating.

Dating in general or dating me?

Please say dating in general, please say dating in general.

K: I know this is going to sound really bad, but I have to be honest. You are great. I really like you. I just don't have the time to invest in something that will lead me down a dead-end road. Does that make sense?

Ouch.

That was the first time a girl had ever referred to my advances as a dead-end road, and it was a kick in the balls. Why was I so damn determined to get this girl to go out with me? She clearly had some deep scars and should be easy to walk away from, but instead of running the other direction, I wanted to scoop her up, clean her off, and make her world good again. I felt defeated.

Yeah, I get it. Friends?

K: Of course! Maybe the girls and I can come see a game sometime. :)

Fuck you, smiley face.

I was annoyed. She closed the door before I even got to it, and then locked it . . . twice. She knew nothing about me. How could she decide that quickly what should and shouldn't be? That day at the inn outside in the rain, there was a moment when we were hovering over a puddle, her arms around my neck, and it was there. She felt it; I felt it, even if I was the only one willing to admit it. I saw it in her eyes. Now here she was, less than a week later, feeding me a line of bull about why it wouldn't work. I wasn't sure if she was trying to convince me or herself.

The stale air in my condo was suffocating, and I needed to get out, work off some of this frustration. I snatched my cell phone from the coffee table. "Hey, you busy? Wanna meet me at The House in twenty minutes? Okay, see ya then."

One of the perks of being a professional hockey player is having a state-of-the-art fitness center and an ice rink available to me just about any time I wanted. In the locker room a few seasons ago, one of the guys referred to the stadium as "The House," and the nickname had stuck ever since. I pulled my truck into the parking lot and made a sharp left, stopping next to Viper, who was sitting in his truck on the phone, his driver's-side door wide open.

"Fine, do whatever the fuck you want!" Viper threw the phone across the cab of his truck, watching as it shattered when it bounced off the other side. "Fuck!" he yelled, running his hand through his shoulder-length blond hair and slamming his door.

"What's up, Murphy?" He shook my right hand and grabbed my shoulder with his left.

"Um, well . . ." I nodded toward his truck. "You're going to need a new phone."

"Yeah, second time this month I've broken one."

"What's going on?" I asked as we walked toward the stadium.

Viper sighed. "Same old shit. Kat thinks I'm cheating, so she's moving out. What else is new? I don't care anymore; she can go."

"Are you cheating . . . again?"

A shit-eating grin spread across his unshaven face as he looked at me out of the corner of his eye. "Maybe."

I reached around and smacked the back of his head. "You really live up to your name sometimes, Viper."

"Hey, I got that nickname because of the smooth way I slither on the ice. It's just fitting in my personal life too." He laughed.

Viper had been my teammate for three years now, and in that time, we'd grown pretty close. He always had my back, no questions asked, and I had his; however, I didn't always agree with his actions. He was too out of control, even for me. Lord knows I've done some stupid shit, but he was just plain old reckless. And he tore through women like a kid opened birthday presents, then tossed them aside when he was done, the same way. Kat had been around for several months, the longest one yet, as far as I knew. I stayed as far away from their drama as possible. I didn't understand their relationship. He cheated on her constantly, yet she kept coming back.

"Okay, Viper, I need you to kick my ass in the gym today. I want to be so sore my brain won't function after this workout."

"Sweet!"

After an hour and a half of dead lifts, shoulder presses, bicep curls, and about a thousand crunches, I cried mercy.

"Had enough?" Viper laughed.

I lay on the gym floor, chest heaving, arms and legs spread out like a snow angel, staring at the fluorescent lights on the ceiling. "Yes, no more arms, but I'm not nearly done. Let's hit the rink, Fabio."

"You're on."

I put my goalie pads on and prepared for Viper to shoot ninety-mile-per-hour slap shots, snap shots, and wrist shots at me. When I was in the net, my brain went somewhere else. I was in the zone, and that's exactly where I wanted to be right now, far away from reality. My eyes zeroed in, focused solely on keeping that three-inch piece of vulcanized rubber from getting past me, by any means necessary.

Two hundred shots or so later, Viper skated over to me and spit his mouth guard into his glove. "How ya feeling? You good?"

"Not yet, let's do some more."

"Brody, now *my* arms are going to fall off. Come on, man, let's call it a day. I gotta get home and make sure Kat didn't destroy all my shit."

I let out a frustrated sigh. "Fine." I took off my helmet and tossed my stick and gloves on top of the net.

"What's going on with you?"

"Nothing. Why?"

Viper looked annoyed. "Well, you missed a third of the shots I hit at you. Clearly, you suck today. Why don't you want to cut your losses and go home?"

I did miss a lot of shots, and Viper pointing it out just irritated me more.

"Eh, I'm off my game today, had a shitty morning."

Viper called out incredulously, "You and me both! What happened?"

I eyed Viper cautiously, not sure I wanted to talk about being turned down with the biggest playboy on the team. Vulnerability wasn't my strong suit.

Oh, fuck it.

"Um . . . a girl. I was into her and she shot me down. Didn't really say why. Seems like she doesn't like what I do for a living, and it's really pissing me off."

"I didn't know you'd been seeing anyone," Viper responded.

"I haven't, just met her last week when I was stuck up north in that damn storm. I wasn't even looking for anyone. I was driving along, minding my own business, and bam! Now I can't stop thinking about her."

Viper was quiet, staring off into space.

I sighed. "Go ahead, asshole. Give me shit about it, I can handle it."

"I'm not giving you shit, I was just trying to remember if in my whole life, there's ever been a girl that I couldn't stop thinking about. There have been girls I thought about for a night then forgot them shortly after I fucked them, but thinking about someone for a week? No way. That's worth fighting for, dude. Season's over, you have time. Turn the tables, prove her wrong. Then make her beg."

Viper was right, and I couldn't say that often. Kacie didn't know me; how could she possibly know that I was a dead-end road? She was making a snap judgment based on what I did for a living, and if I wanted any chance with her, I had to show her who I really was.

13

KACIE

"Now remember, you guys, you have to be quiet in here. Whispering only, okay?"

Lucy and Piper bounced along excitedly next to me as we made our way into the library. It was Princess Day at preschool story time, and while the girls sang about tiaras, I was going to find a quiet corner to do some studying. Even though it was summer, I wanted to try and get a jump on next fall's classes, but I hadn't picked my textbooks up in over a week. Microbiology was going to eat me alive if I didn't get my head out of the clouds.

I left the girls in the multipurpose room with a woman who was way too old to be dressing up like Cinderella and found a secluded table along the window overlooking the lake. I got all set up and cracked open my laptop. Up in the corner of my screen, the search bar still had my last search saved.

Brody Murphy.

My heart sank a little at the sight of his name. My eyes drifted out over the lake, getting lost in the ripples, thinking about our texts earlier that morning. He'd seemed disappointed, and frankly, so was I. If it were just me, I wouldn't have to be so cautious, but every decision I made directly affected Lucy and Piper. That thought weighed on me constantly. I had made enough mistakes in my life. I couldn't afford any more. Dating an athlete who traveled all the time and led a hectic, nonstructured lifestyle was not a luxury I could afford.

"Kacie?"

"Oh my God. Lauren!" I jumped up and threw my arms around my old friend. I pulled back but didn't let go of her hands. "You look fabulous! What are you doing in town? You normally call first—is everything okay?"

Lauren was a walking, talking Barbie doll, but not the plastic kind. She was an all-natural American beauty. I was convinced that her gene pool was made up of magical sparkling stream water from the tippy-top of the Alps. She was taller than me, though that wasn't saying much because most people were. She had long, wavy blond hair, sky-blue eyes, and legs that were two miles long. Her nails were always perfectly polished and no hair was ever out of place. From her looks, she should be a total stuck-up snob, but that was the furthest thing from the truth. She was in our same social circle in high school, but we got really close after I had the girls. When I got pregnant, most of my friends took off and distanced themselves, but Alexa and Lauren were my rocks. Zach was always somewhere else, but those two were constantly by my side, massaging my sore back and painting my toenails.

"Tommy and I are both back, actually, just visiting our parents. I brought my niece to that storybook lady and saw Lucy and Piper, so I had to find you. Boy, Cinderella probably shouldn't be wearing that outfit, huh?"

"Definitely not, but the kids go crazy for her. That's all that matters, I guess. Wanna sit?" I motioned toward the table.

"Sure! I'm actually really glad I ran into you . . . I was going to stop by your house later." Lauren chewed on the corner of her lip, her eyebrows creased nervously as she sat across from me.

"Okay, something's up." It was right then that I looked down at her hands and saw the huge rock on her left ring finger. "Oh my God! You're engaged?" I squealed.

The Mr. Rogers lookalike at the next table glared from under his unkempt, bushy gray eyebrows and shushed me.

"Sorry," I whispered loudly before I turned my attention back to Lauren. "When did this happen?"

"Yesterday. He took me to the park where we had our first date. At first I was annoyed because we were supposed to have dinner with my parents and we were running late. Once I realized what he was doing, I melted. I love him so much, Kacie."

I scooted around to Lauren's side of the table and sat down, pulling her into another hug. "I'm so happy for you guys." That wasn't a lie, I *was* happy for her, but I couldn't ignore the twinge of envy inside me.

"Thanks. That's actually why I was going to stop by later. I know it's sudden and I'm not being very original about it, but I wanted to ask if you'd be a bridesmaid for me?" She had tears in her eyes, tears of pure happiness. Seeing her overflow of emotion was contagious, and my own eyes started welling up for my dear friend.

"I would be honored to be in your wedding, Lauren. Wouldn't miss it for the world."

She let out a sigh of relief and smiled at me nervously. "I'm glad you feel that way, because we gotta get moving. The wedding is in two and a half months."

My jaw almost hit the table. "Are you pregnant?"

Lauren laughed and shook her head back and forth. "No, but Tommy got accepted into the master's photography program at the Liberal Academy of Fine Arts in Florence. We leave at the end of August and we won't be back until late next spring. We didn't want to wait that long to get married, and of course, we want our family and friends there, so . . . we're bumping it up. Big-time."

"You're moving to Italy? That's amazing!" My twinge doubled in size, just the way the Grinch's heart grew. I was ecstatic for Lauren, but she was living the life I wanted. Being a single parent of twins and still living with my mom at twenty-four wasn't exactly what I had planned. My petty jealousy disappeared and guilt took over when I saw the joy dancing across Lauren's face. She was glowing, and I owed it to her to ditch my pity party and be the best bridesmaid ever.

"I know, I'm beyond excited. I'm gonna grab some wedding magazines and we can browse. Be right back."

◆ ◆ ◆

Pulling into our driveway, I was momentarily taken aback by the slew of new cars in the driveway. I had forgotten it was Friday. "Wow, girls, lots of new people today," I said to them, and to myself.

"Mom, Piper got in trouble at story time," Lucy blurted out.

I spun around to face them in the backseat.

"I didn't get in trouble," Piper argued. "Cinderella told me to keep my voice down."

"Why? Were you yelling?"

"No. A second grader thinks she knows everything. She said her mommy was running a marathon tomorrow and I told her she was wrong. People can't run marathons. Marathons are when the same show is on TV all day long." Piper smirked and looked out her window, mighty proud of herself.

There goes my chance of winning Mother of the Year.

"Come on, weirdos. Let's go tell Gigi your story, she'll love that one."

We climbed out of the car and made our way to the front door. I stopped dead in my tracks, my heart leaping into my throat when I saw a familiar black pickup truck parked farther up the driveway. The girls didn't skip a beat, one passing on each side of me on their way to the front porch.

Okay, Kacie, stop being a freak. You saw his truck once and it was during a torrential downpour. No way is that the same truck.

I filled my lungs with crisp Minnesota air and exhaled slowly, urging my heartbeat to return to a normal pace.

The girls made their way through the front door, with me a few hesitant steps behind. I was putting our shoes in the closet when I heard the girls squeal from the back of the house. "Brody!"

My body froze.

Holy shit.

He was here. Why? To torture me? I closed the closet door and turned to make my way toward the kitchen, pausing in front of the mirror, making sure I looked presentable.

My mom was standing in the kitchen, leaning against the island with her arms folded across her chest, while Brody sat on a stool across from her. He had a baseball cap on, pulled down low. His eyes were shadowed so that I could hardly see them, but I knew he was staring at me. Lucy and Piper were kneeling on the ground petting Diesel, who was licking the leftover cookie crumbs from Cinderella off their faces.

"Hi, honey. How was story time?" My mom beamed at me like it was no big deal that the sexiest man I had ever laid my eyes on was sitting three feet to her left.

"Um, it was good. They had fun. What's going on?" I looked back and forth from my mom to Brody.

A small, cocky smile crossed his lips, but he didn't say a word. His stare was too intense. I looked back to my mom.

"Nothin', just hanging out. Brody called this morning to see if we had any vacancies, and we did, so he's staying for the weekend. Fred's a little giddy. He's out back restringing his fishing poles." Mom chuckled. "Come on, girls, let's take Diesel outside and give him some fresh water on the deck."

The girls hopped up and followed Mom to the back door with Diesel on their heels.

"Gigi, Piper got in trouble at story time," Lucy babbled to Mom on their way out the back door.

"So, what? You just needed a weekend getaway?" I said dryly to Brody once the back door closed.

"No, I missed Fred," he shot back with a wicked grin.

I rolled my eyes and turned to the fridge, grabbing a bottle of water and a bowl of grapes. Without turning around, I asked, "Can I get you anything, since you're a paying guest and all?"

He let out a short chuckle. "No thanks, but don't eat too much. We're leaving for dinner in a couple of hours."

I spun around and locked eyes with him. "Dinner?"

"Yeah . . . dinner," he replied confidently.

"But this morning we agreed—"

"We agreed to be friends. Friends have dinner together. I already asked your mom to babysit."

"You . . . when . . ." I sputtered words but no sentences.

"So, like I said . . . don't eat too much." He got up and pushed the stool in, locking eyes with me one more time. "I'd like you to be . . . hungry . . . when we go out later." He winked at me as he turned to head out the back door.

14

BRODY

My room at the inn was painted a calming shade of bluish gray, and thank God I don't mind that color, because I stared at it for two hours while I was hiding from Kacie. Not that I wanted to avoid her, but I knew I had gotten under her skin in the kitchen, and I wanted her thinking about me for a couple of hours before dinner, so I was out of sight. I stretched out on the bed, wondering what she was doing right now. Was she down in the kitchen giving the girls dinner? Was she reading on the back deck? Was she sitting at the island chewing on her bottom lip while concentrating on her nursing stuff? It was killing me to be this close but not talking to her, so I grabbed my phone.

Hey, I would like to pick you up for dinner at 7pm if that's okay?

I tapped my foot impatiently, waiting for her response.

K: 7 is fine. You are weird.

Why am I weird?

K: We are in the same house, yet you are texting me. Like I said, weird.

Just so you know, I'm very busy up here doing all sorts of important things.

K: Uh huh. Fred went up a little while ago to ask if you wanted to fish for a bit and he thought he heard snoring.

That was Diesel.

K: Sure it was. Where are we going tonight, anyway?

That's for me to know and you to find out.

K: Well, you have to give me a hint. I don't know what to wear.

Dress casual. Wear that little black number.

K: What black number?

The one you were wearing in the bathroom when Piper opened the door.

K: Ass :)

Oh, I see you're back again, smiley face. I hope you're ready to get your ass kicked this time. I'm gonna turn that one eye into a wink if it kills me.

I had forty-five minutes until I needed to pick Kacie up for our date: time to get moving. I grabbed my keys, left Diesel sleeping in my room, and headed downstairs.

"Hi, Brody!" Lucy and Piper called out as I passed the kitchen. No sign of Kacie anywhere.

"Hey, Twinkies! I'll be back soon, okay?"

"Shit!" The clock on my truck dashboard read 6:57.

Cutting it a little close, Murphy. Don't blow it.

I rang the doorbell. Sophia opened the door, her face contorted with confusion.

"Hi, Ms. Jensen. I'm here to pick up Kacie."

She giggled and stepped back. "Oh, you're adorable. Come in, Brody."

"These are for you." I handed her a small bouquet of tulips.

"They are beautiful, thank you." She furrowed her brow at me, still trying to figure everything out. "Hang on, I'll get Kacie."

She disappeared around the corner and I stayed in the foyer, waiting for my . . . friend. Lucy and Piper came tearing toward me from the back family room.

"Brody, are you sick?" asked Piper.

"Yeah, do you have a fever?" Lucy asked, tugging on my shirt.

I bent down to her level as she felt my forehead. "Nope, not sick. Why?"

They looked at each other and shrugged.

"Mom was on the phone with Auntie Alexa and she said you were hot. If you're hot, you have a fever. Do you need medicine?" Lucy continued the inquest.

"She said I was hot, huh? Interesting. I promise you, kiddo, I'm not sick, but thanks for checking on me."

I held my hand up and they each high-fived me before they ran off.

Kacie came around the corner and my mouth started salivating. She had on a white, lacy tank top and khaki shorts that showed off more of her legs than I had seen before. Her hair was pulled up in a messy bun with a few random pieces falling onto her collarbone. The closer she got, the more her green eyes sparkled. She looked simple, yet incredibly sexy. I was going to need a fucking straitjacket to keep my hands off of her all night.

"Hey," she said, smiling at me.

"Hey there." I leaned forward, giving her a quick "friendly" hug.

She smelled unbelievable; a lethal cocktail of flowers and her pheromones sent my mind into a goddamn tailspin. I wanted to drop to my knees and beg her to blow off the friend idea right now, but Viper's words kept ringing in my ear. "Turn the tables, prove her wrong, and then make her beg." Still drunk on her scent, the thought of Kacie begging for anything was enough to make me hard right there in the foyer.

"Ready to go?"

A small, skeptical smile splayed across her lips as she nodded at me. I stepped back and opened the door for her, following her out. She turned left off the porch, heading for my truck.

I reached out and grabbed her hand, tugging on it gently. "This way." I nodded to the right.

She looked surprised. "That way? There's nothing over—"

"Shh. Follow me."

She didn't resist again, gripping my hand back and following me around the side of the house. We didn't talk while we walked across the backyard for the couple hundred feet down to the lake. I peeked back at her, silently congratulating myself at the confused look on her face.

When we got to the edge of the yard, I made a slight left, still pulling her behind me. We stepped onto the creaky wooden boards of the pier, and I looked back at her again. Her eyes were fixed on the blanket and candles at the end of the pier. She looked at me and smirked, shaking her head.

"What?" I joked, defensively.

"The candles—those aren't exactly 'friend' candles." She nudged my shoulder without letting go of my hand. Any physical contact with her was a bonus. She could give me a noogie and I'd consider it a win.

"No, they aren't 'friend' candles, they're citronella. I didn't want you to get the wrong idea and start hitting on me or anything."

She laughed heartily and I silently put another tick in the win column.

As we got to the edge of the pier, I regretfully let go of her hand so I could go around to the other side of the blanket. I waited for her to sit first, then I followed suit.

She glanced down at the dinner I'd thought long and hard about. "Pizza and beer, huh?"

"Hey, if we were on a date, I would be trying to impress you. Since we're just pals, this is all you get."

She playfully stuck out her tongue and grabbed a Miller64 out of the cooler. She twisted the cap off and raised the bottle to her mouth, licking her lips before the bottle touched them. My khakis felt tight; I looked out at the water and talked to myself.

Speedboats. Green grass. Pringles. Jay Cutler.

I took a deep breath and looked back at Kacie, crisis averted. Her eyes were narrowed, mouth closed with her tongue running along her teeth. "What were you just thinking about?"

Ripping your clothes off and fucking you right here on this pier.

"Um . . . I'm just wondering how this friend thing is gonna work? I normally talk about beer and sports with my friends. I know that you're clearly not a hockey fan, so what should we talk about?"

She looked down at the pier, embarrassed that I'd reminded her that she didn't know who I was when we met. Little did she know that was one of the many things that attracted me to her.

"Let's talk about you," she said.

I pulled out the paper plates and handed her one. "Me?"

"Yeah, I blabbed enough about me the first night we met. Now it's your turn."

"Okay, what do you want to know?"

"Why don't you tell me about your last relationship?" She grabbed a slice of pizza and started nibbling on the end.

"I've never had a relationship."

"Liar."

"No joke. I've dated, but never anything serious. Hockey has been my life since I was ten years old. In high school, I was too focused on playing in college to date. Once I was in college, I was too focused on playing professionally. Now that I play professionally, I'm wary of every girl I meet." She searched my face, looking for a clue that I was being truthful. "I promise you. Google me; you won't find too many articles about me with girls."

"I already did, and you're right. No articles about girls, but I do know that you love fountains."

"Ah, you read about that one, huh? Did you see the mug shot too?" I scratched my head, wishing I could delete that completely off the Internet. "It was a fun night, but it got a little out of hand."

"That's a story I want to hear . . ."

"Long story short, I was dared. We were playing in Chicago, and my buddy Viper and I went out after the game for drinks. I had too much liquid courage in my system, and Viper dared me to drop trou and splash around for five minutes. I had two minutes left when a couple of bike cops pulled up and dragged my ass out of there and cuffed me. They realized who I was and might even have let me go had I not made some obnoxious remark about them ringing a bell instead of having a siren. They didn't appreciate that too much."

"Viper, huh? Sounds like someone who would definitely be involved in the sport of fountain skinny-dipping."

"Speaking of skinny-dipping . . ." I raised my eyebrows at her.

"Not a chance," she said, shaking her head back and forth.

I grabbed the collar of my shirt and acted offended. "I wasn't asking, geez. Who do you think I am? I'm not that easy."

"Oh, I highly doubt that."

"Someone who is sitting on a pier in a white tank top should be careful of the jokes she makes, don't you think?"

She laughed nervously, wondering if I was brave enough to toss her into the lake. I wasn't.

"Speaking of the pier, how did you pull all this off, by the way?"

"Well, it's not always easy for me to sit in a restaurant or bar and talk in peace, but I wanted to get you out of the house and have you to myself for a while—just as friends, of course—so a picnic was the next best thing. And what better place to have a picnic than on a pier? I looked out the window from inside the house and saw that it was private, so I put my plan into action."

"I've never had a picnic on the pier," she said matter-of-factly.

I reached over and high-fived her. "Me either." I shrugged my shoulders nonchalantly and continued, "I've also never had sex on a pier."

She shook her head again, pushing the pizza box out of the way.

"What are you doing?" I asked, hoping she wasn't cleaning up to go in.

"It's pretty dark. Let's lay on our backs and look up at the stars."

God, yes.

Who knew something as simple as looking up at stars and talking could be so enjoyable? Conversation was easy with her. It felt like we'd been friends forever. We talked for hours about everything and nothing. At one point, probably because of the beer, I got ballsy and reached out for her hand. She didn't skip a beat. She just intertwined her fingers with mine and kept telling me about her and Alexa's crazy high school adventures. What a fucking coincidence that the place I ordered her flowers from was her best friend's shop. That might come in handy later, actually.

A few hours later, she swatted at her leg for the hundredth time and sighed. "We should probably go in. I'm getting eaten up."

I pulled my phone out of my pocket and lit it up to check the time. Twelve forty-five.

"Yeah, I guess you're right. I promised Fred I'd be up by six and out here on the lake with him."

She crawled over and blew out the candles while I folded the blanket. "He's really crazy about you, ya know? He's so glad you're here."

I looked straight into her eyes. "Is he the only one?"

She stared back at me, frozen. Her eyes looked sad and she bit down on her bottom lip. "Don't do that, Brody. We can't go there."

I smiled a sincere, genuine smile at her. "That's fine. I'll let you off the hook . . . for now."

15

KACIE

I lay in bed, listening to the girls giggling in the next room and replaying last night over and over in my mind. I hadn't laughed that hard in a long time and it felt amazing. A day that started out with crappy texts ended with us lying hand in hand on the pier, watching the stars. My head was still spinning, and that was the problem.

Brody was like a drug. When I was with him, my mind was in this hazy, euphoric state, but once the smoke cleared, I realized that I was just setting myself up for disaster. How many red flags did I need?

He was a professional athlete.

He lived an hour and a half away, even when he *wasn't* traveling.

He admitted last night that he'd never been in a serious relationship.

All of those things were the exact opposite of the qualities I needed. Brody and I had chemistry, no doubt about that, but I needed to keep him at arm's length. He was my Kryptonite.

I dragged myself out of bed, reluctant to leave the safety of my own room. I turned into a melted pile of goo when Brody zeroed in on me, and he was going to be here for two more days. I had to try my hardest to stay solidified.

My cell phone chirped. I looked over at the pile of textbooks sitting on my desk with my phone perched on the top, calling my name. I was worried that if it was another charming text from Brody, nothing would stop me from running up to his room, ripping my clothes off as I went. I walked over and peeked at my phone with one eye. It was from Lauren. Thank God!

L: Hey, what are you and the girls up to today?

No plans, just hanging.

L: Sweet! There's a fair over in Lake County, I'm taking my niece. Wanna go with?

Yessssssssss!

L: Sweet! We'll be by in an hour.

An all-day fair was exactly what I needed to keep myself occupied and out of the house for the day. I ran off to tell the girls about our exciting new plans.

Lucy and Piper were in their room filling their backpacks with stuffed animals and arguing over which flavor slushy they were going to have first, while I ransacked the kitchen, packing my bag full of pretzels, Band-Aids, and hand sanitizer.

The back door creaked open, but I didn't turn to see who came in. I already knew. I could feel it.

"Morning!" Brody said cheerfully.

"Hey," I responded without turning around.

"How are you today? I'm exhausted." He yawned.

"I'm okay."

"What's wrong? You're being short with me."

I turned and looked at him. He was wearing a Minnesota Wild T-shirt that showed off his vast, strong shoulders and clung to his biceps perfectly. He had his Wild ball cap on again, facing backward this time. The hunter-green hat made his already dazzling green eyes pop, and I was hypnotized. I had to look away to regain my composure.

"Am I? I don't mean to be." I went to the fridge and grabbed a few juice boxes, tossing them in my bag. "I'm just in a rush. The girls and I are going to the fair over in Lake County today."

"Nice—that oughta be fun. Want company?"

My heart plummeted through my body, through the subfloor, through the foundation, and landed in a patch of dirt and weeds under the house. I didn't want to tell him no, but I couldn't hang out with him much longer and continue dodging his advances.

"Um, well, I was thinking the girls and I need some time alone today. Please don't be upset."

He grinned at me and tilted his head to the side. "Kacie, I would never, ever be upset with you for wanting to spend time alone with your kids. Ever. Go, have fun. Meet you on the pier later?"

"Maybe." I smiled at him, wishing he weren't such a sweet guy. He would be much easier to avoid if he were an asshole.

There was a loud knock at the front door.

"Be right back."

I could feel his eyes on me like a tattoo when I walked out of the kitchen.

I opened the front door and Lauren burst through it, swaddling me in a hug, almost knocking me on my ass. She let go and Tommy stepped up. "My turn."

He wrapped his arms around me with a big bear hug and lifted me off the ground.

"Long time no see, Tommy. Congratulations!" I planted a peck on his cheek.

"Thanks, Kacie. I'm a lucky man." He reached over and squeezed Lauren's hand as they smiled at each other.

"Okay, if you two are going to do that all day, you're gonna make me puke," I teased as I squatted down in front of Lauren's niece, Molly. "Hey, Molly. Piper and Lucy are so excited to play with you today."

She grinned shyly and hid behind Lauren's leg.

"So, who all is going? Did you call Alexa and Derek?" Lauren asked.

"Yeah, she's a sloth. She had a long week and apparently her delivery boy called in sick today, so she had to get up super early and make all the deliveries. She went home and crashed again."

"Bummer. All right, well, let's get moving!" Lauren clapped her hands in excitement.

"Let me grab the girls and my bag from the kitchen." I turned and started down the hall with them trailing behind me.

Brody was standing in front of the fridge, scratching his chin.

I looked at him, feeling incredibly guilty. "We're gonna head out. I'll see you later?"

"Yeah, I'll be here." He turned and smiled at me sweetly, nodding respectfully at my friends.

"Holy shit! You're Brody Murphy!" Tommy exclaimed.

Brody looked over as Lauren smacked Tommy's arm and covered Molly's ears. "Tommy, watch your mouth!"

"Sorry, babe, but he's Brody Murphy." Tommy just stared at Brody, his eyes wide and mouth hanging open.

"Hey, man, nice to meet you." Brody walked over and shook Tommy's hand.

Tommy returned the handshake like an eager kid. "Wait . . . what are you doing *here*?"

"Uh, I'm staying for the weekend. Kacie and I are . . . friends."
Brody looked at me out of the corner of his eye.

"Kacie! How could you not tell me you're friends with Brody Fucking Murphy?"

"Tommy!" Lauren and I both reprimanded at the same time.

"Is he going with us? Are you going with us?" Tommy blurted out, his eyes jumping back and forth between Brody and me.

"Jesus, calm down, Tommy. I hope you're this excited to meet our firstborn one day." Lauren sounded annoyed.

"Uh, well, if our kid comes out as the NHL MVP, then yes."

"Okay, can we just stop all this and go, please? Girls! Come on!"
I hollered down the hall. Lucy and Piper came running and huddled around Molly, hammering the poor girl with questions.

"Yes . . . but . . . is Brody going?"

"Yes, Brody is going. Come on already." I threw my hands up in the air and grabbed my bag off the counter, slinging it over my shoulder.

"I am?" Brody looked at me, utterly confused.

"Yes, you are. Let's go." I started pushing everyone toward the front door.

"I smell like fish," he argued, spinning around to face me.

"You smell great. Hush." I grabbed his shoulders and turned him back around, thoroughly enjoying the view from behind.

Once outside, Lauren turned to me. "Uh, my car isn't going to fit everyone; we'll have to take two."

"No biggie, I can drive too." I shrugged my shoulders.

"Mommy, can we ride in Molly's car?" Lucy asked, sticking her bottom lip out.

Piper stepped up behind her, clasping her hands together. "Pleeeeeeeeease?"

"It's fine with me." Lauren opened the car door, waving them in.

"Can I ride with Brody?" Tommy copied the girls, sticking his bottom lip out and clasping *his* hands together.

Lauren narrowed her eyes and glared at him. "Only if you want him moving to Italy with you instead of me."

Tommy's eyes drifted up toward the sky, pretending to contemplate her offer. Lauren sighed and got in her car with Tommy right behind her.

"Wanna drive *my* truck?" Brody grinned at me.

Before I could answer, he tossed his keys to me and walked to the passenger's side of his truck. I looked down at his keys in my hand, panic-stricken.

"Your truck? No way! I can't drive a truck." I fiercely shook my head.

He peeked his head around the back of the truck and grinned at me. "Get your ass in the truck and turn the key."

I climbed into his truck, my heart thumping so loudly against my sternum I was sure he could hear it.

"What do I do?" I tried to act composed, but my insides were rattling.

Brody's hand reached over and squeezed my knee. "Hey, look at me."

His face was relaxed, with a lopsided smile showing off one of his sexy dimples. His eyes were serene.

"Relax, it's just a truck. It's an automatic. You know what to do. Come on, start her up, they're about to leave without us."

I don't know if it was his warm hand on my knee or his soothing voice, but I felt much better, calm even. My confidence grew with each second as I put the key in the ignition and started the engine. It took me a few minutes to get used to the bigger truck and the engine, which was much more powerful than my little SUV.

"So, what made you change your mind?" Brody asked, propping his foot up on the dashboard.

I turned my head toward him without taking my eyes off the road. "Change my mind?"

"About me coming along."

"Oh, I don't really know." I shrugged. "I thought it would be fun . . . and friends go to fairs together."

"Touché." Brody smirked and looked out the window.

We rode the last ten minutes in silence. Not awkward silence where you feel uncomfortable just being together; it was contented silence. I knew he was thinking about me, and he knew I was thinking about him. That silence was louder than any words we could have spoken.

His hand never did leave my knee, and I liked it.

We walked through the fair gates, and the scent of cotton candy and funnel cakes filled the air.

"Wow! Crowded today; everyone stay together," Lauren said, aiming her attention at the girls.

"I'm gonna go grab tickets, be right back." Brody's hand grazed the small of my back as he walked by, sending shivers up my spine like another hit in my bloodstream.

"Hey, Tommy, can you take the girls over and get them some water before we start with the rides?" Lauren asked.

Tommy grabbed Molly's hand, which was already linked up with Lucy's and Piper's, and off they went.

"What. The. Hell?" Lauren blurted out, spinning to face me. "I've been dying to get you alone. When did this start? Why didn't you tell me yesterday?"

I laughed. "There's nothing to tell, Lauren. We're friends."

"Yeah, okay, whatever. Seriously, what's going on with you two? Hurry, before he comes back."

I looked over toward the ticket booth at Brody, who had been stopped by a small group of teenage boys. He was signing autographs and taking pictures, giving each kid a turn with his undivided attention.

"Really, there's nothing going on. He showed up last weekend when he couldn't get through town because of the flooding at the bridge, and we became friends. That's all."

"I'm not an idiot, Kacie. In that kitchen I watched him, watching you. Tommy would never look at me like that, except maybe if I were walking toward him butt naked carrying a heaping plate of bacon."

"We've talked about this, Lauren. You know what I'm looking for. He doesn't exactly fit the mold, ya know? I'm playing it safe."

"Screw your mold, Kacie. Make a new one. He's completely smitten with you, and you are with him."

I sighed, growing frustrated. "Can we just not talk about feelings and futures and any of that crap today? I just want to have fun with everyone and give my brain a rest for a few hours. Fighting with yourself is exhausting."

She didn't have time to argue again because Brody jogged back over.

"What did you buy?" I exclaimed, gaping at the sheets of tickets in his hand.

"Uh . . . like thirty sheets of tickets? Think that's enough?"

Lauren's mouth hung open. "That's like six hundred tickets!"

"We better get moving then." Brody reached down and grabbed my hand, pulling me toward Tommy and the girls.

We spent the next six hours filling up on hot dogs and nachos and riding every single ride there . . . twice. I wasn't a big fan of fair rides, not the high ones anyway. I had a crippling fear of heights that kept me grounded the entire day. I was perfectly content sitting on a bench while those crazies spun and flipped their day away.

"Okay, guys, one more ride, and then I think it's time to call it a day. Auntie Lauren isn't used to all this. I need a bubble bath and a bottle of Tylenol." Lauren plopped on the bench next to me.

"Whose idea was it to wear the cute wedges to a fair, knucklehead?" I shoulder bumped her.

"Can we do that one again?" Lucy pointed to a bizarre contraption that took them up in the air in a car-looking thing and spun them for four minutes. I would rather have a root canal.

"You guys do whatever you want. I'll be here." I pulled Lucy onto my lap, kissing her cheek.

"Come on, guys!" She hopped off my lap and sprinted toward the ride with Piper and Molly right behind.

Lauren took off after them. Tommy turned to Brody. "You coming?"

"No thanks, I'm gonna sit this one out."

"See you guys in a minute." Tommy jogged to catch up with the others.

Brody sat down next to me on the bench. "You having fun?"

I looked over and smiled. "Yeah, I am. It's been a great day. I'm glad you came."

Brody stared off into space, his eyebrows pulled together, deep in thought.

My curiosity got the better of me. "What?"

"Do you trust me?"

I stared at him nervously out of the corner of my eye, the hair on the back of my neck standing up. I hesitated before answering.

"Do you?" he repeated, leaning forward, his eyes concentrating on mine.

"Yes."

He took a hold of my hand tightly and stood up, nodding to his right. "Follow me."

We walked behind the snow cone trailer and I realized we were walking straight toward the Ferris Wheel of Death. Okay, that wasn't really the name, but it should have been.

I pulled my hand from his, stopping dead in my tracks.

"No way, Brody." All of the cells in my body went hypersensitive and my arms and legs started tingling. My chest felt tight and I couldn't take a full breath.

He turned to face me, grasping my shoulders gently. "Kacie, look at me. You can do this, trust me."

"I can't." I meant that literally. I couldn't will my feet to move even if I wanted them to.

"Look in my eyes. Yes, you can. You said you trusted me, now come on. Jump in puddles with me."

I looked into his eyes, trying to understand the words he was saying, but my brain had sputtered to a halt. Puddles? What the hell was he talking about?

Suddenly, it hit me. Last week in the storm, the puddles. I let go of control a little that day, and it actually felt really good. This, though, was different. I had *no* control up there.

"I don't think I can." My voice was shaky, terror constricting my every movement.

"Yes, you can. One foot in front of the other. Come on, I got ya. Just keep looking at me." Brody started walking backward, still holding on to my shoulders. He never took his eyes off mine, except to peek backward and make sure he wasn't going to bump into anyone.

When we got to the entrance of the ride, everything inside me was screaming to run. Brody still had a gentle but firm grip on my shoulders and wasn't about to let me go anywhere.

He trailed a path from my shoulders to my hands, never losing contact with me as he squeezed my hands tight in his. He turned and nodded at the young, tattooed ride attendant, who opened the silver gate and let us through. Brody didn't let go of my trembling hand as he led me onto the ride. I sat down, already terrified to look to my side, and we weren't even off the ground yet. He let go of my hand and stepped out of the ride, and I panicked.

"I'm not going anywhere, I promise. Just one sec," he reassured me, probably sensing that I was about to climb over the back of the seat and sprint straight for the parking lot.

He stepped away and whispered something into the kid's ear and then handed him something. I was too preoccupied thinking about death to care what it was.

He walked over and slid in the seat next to me. I immediately reached for him, and he put his right arm around me. I snuggled up as close as I could, laying my head on his chest. He took his phone out of his pocket with his left hand.

"What are you doing?" I blurted out, not wanting him to make any movements at all.

"Tommy gave me his number earlier, I'm just letting them know where we are." He snickered.

His laugh vibrated through my body, calming my nerves a bit. My peace was shattered when the fair kid slammed the metal bar down in front of us. I flinched and Brody squeezed my shoulders tight.

"We're okay," he whispered into my hair, his thumb rubbing back and forth on my shoulder.

The ride squeaked as it started turning, and I buried my face deeper in his chest. We went very slowly, stopping about ten seconds later, I assumed to let people off and more people on, though I didn't dare crack my eyes open to look.

We did that about twenty more times before the ride started picking up speed. The faster it went, the tighter I pinched my eyes, my face still buried in Brody's stinky fish shirt. Every revolution, my stomach flip-flopped from my feet to my head, and I was praying for it to be over soon. Up, down. Up, down. Brody had moved his hands from my shoulder to the nape of my neck, and he was stroking my hair, trying to keep me calm. He didn't talk the whole ride and I was thankful for that.

The ride ground to a halt, but I refused to move. I felt us go up, but we never came back down. I knew we were stuck at the top.

What were the fucking odds?

"Okay, Kacie. Open your eyes," Brody said softly.

I didn't respond. I just shook my head no.

"Come on, please?"

I shook my head again.

"I promise we're safe. It's breathtaking. Just a quick peek?"

I let out a deep breath and opened one eye without taking my head off his chest. All I could see were our feet. I opened the other eye, still not lifting my head.

"Take your time, when you're ready." He continued playing with my hair.

Lifting my head so that it was off his chest but still leaning on him, I looked straight ahead. I could barely see over the front of the car, but I could see enough to tell that we were high, really high.

"Don't look down, look out."

The sun was about to go down behind the tall pine trees. The sky was a beautiful palette of pink, orange, and purple swirls. Airplanes left squiggly smoke trails, framing the stunning sunset.

"If you can, look to your right."

I didn't turn my head but strained my eyes over to the right. In the distance was a big lake dotted with sailboats and buoys. The sun glistened off the water like fireworks.

The longer I sat there taking in the view, the more I relaxed. I sat up straight, off of Brody, to get a better look at everything. He was right; it was amazing up here. I could see for miles.

After a few minutes of my eyes dancing all around the county, I turned to him. He was just staring at me, a faint smile on his lips.

"Thank you." It was my turn to squeeze his knee.

"You know why I insisted you come up here?" He leaned back in his seat, not letting go.

I didn't respond, just stared into his eyes.

"You were so scared, Kacie, just like you are about life. I wanted you to see that sometimes, even when something terrifies you, if you just give it a chance, it's actually pretty incredible."

My eyes welled up with tears. This man was amazing, and I . . . was an idiot.

Not wanting to waste one more second, I swooped over and planted my lips right on Brody's. He responded eagerly, taking my face in his hands. He kissed me back slowly, taking his time tasting my lips, expertly pulling each one into his mouth. He sucked gently on my lower lip, and I let out a soft moan that fueled his fire. His tongue gently licked across my bottom lip, and I opened my mouth, giving him access. He sat up straighter, his thumbs gently rubbing my cheekbones as his warm tongue explored my mouth. We moved perfectly in sync, like we had been kissing for years, losing ourselves in our surroundings and each other.

Our perfect moment was interrupted when the Ferris wheel started moving again. My hands fisted his shirt out of fear, and I immediately pulled back and tucked my head back on his chest. He chuckled and started playing with my hair again.

"Do me a favor, Kacie. Just keep your eyes open, okay?"

I watched as we slowly got closer and closer to the ground, relief washing over me when the ride came to a stop at the bottom. My body was exhausted from the combination of tension and lust I had just experienced. I didn't even know if I could walk anymore. As the metal bar lifted and we stood up, I looked around, realizing that there was no one else on the Ferris wheel. We had been the only ones. I looked up at Brody, who enveloped my hand with his and smiled down at me sweetly. He shook the hand of the kid running the ride as we walked by.

"Thanks, kid."

"Thank *you*, Mr. Murphy."

We walked for a few minutes, still hand in hand, while I came down from my latest high.

"What just happened? I don't . . . how did you . . ." I couldn't get the words out.

"Eh, he's young. Most young kids would do just about anything for a hundred-dollar bill."

My heart soared like those airplanes we'd just seen, and I squeezed his hand, when reality hit me.

"Oh my God, the girls. We need to look for everyone." I scanned the nearby benches and lemonade stands but saw no sign of them.

Brody took out his phone.

"Are you texting Tommy again?" I asked, still looking through the herds of people.

"Uh, I will in a minute." He looked up at me with a devilish grin on his face. "After what you just did up there, I'm ordering a Ferris wheel to be installed at your mom's place tomorrow."

16

BRODY

Ever since we got off that Ferris wheel, Kacie had been very different with me—more affectionate. I was ecstatic about it. I offered to let her drive again on the way home.

"No freaking way! I don't think my nerves can handle one more thing today." She climbed up into the passenger seat and snuggled up for the drive home. "I was thinking we could lounge around and watch a movie after I put the girls to bed?"

"Sounds perfect."

She reached over, laced her fingers in mine, and closed her eyes.

Once home, Kacie took the girls to their rooms and tucked them in while I took Diesel out for a long walk. He gave me the cold shoulder, clearly annoyed that I'd blown him off all day for a girl. He'd better get used to it, because if it were up to me, Kacie was going to become a permanent fixture in my very near future.

Diesel and I played some makeup fetch, and then he pranced around the lake for a while, trying to prove his masculinity by biting fish. I was also stalling. I didn't want to smother Kacie. We'd had a monumental day, in my opinion, and I didn't want to pressure her to hang with me and have her freak out again. After a little bit, D and I headed back up to the house.

We walked through the back door. Kacie was already curled up on the couch under a blanket, a sexy, sleepy look on her face as she looked up at me. I walked over and sat down on the other end of the couch near her feet. She immediately sat up and crawled over, lying back down with her head on my lap.

"What are we watching?" I asked her, not even remotely interested in the TV.

"*You've Got Mail*." She looked up at me, nervously awaiting my response, which she got when I rolled my eyes and fake snored.

"Come on," she argued, batting her long eyelashes at me. "It's romantic, the way they fall in love without ever meeting."

"I'll watch anything you want. I'll even suffer through the Kardashians, as long as you stay right where you are."

She beamed up at me, struggling to keep her pretty green eyes open.

"I think we should talk later, you know . . . about stuff. I'm just too tired now," she murmured, cozying up to me.

"I know, we will." I threaded my fingers in her hair, rubbing her forehead with the pad of my thumb. "Not now, though, tomorrow. Just rest."

She didn't resist. The corners of her plump, pink lips curled up in a half smile, and she blinked one last time. I watched her, waiting to see if her eyes would flutter open again. It's a very relaxing thing watching someone fall asleep, that moment when they lose all control of their minds and surrender to their subconscious. They say you often dream about something that happened in your day, good or bad. I was pretty sure I'd be dreaming about Ferris wheels later. I hoped she was too.

I quietly propped my feet up on the coffee table, careful not to disturb her head, and slowly shimmied the remote from her lifeless hand.

Kacie asleep on my lap and SportsCenter on the TV . . . heaven.

◆ ◆ ◆

"Brody. Brody, wake up."

I pried my eyes open and lifted my head to see who was calling my name as pain shot up the right side of my neck. I must have fallen asleep in a funny position, but I was groggy and the last thing I remembered was watching *Baseball Tonight*'s Web Gems with Kacie sound asleep on my lap. Where was she, anyway?

"You okay?" Fred asked in a loud whisper.

I rubbed the pain away. "Yeah, I'm fine, Fred."

"Let's go fishing again." A wide grin crossed Fred's face, making him impossible to turn down, even though I wanted nothing more than to crawl up the stairs to my room and go back to sleep. I grabbed my phone to check the time but all I noticed was the little envelope lit up in the top right corner signaling a text from Kacie.

"Sure, Fred, I'm up for fishing again. Just give me a minute to use the bathroom and grab a quick bite and I'll meet you out there."

His face lit up as he reached down and patted my shoulder. "Sounds good. See you in a few minutes."

I gave him a little wave as he disappeared out the back door, and then turned my attention back to my phone.

Hey! I went to bed but I didn't want to wake you because you looked so peaceful. See you at breakfast. :)

Relief washed over me. I was slightly worried that after her little nap she would wake up feeling like she'd made a huge mistake and possibly regret last night, especially that kiss.

Holy shit, that kiss.

"Thought maybe you'd bailed on me," Fred said as I sauntered down the hill toward his run-down red canoe.

I ran my hand through my hair and forced a smile at him. "Nope, just moving slow this morning, sorry."

"No problem." He hopped out of the canoe and walked around next to me, motioning to his small wooden deathtrap. "Let's push her off and hop on in."

Don't get me wrong, I didn't mind fishing with Fred at all; it was actually really relaxing. We'd just had a really long day yesterday, both physically and mentally exhausting, and I didn't exactly sleep well sitting straight up on the couch overnight.

I liked Fred, but I *loved* sleep.

It really was a beautiful morning out on the lake, though. The fog was still sitting just on top of the calm water; the birds were just starting to chirp, not a soul around. Fred and I paddled about fifty yards from the shore before he spoke again. "This look good?"

"Sure. Looks great," I said in between yawns.

"You're gonna let the flies in," he teased.

"I don't know what's wrong with me today, I'm never like this." I reached down and scooped up a small handful of lake water and splashed it on the back of my neck, hoping the shock of the chilly water would wake me up.

"Well, sleeping on that couch like you were all night certainly doesn't help. I'm glad you came out here with me, though, I want to talk to you." He stared off in the distance and squinted his eyes. "I've known Sophia and Kacie for about ten years now. Sophia and I have grown to be great friends, and Kacie . . . well, she's like a daughter to me, Brody." He looked me square in the eye and I focused right back on his. "I don't know how much she's told you about her past, but when that little prick left her four years ago, it devastated her."

Kacie hadn't filled me in on many details yet, so part of me felt like I was betraying her by listening. The other part of me didn't dare interrupt him, because I wanted every bit of information I could get about her.

He continued, "When she called her mom from Minneapolis and told us that he was gone, we immediately went into worker-bee mode. Painting rooms, putting together cribs, buying stuffed animals . . . all so they would feel at home when they got here. When they did finally arrive a few days later, they weren't ten feet in the door when Kacie set the girls down and collapsed in her mom's arms. She didn't leave her bed that whole first week." Fred took his glasses off and used his pointer finger and thumb to rub his eyes. I wasn't sure if he was tired also, or if he was getting choked up reliving this. "Sophia would make her food and take it in to her. An hour later she would go get it and bring back an untouched plate along with a small trash bag full of tissues. She was crushed, heartbroken." He let out a heavy sigh.

I put my hand up before he started talking again. "Wait, I don't get it. If he was such an asshole, wouldn't she be happy he was gone?"

He looked down at the bottom of the boat, kicking at loose paint with his worn-out leather boots. "I'm sure she didn't tell you anything about her dad either?"

She hadn't said one word about him. I just shook my head, not sure I wanted to hear any more about what she'd gone through.

"I can't say too much about that; I wasn't around when he was. All I really know is that he was Kacie's hero. She followed him around like a shadow her whole life, a real daddy's girl. Then one day, he up and left Sophia and Kacie when Kacie was ten. Divorced Sophia and left her for another woman, never really kept in touch with Kacie either. When Kacie found out she was pregnant, she was hell-bent on keeping her family together and giving the girls all that she didn't have. Then when Zach left, she felt like she was not only reliving everything with her dad again, but she'd somehow failed Lucy and Piper too."

We both sat in silence for a minute, staring at our feet, taking it all in.

"Anyway, the reason I'm telling you all this is because I made a promise to myself during that time that I would never allow someone to hurt Kacie like that again. She's an amazing girl, as you've seen. She's smart, she's beautiful, and she's an outstanding mom. Those girls are her life and she protects them fiercely. Sophia and I both agree, though, she does deserve more—she deserves to be happy." He looked up from his boots and stared at me again, his eyes softer now. "I haven't seen her look at a man like she's looking at you . . . ever. Not even Zach. In all honesty, Brody, it scares the hell out of me."

"Let me stop you for a second, Fred. I don't know what you've heard or read about me, but I'm not a bad man. I'm not a love-'em-and-leave-'em man. I'm not a playboy. I've never been in a serious relationship, though I'm not sure that's a good thing." He let out a nervous laugh as I continued. "What I *do* know is that I like Kacie. I like her a lot. Am I in love with her? No, I just met her a week ago, but there's something about her that just gets to me. Something that keeps me wanting to spend more and more time with her, and I'd like to explore that."

Our eyes were locked, and a faint smirk teased the corners of his mouth as I kept going.

"I know that what I do for a living is hard for some people to grasp. It's not typical, and it's not always an ideal situation, but I'm really hoping that it won't interfere with Kacie and me. I also hope *no one* will interfere."

His eyebrows shot up in surprise, but his smile remained.

Crap, I didn't meant for that last part to come out so aggressive.

"I like you, Brody. I don't know why yet, but I like you. Please be gentle with her. She acts like a tough, stubborn little shit, but she's fragile." He extended his hand out to me, and I grasped it with my right hand, then clapped his with my left.

"You have my word, Fred. No games."

The corners of his eyes crinkled as he smiled and nodded once at me. "Good, 'cause this lake is pretty deep out there in the middle, and I have a lot of old weights from my military days just laying around, looking for a new purpose."

17

KACIE

"You look like hell." I stared wide-eyed at Brody as he closed the back door and dragged himself across the family room, collapsing on the kitchen table.

"I feel like it," he responded as his head fell onto his folded forearms.

"Have you been out with Fred *all* morning?" I walked over and stood across the table from him.

He lifted his head and rubbed his eyes. "Yeah, since about six. We probably would have stayed longer, but it started pouring on us."

I looked out the oversize family room windows at the rain, bummed that the girls and I would be stuck inside for the day.

"Did you catch anything?"

He laughed, seemingly amused by my question.

"What?" I asked defensively.

"Nothing," he said, shaking his head, a slight grin still apparent on his face. "Yeah, we caught a few bass and we talked . . . a lot."

Panic flared in me. "Uh-oh, what does that mean?"

He looked at me without saying anything, and his eyes danced around my face. When he stared at me like that, he made me feel like I was under a microscope. Instead of metal clips holding me down, it was his two piercing green eyes.

"It means that Fred really cares about you. You're a lucky girl." He took my hand, gently kissing the top of it. My skin tingled where he'd kissed it, even after he pulled his lips away.

"Mom, what's for breakfast?"

I pulled my hand back quickly when Lucy came in the room. Looking at Brody, I was relieved when he smiled and winked at me, not at all offended that I hadn't wanted her to see his affection for me.

"I don't know. What should we make today?" I scooped up Lucy and sat her on the island, eye to eye with me.

Her father's brown eyes looked up toward the ceiling as she contemplated what she wanted to eat. "Chocolate chip pancakes!" she answered excitedly.

"Coming right up." She wiggled to get down, but I caught her knee before she was able to get away. "Uh . . . pay the toll."

She giggled and gave me a big smooch before hopping off the island and disappearing back down the hall.

I grabbed the pancake mix and chocolate chips out of the cabinet and tossed them on the island, glancing over at Brody, who was still sitting at the table with his elbows bent, hands clasped together, staring at me.

"What are you looking at?"

Without moving his folded hands from in front of his mouth, he raised one eyebrow in response to my sarcastic tone. He stood up from the table and slowly stalked over to me, stopping just inches from my chest. His left hand rested on the island to my right, while his other hand purposely grazed my elbow as he leaned in, reaching for the bag of chocolate chips and pinning my hips to the island.

"Just thought I'd help you make pancakes." His taunting tone was husky with underlying meaning as he bent down, his lips nearly touching mine. "My specialty is licking . . . the spoon when you're done."

My heart was pounding against my rib cage, my pulse off the charts. The edge of the granite counter was digging into my lower back, but all I could concentrate on was trying to slow my breathing, and I was failing miserably. He was intimidating, playing with me like a cat played with a mouse, but I wasn't going down without a fight.

I leaned up on my tippy-toes and softly kissed his lips, barely making contact, and then pulled back. When he came forward for another taste, I spun around, giggling. "You stink, Fish Boy, and I don't let smelly men lick my spoon. Go shower, then we'll talk."

He groaned from behind me and dropped his head on my shoulder. "You're dangerous, Kacie Jensen, you know that?" He gave me a tap on the butt as he turned and headed upstairs to the shower.

Dangerous, huh? I'd never been called dangerous before. I kinda liked it.

After breakfast, I finished cleaning up the kitchen while Mom was up front, seeing a few guests out. Fred snored off his pancake coma on the couch. Lucy and Piper were in the family room by Fred, quietly coloring pictures of the horses from the fair yesterday. Brody went upstairs to pack up his bags. This was the part about this whole thing that was going to suck, saying good-bye. Less than twenty-four hours since our first kiss and I was already having doubts. There were just so many things that could go wrong. Was this really going to be possible? Were *we* going to be possible?

I wiped off the place mats and carried them to the pantry. Reaching up to put them on the shelf, I was startled when Brody's strong arm wrapped around my waist, pulling me in close. I quickly looked past the pantry door.

"Relax, they're still coloring," he whispered into my ear as he leaned over and gently kicked the pantry door closed with his foot.

I closed my eyes and took a deep breath, inhaling his freshly showered scent. He smelled clean, yet outdoorsy. I let myself relax into his hug, losing myself in his comfort. His strong arms wrapped around me like a warm cotton sweater, making me feel tiny and protected. He loosened his grip just enough for me to turn to face him. I laced my fingers together and swooped them around his neck, his hands resting on my hips.

"This has been an interesting weekend, huh?" I asked coyly, staring into his mesmerizing eyes. He grinned, flashing me his champion smile.

"To say the least. I don't want to leave, but I have some things I have to take care of this week."

"That's okay, it's probably good that you're going. I need to clear my head." I sighed.

Concern rolled across his face. His brows pulled together as he tightened his grip on my waist.

"Are you having second thoughts?"

"No, nothing like that. It's just all happening so fast, I need to breathe." I smiled to reassure him and myself.

"Kacie, I like you, there's no doubt about that. When I went home last week, I couldn't stop thinking about you. That's why I came back. The more I know about you, the more I *want* to know." He bit his lower lip and paused for a second, thinking about what he was going to say next. "I'm in no rush; I'm not looking to get married tomorrow. Hell, I wasn't even interested in having a relationship until I met you. And now that I've met you, walking out that door with no plans to see you again isn't an option. We can take this as slow as you want. Just give it a chance."

My heart raced around my chest, probably in an attempt to leap out of my body and land at his feet as an offering. I closed my eyes and took a deep, cleansing breath before responding.

"I like you too, Brody, more than I want to, actually. I'm not used to this feeling. It scares and excites me at the same time. We're so different—our worlds are *so* different. And the thought of putting myself out there to be hurt again—"

"Stop right there." He cut me off as he took my face in both hands, squatting to be eye to eye with me. "You're not a conquest and I don't play games. I told you I haven't really ever done the girlfriend thing, and you haven't done the boyfriend thing in a long time. Let's figure it out together."

His persistence beckoned me. The way he sounded so sure, so certain . . . maybe this would work.

I smiled at him and clasped my hands over his. "You're right, it's silly not to try. But . . . under a couple of conditions."

He let go of my face and stood up tall, crossing his arms across his chest. "Conditions, huh? Interesting. Hit me."

"Well . . . first, the girls can't know anything is going on. I always said if and when I dated someone, he wouldn't meet the girls until we were very serious. No way was I going to have a bunch of guys floating in and out of their lives. I know this thing between us wasn't exactly planned, and you've already met them. Hanging with them is okay, but no kissing, holding hands, or anything like that when they're around. Deal?"

He flared his nostrils and narrowed his eyes at me, contemplating what I'd just said. "Deal. But . . . that just means when I'm alone with you, I'm going to be *extra* . . . attentive. Double deal?"

Every vein in my body damn near exploded from the surge of excitement that jolted through me with that sentence. I had no idea what he meant, but I wanted to. The possibilities were endless.

"Deal," I replied, my head held high and my voice deceptively confident.

"Is that it?"

"One more," I answered, biting my lip. "No pressure."

He looked confused as he arched a brow at me. "No pressure?"

"Yeah, you said we're taking this slow, and I'm good with that." I looked into his dark green eyes, wondering if I would be able to keep my own deal. "Nothing serious. Let's just have fun. No pressure. Get it?"

"Got it. No pressure." He smirked, entertaining me.

Swallowing the lump in my throat, I suddenly needed air. Being this close to Brody, with all of his energy focused on me, was intense, overwhelming. "All right, I gotta check on Lucy and Piper."

I walked over to the pantry door, and just as my hand grabbed the knob, Brody's arm shot in front of my face and grabbed the doorjamb on the other side of me, blocking my path.

Baffled, I looked up at him, butterflies swarming my stomach.

He licked his lips as a sexy grin spread across his face. His gaze burned down on me.

"Pay the toll."

Instantly, my butterflies morphed into pterodactyls.

18

BRODY

"Where'd you disappear to this weekend? As if I didn't already know," Andy badgered sarcastically on the other end of the line.

"Uh . . . Kacie's." I yawned, still half-asleep.

"No shit, Sherlock. How did that go? Did you two crazy kids profess your undying love for each other? Will I be getting a wedding invitation in the mail?"

"No, asshole. We just hung out," I snapped back, slightly irritated at his teasing.

"Wow! Little defensive, aren't we? Okay, okay. I'll back off. I do have a question for you, though—actually, a favor." Hesitation rang loud in his voice, and I wasn't sure I wanted to hear what this favor was.

I sighed. "This is gonna piss me off, isn't it?"

"Probably."

"What is it?"

"Remember I told you last week that Blaire is trying to turn into Suzy Homemaker? Well, she's hosting a party and doing all the cooking to show off her new . . . skills."

"No," I shot back before he had a chance to continue.

"Come on, Brody. Don't make me suffer through this by myself," he begged.

Driving all the way out to Andy and Blaire's house was bad enough, but having to fake through an evening of pleasantries *and* eating her cooking was going above and beyond.

Before I could answer him, he sweetened the pot. "Why don't you bring Kacie with you? I'd like to meet the girl who has turned my best friend's brain into a pile of shit anyway."

Smiling at the sound of her name, I responded, "When is this grand dinner?"

"Next Saturday night. My house. Cocktails and hors d'oeuvres at six, dinner at seven. You in?" He sounded excited, clearly expecting me to say no.

I sighed. "Yeah, I'm in."

"Kacie too?"

"Yes. It's going to take some convincing on my part, but I'll get her here."

Convincing, begging, whatever.

"Awesome. Thanks, bro. It means a lot to me. By the way, you might want to eat before you come out here, but don't tell Blaire I said that."

"You busy?" Kacie's voice was soft and sexy, tempting me to jump into my truck and drive back to her house right then, just for one more kiss.

"I *am* busy, actually, but I'd drop just about anything for you."

Wow. Okay, way to sound like a lame teenager, Brody.

"You're sweet, but stop it or you're gonna make me like you even more." She giggled.

Challenge accepted.

"How's your morning been?" I asked.

"It's been full of Lysol and laundry detergent." She sighed. "Both girls have the stomach flu. I was actually calling to warn you. I hope you don't get sick."

"Eh, don't worry about me. I'll be fine. I'm more worried about *you*."

Hmm, getting sick might be a blessing. It would get me out of Blaire's fake-ass dinner.

"I'm okay. I think between the girls and all the people I'm exposed to at the inn, my immune system is made of steel. I almost never get sick."

"Never say never," I teased her. "So, let's assume for a minute that I did end up with a raging case of the stomach flu. Would you come down here and take care of me?"

Silence on the other end of the line.

"I'll take that as a no." I laughed, trying to break the tension.

"No, that's not a no. I just haven't really thought about the whole coming-to-your-house thing yet. It caught me off guard," she said quietly.

"Funny you should mention that . . . ," I said matter-of-factly.

She inhaled quickly. I could feel her anxiety through the phone.

"Before you freak out, nothing has changed, we're still taking things slow . . . but I have a dinner party to go to next weekend and I was hoping you'd be my date."

"Oh. Wow. Coming to your house . . ." She paused. "Um, I don't know."

"That's not the answer I was hoping for. I was looking for something more along the lines of: 'Why yes, Brody, I'd love to spend the weekend at your house having copious amounts of crazy, sweaty monkey sex.'"

"Kacie, I'm kidding. Look, if sleeping here makes you nervous, I have a spare room with its own bathroom. You are more than welcome to sleep in there. I won't be offended. No pressure, remember?"

"Okay."

I could tell she was smiling now, thank God.

"I have to run it all by my mom and see if she minds watching the girls for the night."

"Maybe you could come down on Friday and go home Sunday?"

"I don't know, Brody, that's a long time to be away from them. I've never been away longer than a few hours." She sounded unsure, nervous even.

My jaw was on the floor. "You've never been away from them overnight?"

She giggled. "Nope, they're my life. I hate to be away from them. Besides, where would I have gone?"

I hadn't thought of that. "True."

"How about we compromise . . . I'll come Saturday morning and stay until Sunday afternoon sometime. Okay?"

"Kacie, I'll take what I can get with you."

"You're doing it again." She laughed.

"I can't help it."

"Hang on . . ." I could tell she put her hand over the phone and was hollering at someone. "Brody, I gotta go. Lucy is getting sick again. I'll text you later?"

"Go. Be with them, I understand. Text when you can."

To say I was excited for Kacie to get here was putting it mildly. All week, Kacie and I had texted throughout the day, and at night after she put the girls to bed, we talked well into the morning. I felt kinda bad about that. I could sleep in, but she was functioning on only a few hours of sleep each night. She never once complained, though, and each night on the phone, we got more and more comfortable with each other.

Friday afternoon, I decided to tackle my ghost town of a guest room. No one had stayed with me in a while, and she'd slept in my bed, not in here. I spent the better part of the day washing sheets and dusting bookcases, doing whatever I could think of that would make Kacie as comfortable as possible while she was here.

A little while later, my phone chirped. It was Viper this time.

V: Dude. Shit hit the fan again today. Can I crash at your place tonight?

You've got to be fucking kidding me. Of all nights he wants to stay here *tonight*?

Yeah, that's fine, but you have to sleep on the couch.

V: Totally cool with that. I'm going to grab a pizza and I'll be over.

Get two. I'm starving.

An hour or so later, I was kicked back on my couch watching baseball when my front door flew open and Viper came strolling through, pizza and beer in hand.

"'Sup, my man?" he bellowed as he dropped the stuff on my kitchen counter and came over to shake my hand.

I stood and shook his hand back.

"I'm clearly doing better than you. What's going on at your house?"

He groaned and rolled his eyes. "Kat came home and the cleaning lady was still there."

I stared at him, confused. "Why would that piss her off?"

"Well, Kat came in and I was relaxing in my chair. The maid was on her knees . . . sucking my dick." He laughed. "Apparently, that was not an approved chore. Kat ran over and grabbed her by the ponytail and started whaling on her. I'm not gonna lie, it kind of turned me on at first, those two going at it, but I wrapped my arms around Kat until what's-her-name could get out of the house. Needless to say, she's fucking pissed, and I didn't want to sit there all night listening to it."

Shaking my head, I asked my next thought out loud. "Why do it? Why go through all of this? Is it worth it? Why not just break up with her and live your life however you want?"

Viper narrowed his eyes, contemplating my question. "I don't know. She's always there when I need her. It's nice to have someone there for me all the time. I know she'll never really leave. Plus, she's a fucking animal in bed." His eyebrows wiggled up and down. "Clawing, biting, screaming. Who bails when you get to fuck that every night?"

"You . . . make my brain hurt." I smacked him hard on the back of the neck as I walked into the kitchen to grab the pizzas.

"Speaking of fucking, what's up with you? I haven't talked to you all week. You fuck that girl yet?"

I turned around and locked eyes with him. "Dude. Don't."

He held his hands up in front of him defensively, his eyes wide. "My bad, man. Sorry."

I picked up the pizza boxes from the counter and turned back to the living room, nodding toward the kitchen. "Grab the beer, will ya?"

"Got it." Viper grabbed the six-packs of beer and carried them over to the coffee table. "This girl really has you all fucking crazy, huh?"

"Yeah, she does. And I'm totally okay with that."

"What is it about her? I don't think I've ever met a girl who has made me act as idiotic as you are," he said as he shoved a piece of pepperoni in his mouth.

"Nothing. Everything," I said, smiling to myself.

"Oh my God. Did you grow a pussy while you were up there?"

I reached over and punched him on the arm, hard.

"Seriously, dude." He looked at me incredulously. "What is it about her? I've never seen you like this."

"I don't know . . ." Moments I'd had with Kacie started running through my head as I tried to pinpoint exactly what it was that had me so crazed. "It's the way she looks when she's playing with her daughters. It's the way she crinkles her cute freckled nose when she smiles really big. It's the way her hair looks sexy all the time, even when it's in a ponytail. I could sit here listing things for hours and still not tell you all of the amazing things about her."

Viper stared at me, his eyes wide open in disbelief.

"Whoa."

Whoa was an understatement: I was beyond crazy about her, and it was completely foreign to me. Ever since I was old enough to form memories, hockey had been my life. I thought about it constantly, obsessed about it. I dissected plays from past games in my head, watched thousands and thousands of hours of highlight reels, anything I could do to improve my game. Kacie was the first person to pull me out of a lifelong hockey haze and consume my thoughts with something I'd never expected. Something far better. My mind often wandered to thinking about her and what she was doing right that minute, what she was wearing today, if she was thinking about me too.

"She's coming here this weekend," I said nonchalantly.

"She *is*?" He grinned wildly and licked his lips like a wolf on the prowl. "Do I get to meet her?"

"Hell no."

"Come on," he begged.

"Not a chance." I shook my head. "You can crash here tonight, then get your ass up and out early before she gets here."

He smirked at me like he had other plans. "We'll see about that."

19

KACIE

"Stop stressing, we'll be fine." My mom smiled reassuringly as she wrapped her arms around me in a tight hug. "Go. Have fun. Relax."

She knew me too well, sometimes better than I knew myself. My stomach was full of tiny little knots, each one representing something different that could go wrong over the next thirty-six hours. "I know, Mom. Thanks . . . for everything."

Cupping my cheek lovingly with her hand, she said, "For you, anything. Now hurry, before traffic gets too bad." She grabbed the plastic dress bag from the front hall closet and handed it to me. "Don't forget this."

Due to my complete lack of fashion sense, Lauren had stopped by that morning with a dozen dresses for me to try on for the dinner with Brody. She and my mom squealed and giggled louder with each dress I tried on, discussing how the ice-blue one made my butt look perfect and the salmon-colored one complemented my skin tone. I just stared at them like a deer in headlights and turned when they told me to.

Obviously, I picked the ice-blue one.

I tossed my duffel bag in the back of my Jeep and hung the dress on a hook. Butterflies slammed against my rib cage as I pulled out of the driveway, waving at the two little smiling faces on the porch. Not quite ready, I pulled back up the driveway, threw my Jeep in park, and dashed to the porch for one last kiss.

God, I'm going to miss them.

My phone beeped as I turned onto the main road. I looked down and saw it was a text from Brody. Rather than text back, I dialed his number.

"Hey!" he enthusiastically answered the phone.

"Hey, you."

"I was just checking to see where you are. Have you left yet?"

"Nope, bad news. I have the flu, I'm not gonna be able to make it."

A heavy silence hung on the other end of the line, followed by a sigh. "Really? That totally sucks." His deflated tone filled me with guilt . . . almost.

"No, not really." I giggled. "I'm in my Jeep, just left."

"Oh, you think you're funny, don't ya?" His voice relaxed again. "You're gonna pay for that one . . . I promise."

Two hours later, I finally pulled into the underground parking lot at Brody's building. I typed the code he gave me on the digital security screen and the metal gates swung open. I pulled my Jeep into the open spot next to his truck where he'd instructed me to and went to the back to grab my bag.

"Nice back end."

Spinning around, my eyes rested on Brody leaning up against a concrete pillar, his arms folded across his chest with a suggestive smirk on his face. I looked him up and down, head to toe, taking in every sexy inch. He had on a Wild T-shirt that hugged his biceps tight and made his eyes look extra intense. Loose curls peeked out from under the baseball cap he was wearing backward, as usual. I almost forgot how ridiculously handsome he was, and he was smiling at *me*.

"Hey," I replied shyly, not quite used to his compliments yet.

Not wasting any time, he walked over and wrapped his arms around me tight, picking me up off the ground. My whole body tingled as I squeezed him back just as hard.

"I could get used to *this*," I said into his T-shirt, inhaling the scent of his cologne.

He put me down and hooked a finger under my chin, pulling it up to him as he put his lips on mine. It was a sweet, gentle kiss that melted my reserves away and instantly put me at ease.

"Good," he replied as he pulled back. "Let me get your stuff."

He snatched my duffel bag out of the backseat with his left hand and reached for mine with his right. He pulled it up to his lips and kissed my fingers.

"I'm glad you're here."

My heart swelled as I smiled up at him. "Me too."

As we got to his condo door, he stopped and turned to me. "I have to warn you . . . my friend Viper is here. He had a fight with his girl-friend yesterday so he crashed here last night, but he's leaving. He was supposed to be gone already, but he slept late."

"I can't wait to meet him," I said, ignoring the twists and turns happening in my stomach again.

He turned the knob and grimaced at me. "You might regret saying that."

All week long, I had been picturing Brody's condo in my head. Lawn chairs in the living room, the garbage can overflowing with empty beer cans, and takeout containers covering every surface.

I couldn't have been more wrong.

Not only was it spotless, it was warm and cozy. Decorated with leather furniture, funky artwork, and of course a TV bigger than I'd ever seen in my entire life.

Jumping up from the couch, Viper bounded over to us, throwing his arms around me. A little overwhelmed, I politely returned his hug. He pulled back and looked at me. "So, you're the girl that tamed the beast, huh?" He looked over at Brody and nodded. "Nice choice, man. I approve."

Brody narrowed his eyes at Viper, issuing a simple warning. "Easy."

"I'm just giving her a compliment. Here, I'll start over." He took my hand in his, kissing the top of it as he bowed in front of me. "I'm Viper, very nice to meet you."

"Hi, Viper." I smiled warmly and shook his hand back. "Nice to meet you too."

Viper was intimidating. He was as tall as Brody and muscular like him, but that's where the similarities ended. Tattoos of dragons and snakes and God knows what else covered his arms and crept all the way up his neck from under his T-shirt, stopping at his strong jawline. His shoulder-length blond hair was pulled back in a messy, low ponytail, and his lip was pierced in two different places. Scary biker look aside, something about him was comforting. I liked him, a lot.

Brody smacked Viper hard on the back of the shoulders and put his arm around him. "He was just leaving."

Viper looked surprised. "I was?"

"Yes, you were." Brody walked over to the coffee table and gathered his keys and phone and handed them to him.

Viper winked at Brody. "Ooooh, I get it. You want to be alone with her. I feel ya, man."

I laughed as Brody sighed, took his hat off, and ran his hands through his hair.

Viper started past me toward the door, stopping to plant a kiss on my cheek.

Brody pushed him from behind. "Keep walking, Casanova."

As they got to the door, Viper turned and looked over Brody's shoulder, waving at me once more. "Dude, if it doesn't work out, will you give her my number?" he asked.

"Good-bye." Brody closed the door as Viper continued from the other side.

"I was just asking. She smells really fucking good!"

Brody clicked the dead bolt and turned back to me. "Sorry about that."

"It's okay, really." I laughed. "I thought he was sweet."

"Sweet?" He scratched his head. "That's not usually a word I hear used to describe Viper, but okay."

He walked over to me and wrapped his arms around me again. "He was right about one thing, though. You do smell amazing."

"You smell pretty delicious yourself," I replied, feeling bolder now that we were alone. I wrapped my arms around his neck, planting my lips right on his. He responded eagerly, sucking my bottom lip into his mouth, running his tongue along it.

In that moment I wasn't thinking about being a mom or what the girls were doing back home, nor did I care that I hadn't studied at all since I'd started talking to Brody. In his arms, I floated higher and higher into the clouds, swirling around in a dizzying, euphoric haze. All that mattered was that kiss, and I threw myself into it wholeheartedly, holding nothing back. His hands flowed smoothly down my back, his fingertips digging into my hips.

Our tongues continued their seductive dance as Brody walked me backward toward the living room. Giggling as I fell back on his couch, I pulled him down on top of me, where I was able to *feel* just how happy he was that I was here. Knowing that I could do that to him only made me want him more. Slipping my hands up the back of his shirt, I ran my fingers over the ripples of his strong back muscles as they flexed under my touch with each slight movement he made. He reached up and fisted a handful of my hair, gently pulling it to expose my neck. I couldn't contain my moan any longer when his lips finally connected with my skin, kissing and sucking their way down to my collarbone.

"Can I show you the rest of my condo?" Chills blanketed my body as his lips grazed my ear. "My bedroom is just past that door."

All at once, my senses came flooding back to me. "Wait, no . . . slow. Remember?"

His head dropped to my shoulder as he sighed. "I should've kept my mouth shut." He sat up and grinned at me, holding his hands out. "Come on, I'll actually give you the grand tour, slowly."

I took his hands, stood up, and adjusted my top. "You're not mad, are you?"

"At you? Never." He kissed my hand again and led me down the hall.

Brody's bedroom was simple, sparse even. A king-size bed, topped with chocolate-brown-and-tan plaid bedding, was against the wall to the left, each side anchored with a chunky black nightstand. A black leather chair sat in the far right corner next to a bookshelf, which I was immediately drawn to. I walked over, eager to see what types of books would grab Brody's attention.

"Don't waste your time, nothing but magazines." He sounded embarrassed. "Mostly *Sports Illustrated*."

I turned and smiled at him. "Nothing wrong with that." Half a dozen pictures hung on the wall on the other side of the chair. A middle-aged woman with Brody's features was in most of them. "Is this your mom?"

He walked up behind me and curled his arms around my waist. "Yep. Beautiful, isn't she?"

"Very." My fingers traced each frame as I looked at her closely. The resemblance was astonishing, from their same dark brown curls to their award-winning smiles. She was an older, softer version of her handsome son. "You have her eyes—beautiful and sincere, very expressive. You have the ability to tell a whole story with just one look. You know that?"

He hugged me tighter, resting his head on top of mine while I continued studying the woman responsible for his existence.

My heart sank when I came to a picture of her sitting in a big chair, curled up under a blanket. She had a pink bandanna wrapped around her head and was very thin, her face drained of all its color. Despite all that, her beautiful, contagious smile spread wide across her face as she gave the camera two thumbs up.

"What about this one?" I asked cautiously.

"I took that," he said proudly. "That was about three years ago, the morning of her last chemo treatment. She was diagnosed with stage three breast cancer, but she beat it. I keep that picture up there to remind me how far she's come. I'm so proud of her."

"You guys are really close, huh?"

He sighed, his breath warming my neck. "What can I say? I'm a mama's boy."

"Hope she doesn't mind sharing." I turned to the right and kissed his cheek. The instant my lips left his face, he grabbed my hips and spun me around to face him.

"I'm about to throw you on the bed and have my way with you. Can we please stop talking about my mom?"

20

BRODY

"Ready to go?" Kacie called from the living room.

"Almost," I hollered back. "You can come in. I'm just changing my shirt."

My bedroom door creaked as she opened it, peeking around the corner. "You sure?"

I couldn't take my eyes off her as she walked over to the leather chair, her wavy, auburn hair flowing around her bare shoulders as she went. She had on jeans shorts that were long enough for public but short enough to drive me batshit crazy all afternoon, a hot-pink tank top that showcased every single curve perfectly, and black flip-flops. Never in my life had I known little pink toes could be hot until right then. She curled up in the chair and grinned at me, crinkling her nose. Her pink lips were still swollen from the twenty minutes we had just spent rolling around on my bed before she halted things . . . again.

I'd meant what I said when I told her I was in no hurry to rush things along. I wanted to be inside her as bad as I wanted a Stanley Cup ring, but I could be patient.

I'd also be spending a lot of time in the shower—a cold shower.

I walked out of my closet with a navy-blue-and-green-striped polo and tossed it on the bed, watching Kacie watch me. Her all-consuming stare was a form of torturous foreplay, something that should be used on prisoners. When I locked eyes with her, it was just that, a lock. I couldn't look away. I didn't want to look away. I wanted to walk over, scoop her up, and lay her back down on my bed, after I texted Andy to tell him he could take his dinner party and shove it up Blaire's ass. I would much rather spend the evening tangled up in bed with Kacie.

I pulled my T-shirt over my head and she gasped. "You have a *tattoo*?"

I laughed. "Yep. It's the Murphy family crest . . . got it on my eighteenth birthday. My dad has the exact same one."

"It's huge!" She hopped up and came over to me for a closer look. She ran her hands softly over the skin in between my shoulder blades where my tattoo started and traced the outline all the way down my back. "Wow. This is amazing," she said so quietly I almost didn't hear her.

"What's wrong?"

She didn't answer, and I turned to face her. The shimmer in her green eyes had been replaced with sadness, and she was staring at the ground.

"Kacie, what is it?" I asked, cupping her face in my hands.

"Nothing." She sighed, looking up at me. "I just feel like an ass."

"Why?"

"When you left the inn that morning and I found your jersey on the fireplace, I jumped to conclusions." Her shoulders drooped as she continued, "I assumed that since you were this single, big-shot athlete, you must have been a selfish playboy who didn't give a crap about family, or anyone for that matter. After hearing you gush about your mom, then seeing all your family pictures, and now this . . . I was wrong, Brody. I'm so sorry." She looked back down at the ground and let out another sigh.

"Hey, it's okay. You didn't know anything about me." I tilted her head up so she was looking at me again. "It probably just looked like I was some dude trying to get in your pants, and that part I can't completely deny." A tiny smile crossed her lips, but I wasn't convinced. "It's really okay. Come here." I pulled her in close and wrapped my arms around her, holding her head tight against my bare chest.

"Hey, we have a couple hours until we need to get ready for this dinner tonight. Wanna grab some coffee? I'll show you around?"

Kacie smiled up at me. "Fantastic. You should probably put a shirt on first, though, huh?"

"Or you could take yours off so that we're even?"

She rolled her eyes and left my room with a grin on her face.

The weather was perfect. Kacie's hand was in mine, and we were strolling around my neighborhood. I showed her the Bumper and my favorite Polish deli, which makes the most amazing pierogi casserole. It took us less than ten minutes to get to the coffee shop I went to almost every single day.

Scooter Joe's Café.

"Cute name," Kacie said as we walked up.

"Wait until you meet Joe." I winked. "I think you'll like him, but be careful, he has wandering hands."

She narrowed her eyes, thoroughly confused as Joe walked up behind her and put his arm around her waist. "Brody, who's your little friend?"

Joe was harmless, a little old man who refused to slow down after he retired from the plumbers' union, instead dumping all of his savings into this place. It was always packed too—not a bad investment.

Kacie's posture stiffened as she looked from Joe to me with wide eyes. I chuckled and held my hand up toward Kacie. "Joe, this is my girlfriend, Kacie."

"Hi, Kacie," Joe said, pulling her in tighter. "Nice to meet ya."

Kacie slipped out of his grip and spun around, holding her hand out. "Nice to meet you too, Joe."

"We're gonna sit in my usual spot, okay?" I said.

"Sounds good, boss. I'll bring you a couple of menus." He grinned at Kacie and hurried behind the counter.

"I usually sit at the bistro table outside—that work for you?"

Kacie tried to hide her grin. "Sounds good."

"What's that smirk about?" I asked as we walked to the patio.

"Nothing," she said with a small giggle.

"Liar."

"I just thought it was cute that you knew what a bistro table was."

"You can thank my mom for that. I brought her here once when she came to stay with me." I pulled out her chair and had to fight the urge to stick my nose in her hair as her scent washed over me. "I called it a two-seater. She corrected me."

Kacie scooted her chair a little closer to mine. "I love hearing you talk about your mom."

"She's wonderful—a lot like your mom, actually."

"What about your dad?" she asked as Joe brought our menus over.

"We're close, just not as close as my mom. My dad worked a lot of overtime when I was a kid to pay for all my hockey camps and leagues, so I spent most of my time with my mom."

She leaned in close, resting her chin on her hand.

"When I got my signing bonus, the very first thing I did was drive straight to their house, pay it off, and force my dad to retire. Then a couple years later, I built their dream house out in the country."

"Wow. That's amazing."

"Yeah, I've been very lucky. What about your dad?" I asked cautiously. "I've never heard you really talk about him."

She picked up the menu and shrugged her shoulders. "Nothing really to tell. He and my mom were married for like fifteen years, then one day he decided to leave. No warning; that was it."

"Interesting . . . did he say why?"

"Apparently he'd been seeing someone, got her pregnant, and wanted to be with her instead. I haven't talked to him since that day."

"I'm so sorry," I said sincerely.

"I'm not." She forced an uncomfortable smile and looked around. "Where is our waitress? I want a scone."

A scone or a distraction?

21

KACIE

Being with Brody was relaxing, natural. When he looked at me with his piercing gaze, my stomach fluttered like a teenager's in a brand-new relationship, yet we could sit comfortably like an old married couple and hold hands, chatting for hours about nothing at all. We spent the day walking around the city, and way in the back of my mind, I wished it were my everyday life. I could picture us getting up on a Sunday morning and strolling to that little coffee shop, contemplating which movie we wanted to see later, while the girls ate cinnamon scones and danced to the trumpet player on the corner.

I forced that daydream out of my head because that's exactly what it was . . . a dream.

This . . . *thing*, whatever it was, had no chance of going anywhere special; we were too different.

My relationship with Brody had an expiration date, and I was doing my best not to look at the calendar, and just live in the moment.

Right now, though, I was supposed to be showering and getting ready for this dinner tonight. I opened the bedroom door and hollered out to him, "Hey, do you by any chance have any extra shampoo and conditioner? I forgot to bring mine."

"In the linen closet in the bathroom."

"Thanks!"

"No problem, babe," he called back nonchalantly, like it was just any other Saturday, but those three tiny words sent my heart into a tizzy.

Leaving the bedroom door slightly ajar, I walked into the guest bathroom and slid the linen closet door open and laughed out loud. On the shelf there must have been thirty different shampoos and conditioners—fruity ones, flowery ones, extra-strengthening ones—made by every imaginable salon company. Still snickering, I called out the door again, "Did you rob a beauty supply store or what?"

He chuckled in the living room before yelling back, "No, I had no idea what you used, so I bought every one they had."

My mouth hung open, shock coursing through my veins as I stared incredulously at the shelf. It was such an innocent, silly gesture on his part, but it meant more to me than he could possibly comprehend.

Freak out about shampoo later, Kacie. Pull yourself together and get your ass in the shower.

Tonight I was meeting several new people, most of whom would know me as nothing more than "Brody's date," so it was imperative that I didn't embarrass him or make him look bad. More importantly, one of those people was his best friend since childhood, and his wife, who according to Brody made a piranha look like a teddy bear. My stress level was at an all-time high; I desperately wanted everything to go perfectly. I wanted them to like me.

Screw that, I wanted them to love me.

When you've spent the majority of your adult life in jeans and T-shirts, an event like this was beyond intimidating. Lauren helped me in the style department with the dress and the shoes, but I was on my own with makeup. The last thing I wanted was to look like a cheap hooker he'd picked up on his way over. And don't even get me started on table manners.

Salad fork, dinner fork, soupspoon, regular spoon . . . it was all so damn overwhelming.

An hour later, I stood in front of the full-length mirror, inspecting every last detail of my appearance. I'd put my hair up and then taken it back down six different times, changed my eye makeup three times, and cursed out loud twice that I hadn't brought that damn salmon-colored dress with me as a backup.

It is what it is. Showtime.

I slipped my feet into Lauren's not-too-high silver heels, took a deep breath, squeezed every drop of confidence I could muster out of my soul, and strode into the living room.

Empty.

"Holy shit," Brody muttered from behind me, where he stood frozen at the kitchen sink.

My heart rocketed into my throat and stuck there as I spun to face him. "Is that a good holy shit or a bad holy shit?"

He didn't respond with his mouth, but his eyes spoke volumes as they raked slowly all the way down my body and back up again. "It's the best holy shit ever."

Proudly, I looked down at myself and beamed up at him. "I cleaned up okay, huh? On a scale from one to ten—"

"Six hundred fifty-two," he interrupted as he stalked over, gripped the back of my head, and pressed his mouth to mine hard.

That kiss was different from all the other ones he'd given me. His tongue delved deep into my mouth with the delicious promise of things to come for the night. It was getting harder and harder to resist letting him do whatever he wanted to me. He pulled back just enough to press his forehead against mine, still cupping the back of my head.

His tone was rough; if sex ever had a voice, this would be it. "We need to leave, because I'm about to blow this thing off, throw you over my shoulder, and take you straight to bed."

Just that sentence alone caused a fire to start between my legs, and I started to wonder if sleeping over was a good idea after all.

A security guard waved us through the gated entrance of an exclusive golf course community. The winding streets were lined with antique lampposts and perfectly shaped hedges, each house bigger and more lavish than the one before.

"What is this? The Stepford subdivision?" I asked in awe as Brody drove us to the back of the neighborhood, easing his black BMW 740i into a wide, stone-paved driveway that curved up into a half circle in front of what could have easily passed for a castle.

"Something like that." He put his car in park as my mouth fell open and I stared incredulously at the two parking attendants heading our way.

"They have valets for dinner parties? At their *house*?"

Brody looked over at me and rolled his eyes dramatically. "Only the best for Blaire."

My door swung open and one of the young men took my hand, helping me out of the car. "Thank you," I said, smiling up at him.

Brody handed the other man his keys and met me at the front of the car. He offered me his arm, which I eagerly accepted before I broke a heel on Lauren's shoe, or my ankle, on this fancy cobblestone driveway.

"You're not a big fan of Blaire, huh?" I asked as we slowly walked up to the house.

He looked me dead in the eye. "Not in the slightest. We haven't really liked each other since college. I've always thought she was a gold digger, and she thought I was a bad influence on Andy. I'm here only as a favor to him. Plus I'm excited to see the kids, assuming she hasn't shipped them off for the night."

"They have kids?"

"Yep, Logan is four and Becca is almost two."

Perfect!

That would be my in with Blaire; all moms love talking about their kids and telling those really embarrassing tantrum stories or comparing little tips and products. This would be easier than I thought.

Their house was even more amazing up close than it was from the street. The oversize arched front doors were made of dark chestnut wood with wrought-iron accents. Waist-high vases sat on either side of the porch with bright hot-pink flowers cascading down the sides. Brody reached over and rang the bell, and within seconds, a sunny woman in her early sixties answered the door. Her short, gray bob curled around her plump cheeks as they rose with her cheery smile.

"Welcome, please come in." She stepped back and nodded politely as we walked through the doorway.

We were barely through the door when a little boy leaped from the widest staircase I'd ever seen, straight into Brody's arms. "Uncle Brody!"

The cute little guy with sandy blond hair and bright blue eyes, dressed in Angry Birds pajamas, wrapped his arms and legs around Brody's torso like a monkey. Not that I could blame him; I'd wanted to do that to him myself a few times.

"What's up, my man?" Brody peeled him off and tossed him up high in the air over and over. Logan's squeals echoed through the cold stone foyer. A chill passed through me as I looked around. You couldn't even tell kids lived here.

She probably keeps them locked in the dungeon.

I chuckled to myself as a little girl with a head of white-blond ringlets wobbled up to Brody and held her arms up.

"Becca!" he cheered as he reached down and scooped her up in his other arm, covering her tiny face with kisses as she squirmed and giggled.

"Figures the first thing you'd do when you get here is make the kids wild," a soothing voice from behind me called out.

A distinguished-looking man, dressed in what I was sure was an expensive jet-black suit, appeared from the back of the house. I was shocked by his resemblance to Logan, who was an exact replica of him, just a smaller version. Same sandy-blond hair, same bright blue eyes.

He walked over and offered his hand, which Brody awkwardly shook around Becca, pulling him in for one of those man hugs where they don't really embrace each other, more like backslapping.

"Glad you made it. I wasn't so sure you'd actually show." He reached for Becca, who eagerly dived for her father's chest, laying her head on his shoulder while she eyed me cautiously.

"Trust me, I didn't want to, but Kacie here was dying to try Blaire's cooking," he joked sarcastically as he draped his arm over my shoulder.

"Hi, Kacie, I'm Andy." His smile was warm and familiar as he gently took my hand in his.

"Hi, Andy, thanks for inviting me." I couldn't resist the cute little thing clinging to his neck any longer. "You must be Becca. Aren't you the cutest little thing I've ever seen? Is that your baby?" I pointed at the floppy doll tucked under her arm.

She sat up straight, her eyes lighting up as she lunged for me.

"Becca, sit nice, honey. Not everyone wants to hold you." Andy kissed her cheek.

"It's okay, I'd like to . . . if you don't mind."

"Of course not," he said as he handed her over to me. "I have to attempt to pry Logan off of Brody anyway. That's a task in and of itself." He reached over and tickled under Logan's arms in an attempt to get him to loosen his grip around Brody's neck, but Brody squeezed Logan tight and defiantly ran the other direction. Andy looked back at me and sighed. "As you can see, they have the same mental capacity. It's why they get along so well."

Becca held her baby up to me, pointing at its face. "Nose."

"Is that the baby's nose?" I cooed at her. "Where's your nose?"

She giggled and shoved her chubby little finger in her nostril. Andy reached over, quickly plucking it out. "She probably learned that from Uncle Brody too."

I laughed, feeling instantly relaxed with Andy and wondering how such a nice guy could be married to the witch Brody had described. Clearly he must have exaggerated. Andy held his hands out to Becca, but she swatted them away and laid her head on my shoulder.

"Wow, looks like I've been replaced," he teased.

"Fine by me," I said. "She's cuddly." The smell of baby shampoo in her hair made me ache for my girls. I'd been so distracted with Brody today that I thought I was handling being away from them just fine, until this little reminder hit me square in the face.

"Oh, I'm so sorry!" a woman bellowed as she came into the room. She looked like a supermodel, tall, ultrathin, and dressed like she'd just walked out of a magazine. Her large platinum curls swayed like a pendulum when she moved. I was sure there was a dentist somewhere who was putting his kid through college, thanks to all she'd spent on teeth whitening.

"Becca, come here. Stop bothering people." She roughly took Becca from me, while Becca fussed in protest. "Gloria, could you come here, please?" she yelled toward the back of the house, sounding annoyed as her turquoise earring violently swung back and forth.

"Coming." A young lady briskly walked to the foyer. Her hands were folded neatly in front of her while her eyes were plastered to the floor like a child who had just been reprimanded.

"Gloria, what am I paying you for? You're supposed to be watching the children!" she scolded as she pushed Becca into Gloria's arms. In the handoff, Becca dropped her baby on the floor and I bent down and picked it up, quickly handing it to Blaire, who rolled her eyes. "Here. Don't forget her stupid doll."

She looked over at Brody and Logan and snapped her fingers. "Logan. Go. Now."

Brody glared at Blaire and gently pulled Logan off his shoulders, setting him on the ground. "We'll catch up before you go to bed, okay?" Brody high-fived Logan as he walked off with Gloria and Becca, his shoulders slumped in disappointment.

"I'm so sorry about that." She locked eyes with me, grabbing my hand in hers. "I'm Blaire, so nice to meet you."

"I'm Kacie, nice to meet you too."

Brody walked up behind me and put his arm around my shoulders again. "Kacie is my date," he announced proudly.

She looked him up and down, scrunching her nose in disgust. "I'm sorry for that too," she said, leaning in close to me. "You guys wanna come in or what?" With that she turned and disappeared as quickly as she'd entered.

Andy sighed at us, holding up his glass. "I'm gonna go refill this with something much stronger. You guys want one?"

"Absolutely," Brody answered for both of us, noticing I was still too speechless to talk. "Nice tie choice, big shot." He reached over and flicked the sky-blue tie on Andy's chest, which was decorated with little yellow Angry Birds all over it.

"Hey, lay off, man, Logan picked it out." He looked at me and winked. "Plus it really pisses her off when I wear it."

We followed Andy to the back of the house, Brody groping my butt the whole way. In shock at his brazen behavior, I turned and stared at him in disbelief. He grabbed my hand and stopped walking, allowing Andy to go on without us as he pulled me in for a tight hug.

"Don't look at me like that, I can't help it. This dress, my God," he growled into my neck.

Twice today Brody had a moment of animalistic intensity, and holy shit, I loved it. If he could turn me on like that with just his words, I was dying to see what he could do with his body . . . or his tongue.

I bit my lip as he sucked on my earlobe. "Maybe if you play your cards right, it'll be in a heap on your bedroom floor tonight."

He groaned as he kissed his way down my jawline.

"Hey, you two need to borrow the guest room, or can you hold off until after dinner?" Andy teased, grinning from the kitchen doorway. I pulled back from Brody and straightened my dress, following him into the kitchen.

"Sorry," I apologized half-sincerely as we passed him.

"Don't apologize, I was just kidding." Andy leaned in close to my ear. "Besides, I've never seen him like this, it's kinda nice." He smiled, squeezing my hand as he walked away.

From across the kitchen, Blaire narrowed her eyes, glaring in my direction. I swung around to see if there was anyone behind me but no one was there.

"You okay?" Brody's brows were crinkled, concern in his voice.

"Yeah, I just thought . . . nothing. Yes, I'm good." I shook my head, laughing nervously, thankful when someone called his name and distracted him with hockey talk.

Turned out it wasn't as big of a party as I thought it was going to be; only eight couples were invited. Before the meal some of Blaire's staff brought in an extra table in the dining room and we split up, four couples per table. Thankfully, Brody made sure we weren't sitting at Blaire's table.

Dinner was actually really good. She had made lamb chops topped with gorgonzola butter, garlic mashed potatoes, and crisp asparagus. It wasn't something I would have thrown a party and hired valets for, but she was trying and deserved a little credit. During the meal, I met a really sweet woman named Chelsea, who also happened to have twins.

Apparently she and Blaire were in the same book club. We hit it off really well. It was nice to have someone else to talk to while Brody was busy arguing about the upcoming football season with the other guys. Talking about the girls made missing them a little easier to handle.

After dinner, I noticed people started clearing out quickly, partially due to Blaire's escalating tone. I could hear her getting louder and louder in her storytelling, and that witch cackle she had was impossible to ignore. Twice I saw Andy whisper something in her ear while trying to take her wineglass, to which she objected by pushing him off and laughing.

Before I knew it, Andy, Blaire, Chelsea, her husband, James, Brody, and I were the only ones there. While the guys were talking in the den, Chelsea and I moved to the kitchen and were standing at the island, chatting and sipping coffee, when Blaire came clomping up.

"What are you two blabbing about?" she slurred as she swished her wineglass around.

"Books . . . and kids." Chelsea looked my way and smiled sweetly, then turned back to Blaire. "We both have twins—how cool is that?"

Blaire's jaw dropped as she focused on me. "*You* have *kids*?"

My whole body tensed; my heart raced around in circles inside my chest as I silently begged for Brody to come in and tell me it was time to go.

"Yep," I squeaked out, my voice shakier than I meant for it to be. I cleared my throat and continued, "My twins are five. Both girls."

"Where's their father?" she demanded boldly.

"Uh, not sure."

"You're not sure?" Her voice raised in accusatory disbelief. "What the fuck does *that* mean?"

Oh God, Brody, where are you?

"Oh . . . I get it." Her eyes grew wide as a smirk crawled slowly across her face. "Single mom hits the jackpot with professional athlete."

Chelsea interrupted, "Come on, Blaire, that's not fair."

"Oh, shut it, Chels," Blaire snapped. "You know nothing about this girl, neither do I—other than she has terrible taste in men."

"Blaire . . . ," Chelsea continued halfheartedly, while I stood wishing I could morph myself into one of the flat slate tiles beneath our feet and disappear forever.

"It's a good idea, I don't completely blame you . . ." Blaire walked over to the bar and topped off her wineglass, continuing her onslaught. "But seriously, you couldn't find a better guy? Did you just grab the first one you found, or what? If it were me, I would have picked one that hasn't fucked half of Minneapolis."

Her words punched me in the chest like a champion boxer forcing me to hold on to the counter to keep from reeling backward toward the ropes. What was she talking about? Brody said he'd never really ever done the girlfriend thing.

She seemed to notice my panic and fed off of it. "Did you know that? You're not the first girl he's taken somewhere, honey. Did you think you were special? It'll be someone else next week." She took a long swig of her vodka cranberry, her eyes locked on me. "Hell, it was someone else just a couple of weeks ago. He's been screwing my friend Kendall on and off for years. She told me she texted him this weekend, but he didn't answer . . . guess now we know why, huh?" She cocked an eyebrow and raised her glass at me.

Chelsea reached behind the counter and apologetically squeezed my hand as she called into the den. "James, think we better get going!"

Please, Brody, follow him in here. Please.

I should have said something. I *know* I should have said something, but the fact of the matter was that I *didn't* know Brody that well yet, so defending him was pointless. I had nothing to argue back. Plus, a little part of me still wanted to win Andy over, and screaming at his wife wouldn't earn me any points.

"Oh, don't leave because of me, Chelsea. I'll stop. I just thought she should know who she's getting involved with. Crawling into bed with a rattlesnake might be safer." She laughed to herself, looking down at her drink as she swirled it around.

The guys came into the room, and Brody looked at me curiously, instantly sensing something was wrong. I quickly shook my head to prevent him from asking anything and nodded toward the door. He pulled his brows together in a frown and walked over, pulling me in close.

"You okay?" he asked quietly in my ear.

I couldn't answer; I just nodded again.

"So, Brody . . . how's Kendall?" Blaire cackled.

Brody's face reddened with anger. "What the hell's going on here?" he said, looking back and forth between Blaire and me.

"Nothing," I pleaded, laying my hand on his heaving chest. "Can we just go, please?"

Blaire hiccupped. "I was just having a nice little chat here with Katie, or whatever her name is, about what and *who* you like to do in the off season. Thought she might want to know all that before she and her little darlings get too involved."

"Okay, that's enough," Andy ordered, lunging for her glass, but before he could grab it, she snapped her hand back fast, sending the burgundy liquid dripping down the front of my ice-blue dress.

"Oh no!" Chelsea gasped as she ran to the counter for paper towels.

"Are you okay?" Brody turned, trying to brush the excess liquid off of me, onto the floor.

A lump formed in my throat, and I knew the tears wouldn't be far behind. "I just want to go, okay? Can we please go? Now?" I begged.

"Oh God, she's fine!" Blaire rolled her eyes as she walked over to her purse on the counter. "Here," she said, pulling a wad of money out of her wallet. "This should cover the dress, okay?" With that she tossed a twenty-dollar bill across the counter and winked at me.

Brody snapped. "Listen to me, you miserable bitch . . ." He took a step forward, shielding me from any more of Blaire's looks or words.

"You can say whatever you want *to* me or *about* me, but *Kacie* is off-limits. Got it?"

Her eyes blinked rapidly as she stared at him with a blank expression on her face. He grabbed my hand and pulled me toward the door before he turned back one more time.

"And you might want to remember when you're looking down your fake, plastic nose at her, that it's *her* boyfriend's hockey contract that pays for this fucking house of yours. Your husband will always be my best friend, but that doesn't mean he has to be my agent. Consider yourself warned."

22

BRODY

The drive home from Andy and Blaire's was the longest forty minutes of my life. I apologized to Kacie about a thousand times, and while she smiled at me, all she kept saying was "It's fine." Growing up, my mom and dad would occasionally go at it, and every time she told him "It's fine," he either slept on the couch or bought flowers the next day. When it comes to women, "fine" is bad. Very, very bad.

She wasn't fine; I knew that. I could tell by the way she stared out the window the whole way home but never really focused on anything. She was avoiding eye contact with me, and I didn't blame her one bit. What the hell had Blaire said to her *before* I went into the kitchen, and more importantly, what the hell was I thinking taking her over to Blaire's house in the first place? That was the stupidest thing I had done in a long time. I'd dealt with Blaire and her bitchiness before. Why did I think Kacie would be immune?

We pulled into the parking space in my garage, and Kacie picked up her purse off the floor. Just as she was about to reach for the handle, I locked the door.

She spun and looked at me, her brows pulled together, making the cutest little confused crinkle marks appear on her forehead. "What are you doing?"

"Talk to me," I pleaded with her.

A fake smile crossed her face and she put her hand on mine. "There's nothing to talk about, okay?"

"Yes, there is. What did Blaire say to you before I came into the kitchen?"

Her voice was soft as she stared down at her hands. "She basically warned me about you, to stay away. Listen, Brody . . . I think maybe coming here this weekend was a mistake, like maybe I should just go tonight. Our lives are *so* different."

"Don't say that," I tried arguing, but she didn't give me a chance.

"It's true. My typical Saturday night consists of Disney movies with the girls, maybe an ice cream sundae if we're feeling adventurous. Tonight was . . . rough." She sighed, her eyes bouncing wildly around the car as she started rambling. "But then you look at me like you do, and you kiss me like you do, and I think that it's worth the risk . . . that *you're* worth the risk. A few shitty remarks from Blaire later and not only do I realize I really *don't* know you, but now I'm back to questioning what I was already questioning—"

"Wait, wait. Hold on a minute." I held my hands up in front of me in a desperate attempt to derail the train wreck about to happen in her brain. "First of all, you're confusing the hell out of me. Second, this car is really fucking uncomfortable. What do you say we go upstairs, put some sweats on, open a bottle of wine, and have an 'Ask Brody Anything' session? Nothing is off-limits, okay?"

She raised a curious eyebrow. "Nothing?"

"Absolutely nothing. For you . . . I'm an open book."

She warily looked at me and reached for the door handle again. This time I released the lock, hoping to God she didn't get out and head straight for her Jeep. Even if she did, I wasn't opposed to lying on the hood to force her to talk to me.

She met me at the back of my car and used my shoulder as a crutch as she pulled one of her sexy legs up and removed her heel. I tried really hard not to drool in her hair as she did it again with the other leg. How could someone make such a simple action so damn sexy? She did that with everything, I'd noticed . . . making breakfast, reading to her girls, breathing. She was slowly cementing herself into my heart. I'd be damned if Blaire and her big obnoxious mouth were going to ruin any of that for me.

We walked into my condo and Diesel ran to greet us. After giving Kacie a thorough once-over with his nose, he rushed over to me and whimpered pitifully.

"I'm gonna take him out before he embarrasses himself and makes a mess for me to clean. Wanna go with us?"

"Yeah," she replied quickly. "Can I just change real quick?"

No, please leave that dress on every damn day for the rest of your life.

"Sure," I replied as she turned and headed down the hall. "Need help?" I called out after her.

She glanced back at me and rolled her eyes, continuing down the hall.

A few minutes later, I left my room and walked to the family room. Kacie was squatted down playing with Diesel, her hair falling down around her face. She looked adorable, even just in jeans and a hoodie.

"Ready?" I asked as I grabbed his leash from the closet.

She stood, giving me that crinkle-nose grin that brings me to my knees.

"Yep, let's go."

The sharpness of the evening air slapped us in the face as we stepped out onto the street. Kacie hugged herself. Mid-June was pleasant in Minnesota during the day, but the nights were hit-or-miss. Tonight's chilly weather gave me an excuse to put my arm around Kacie, so I wasn't going to complain.

"Okay . . . ready when you are," I said, wanting her to know that I hadn't forgotten what I'd promised her in the car, because I meant it. Anything she wanted to know, I would tell her, good or bad. Some things would probably be tough to talk about, but if she wanted to know, I'd tell her.

She sighed and I thought maybe she'd changed her mind about wanting to have the conversation, but then she jumped right in. "Who's Kendall?"

"Kendall is a friend," I answered truthfully, without hesitation.

She eyed me for a second and then looked away. "Just a friend?"

"I'm telling the truth, I promise. We've been out a handful of times, but it was never more than a friend thing. We never put any label on it. I wasn't interested."

"Did she text you while I was here?"

Shit.

"Yes. I didn't answer her; I didn't even read them. I just deleted them."

She looked at me out of the corner of her eye, gauging my honesty. "When was the last time you hung out with her?"

"Um . . ." I had to think about that one; my time with Kendall never really stuck out to me. "About a month ago, I think."

Kacie bit her lip, looking at the different storefronts as we walked. I could tell she was nervous and her brain was spinning.

"Did you sleep with her?"

I didn't want to answer this, but I'd promised honesty.

"Yes.

"Here . . ." I motioned toward the wrought-iron bench behind her. "Let's sit for a minute and I'll explain." I hooked Diesel's leash around the armrest and faced Kacie. She sat as far away as possible, her arms folded in front of her, completely closed off from me.

"Remember a couple weeks ago when I told you that all through high school and college I never really dated?"

She nodded, her beautiful green eyes staring straight ahead, digesting everything I was saying. I wanted nothing more than to pull her in my arms, relax back on this bench, and just let life happen around us, but that wasn't an option . . . yet.

"That was the truth. High school, college, up until now, I haven't had a girlfriend. Someone I would take home to meet my parents, someone I would drive an hour and a half just to see her cute smile and freckles."

She pressed her lips together tight, trying to hide her grin when she realized I was talking about her.

"I've never had anyone like that . . . but that doesn't mean I've been alone all this time."

Her eyes lost their sparkle as the color drained from her face, but I needed to continue. "Part of the territory that comes along with my job is fans. That's also my favorite part of the job . . . sometimes. There's nothing I love more than coming out of the locker room to a dozen kids waiting for me with posters and jerseys to sign. The other kind of fans are the obnoxious, overbearing women who are shoving their tits in my face, asking me to sign them and begging for my phone number as I do."

Her mouth dropped open. "Women ask you to sign their breasts?"

"More often than you'd think." I sighed. "Anyway, once I signed my contract and started experiencing all this, I swore I'd never be with a fan, and I've held true to that. But . . . I have . . . friends. Girl friends, women, who I've trusted over the years to hang out with, to . . . be with." Kacie closed her eyes and cringed when I stumbled through that last sentence.

"They are just that, though . . . friends. I trust them not to run to the media with details, not to sell our story to one of those fucking gossip magazines. That's who Kendall is . . . was." I reached out and put my hand on hers. She still stared straight ahead, no emotion. Or so much emotion that she didn't know how to process it all. Silence filled the empty space around us. I said nothing, giving her time to feel whatever it was she was feeling.

After what felt like an hour of her eyes darting around, thinking, I couldn't take it anymore.

"Kacie, you okay?"

Her head cocked to the side, her eyes still fixated on the brick brownstone straight ahead. "I think I am."

"You are?" I asked cautiously, not expecting that response.

"Yeah, I am." Her gaze floated over to me, and her face looked peaceful. "I get it. You have such a public job, it's gotta be hard to trust people with that side of you."

"Exactly!" It took all of my restraint not to scoop her up in my arms and dance around the street with her for being so understanding.

"But . . . I can't be a part of that," she said, shaking her head slowly.

"Wait, what?" Anxiety spread through my chest like wildfire.

"Your past, I get it, completely. The fame, the women, not being able to trust anyone . . . it makes total sense. I don't want that, though . . . that casual, friends-with-benefits thing. I know we said we were keeping this light and fun, but that's a little too light for me." She stood up and shoved her hands in her jeans pockets. "I can't let myself get any more attached to you, Brody. I think I'm gonna go."

"No, you're not." I hopped up and gripped Kacie's shoulders, forcing her to look at me. "I'm done with that, Kacie, all of it. When I stopped at your inn for the night, my life was normal—my life was hockey. Nothing important existed outside of the rink; it was all just filler. Then I met you, and now I can't stop thinking about you. You did something to me, changed something. And now, all I want is you . . . just you. And the Twinkies."

She looked off across the street and shook her head slightly. "How do you know that, Brody? How do you know that this is what you want? How do I know that in a month, *I'm* not gonna be tossed aside like the others?"

"I could ask you the same question," I replied.

"What?"

"You said yourself you haven't dated in four years, but I know you've had offers, so I'm asking you the same question. Why me? What is it about me that makes you want to take a leap of faith?"

"I don't know." She searched my face. "There's not one exact thing, it's just . . . you."

"That's how I feel too, Kacie. It's a million little things about you that pile up together and have created this one amazing woman who I'm certain has changed my life. I can't explain it; it's just there. We're gonna have to learn to trust each other on this one." I cupped her face with my hands and looked straight into her eyes. "This is one big puddle for both of us."

Her green eyes softened as she wrapped her arms around my waist, laying her head against my chest. I embraced back, resting my chin on her head.

"Life is a sum made up of small parts, Kacie. Some are good; some are bad. You and the girls are definitely one of the good. The best good there is, and I'll fight like hell to keep you here."

23

KACIE

I didn't sleep a wink all night. Actually, all morning.

Brody and I stayed awake until the sun came up, curled up in each other's arms on the couch, talking more about his past. Admittedly, I'd judged him when he told me how he'd been having relationships the past few years, and I was wrong for that. I would never understand his situation because I'd never been a professional athlete with women chasing after me, but I could accept it. It wasn't fair of me to hold how he'd been living against him, especially when we hadn't even met yet.

He'd been so honest last night, so sincere, not to mention irresistible. When he talked, the way his mouth moved, the way he licked his lips, the way his eyes brought whatever he said to life. Intoxicating.

He looked pretty damn cute when he slept too.

I rolled over and looked at him, stretched out on his stomach next to me, sound asleep with his arms pulled under his pillow. His firm back rose and fell with each breath, accentuating each muscle individually. I stared at his tattoo: it was vibrant and clear. I felt like it was glaring back at me, challenging me to doubt his sincerity and character.

It was never the plan for him to sleep in here with me, but after we were done talking in the wee hours of the morning, I'd gotten up to head to bed when he'd jumped in front of me and blocked the hallway.

"Listen," he'd said, "after today, I know you're exhausted and have a lot to process. I told you, I'm patient, and I don't want to push you into anything you're not ready for, but . . . will you sleep with me tonight? Sleep, nothing else. I'm just not ready to let you go yet." His eyes were forthright with no underlying meaning, hard to resist.

"Yes," I replied, pointing down the hall, "in there."

He didn't argue, he just turned and walked toward the guest room while I followed.

Here we were, a few hours later, and I hadn't slept at all. I knew I'd pay for it later, but lying there, watching him, just felt perfect. I studied every movement he made, the way his eyes fluttered while he slept, the way the corners of his mouth twitched into a slight grin when something in his dream pleased him.

Hopefully it's me.

I quietly snuck out of bed and tiptoed to the bathroom.

"Ugh," I mumbled, looking at my appearance in the mirror. My hair was going a thousand different directions, my eyes were puffy from lack of sleep, and my cheeks had no color.

I hope he likes zombies.

I tamed my hair into a low ponytail and did a quick mouthwash swish, thinking I'd creep into the kitchen and surprise him with breakfast in bed and hopefully get a kiss in return. My hand was on the bedroom doorknob when I heard him stir behind me.

"Sneaking out?"

He had flipped onto his back and was groaning as he stretched. His body was lean and long, every muscle contracting as he reached out far.

"Nope, I was gonna make you breakfast," I responded, trying not to drool as I stared.

"Uh-uh, come here." He lifted the corner of the blanket, insisting I climb back into bed. I didn't argue.

As I curled into his side, he tucked his bicep under my head and took my hand in his, resting it on his chest.

"How are you feeling today?" he asked, kissing the top of my head.

"I feel bad for judging you so hard last night, but I think I'm good. I think *we're* good." I rubbed my thumb back and forth across his chest.

"Good. I don't want anything from my past to affect us." He sighed contentedly.

"That's unrealistic, though," I said. "Everything from our past is going to play some role in how we treat each other, and how we respond to the way we're treated."

"What do you mean?"

I sighed, deciding since he'd been so honest last night, it was time I started sharing too, at least a little.

"Yesterday, when I came in to shower and I asked you about the shampoo?" I slid my face along his chest, looking up at him. He nodded, waiting for me to continue.

"You said you didn't know what I used so you bought every kind they had. To you, that seemed like nothing, you laughed it off, but to me, that was huge. I'm not used to being cared for like that. It was really sweet."

He chuckled, his laugh vibrating through my body. "It was just shampoo."

"Once, when the girls were about six months old, I had just gotten home from working a double at the hospital. It was after midnight when I got home and my car was almost out of gas. I would've stopped for it myself, but Zach didn't let me have the debit card or any credit cards. He controlled the money. Anyway, I asked him to please get up five minutes early the next morning and get me gas, so I'd have enough to get to work the next day." Brody squeezed me tight as I continued. "I went out in the morning, and naturally, he'd blown me off. I went back inside and opened the girls' piggy banks, but he'd already cleaned those out. My choices were call in sick to work, which we couldn't afford, or drop the girls at day care and take the bus from there. So, I hopped in my car and prayed the whole way to the babysitter. About six blocks from her house, my car sputtered to a stop, right past an intersection. I coasted to the side and called him, seven times. The first couple of times, it rang before the voice mail picked up. Eventually it just went straight to voice mail. He'd turned it off."

Brody inhaled loudly as his arm muscles tensed under my head.

"Just as I was pulling Lucy and Piper's infant carriers out of the car, as if God himself were testing me personally, the skies opened and it started downpouring on us. Thankfully I had two blankets in the car, and I threw them over the girls so they wouldn't get wet. I walked the rest of the way to the sitter, borrowed change from her, and took the bus to work, soaked to the bone and freezing."

Brody was smashing his teeth so hard, the muscle in the corner of his jaw was popping.

"That's how our relationship was; that's all I've ever known. So for you to do something for me like fuss over a tiny thing like shampoo was . . . big."

"Why did you stay with him?" Brody asked after a moment, shaking his head.

I shrugged. "I wanted my girls to have a family, and I was willing to sacrifice my own happiness to give it to them."

"Your happiness is just as important as theirs, Kacie. Please tell me you've learned that?" He reached down and brushed my cheek with the back of his hand.

I closed my eyes and relaxed into him. "I'm getting there."

"Good, because if someone ever treats you like shit again, they're going to have to answer to a very angry hockey player who's done a good amount of fighting in his career."

The rawness in his voice, the way he threatened and meant it, stirred something in me. I'd never had someone who wanted to protect me before, and it was the single biggest turn-on ever. Suddenly, I was overcome with the need to kiss him.

I rolled onto my side and nuzzled my nose into his neck, gently pushing his jaw up. He tilted his head to the left and eagerly let me have access. I started at the top of his collarbone and licked my way up to his jawline, running my tongue along it.

He moaned and wrapped his arm around me, pulling me in tighter. As fast as he pulled me in, he let me go and sat up. "Hang on a sec."

I propped myself up on my elbows, watching as he jumped out of bed and fumbled his way down the hall in nothing but blue-striped pajama pants. A few seconds later, his footsteps pounded along the hardwood floor as he hurried back into my room.

He leaped from the doorway and landed in bed with a thud, almost jarring me off the other side.

"Sorry about that," he growled, climbing on top of me.

"Where did you go?" I giggled in between kisses.

He sat back and flashed that heart-stopping grin at me as he wiggled his eyebrows. "Brushed my teeth."

I threw my head back and laughed hard. Brody, taking full advantage of my exposed neck by pressing his lips against my skin, planted kisses as he made his way up to the sensitive spot where my jaw met my ear. It was as if someone swept in and took over my body, as I was filled with a neediness I hadn't ever felt in my life, not even with Zach.

"I want you," I whispered as I fisted my hands in his hair, tugging at the roots.

He froze and I immediately thought I'd done something wrong.

"What?" I breathed in a panicked tone.

He pulled back slightly and leaned his forehead against mine, breathing hard. "Kacie, I promised you we'd go slow. If you want me to go faster, you're going to have to tell me."

His words dripped with sensual promise and I wanted to bathe in it. I ached for his hands all over me, reminding me that I wasn't just a mom but a grown woman with a thirst that he was more than capable of quenching.

I looked him straight in his eyes, matching him breath for breath, willing the words to leave my mouth.

"Touch me, Brody. Please?"

His eyes grew wild as he licked his lips, still panting. "I said you had to ask, not beg." With that he crashed into me, pushing me back on the bed. Within seconds, we were a mess of tongues and roaming hands and I couldn't drink him in fast enough.

He grabbed my hands and pulled me up to a sitting position, dragging my tank top over my head. His mouth was back on mine the minute the fabric crossed us, and he gently pushed me back down on the bed. He sat back and slowly pulled my pajama bottoms off. I felt so exposed, so vulnerable lying on the bed in nothing but panties. My knee-jerk reaction was to cross my hands over my chest, but before I could, Brody grabbed my wrist, stopping me.

"Don't," he said, pulling my hand away. "You're so fucking gorgeous, don't you dare cover yourself. Let me look at you for a minute. I've been dreaming about seeing this again since I saw you in that bathroom." He bit his lip, slowly looking up and down my body, his eyes lingering longer than I would have liked, but he made me feel so comfortable. So beautiful.

He laced his fingers with mine and lay back down on top of me, his own excitement digging into my hip. His hot mouth connected with my nipple, and I cried out instinctively from the jolt of absolute pleasure that coursed through my body. It had been so long since I'd been with a man. I'd almost forgotten what it felt like to have hands other than my own on me.

His mouth sucked and tugged on my nipple as his hand slowly made its way down to my panties. Just as he was about to cross the threshold inside, he paused and kissed my lips sweetly. "You okay?"

"God, yes," I moaned into his mouth. "Don't stop."

He laughed softly as he kissed me again. "Yes ma'am."

It felt like it took hours for him to trail his hand back down and reach my sweet spot, but when he did . . .

Oh. My. God.

His fingers were *so* much better than mine.

I don't know if it was the expert way he swirled them around or the fact that it had been so damn long, but within seconds, something stirred in my core.

"Brody, stop," I panted, clawing at his strong forearm.

"Stop? Are you serious?" he asked in disbelief.

"No, not stop for good, just for a second." I giggled. "I'm . . . close . . . and your pants aren't even off yet."

"That's okay, I want you to go first. I wanna watch your face." He didn't wait for my okay before he thrust his hand back in between my legs, rubbing and teasing me until my body bucked underneath his hand. Guttural noises that should have embarrassed me passed through my lips while I squirmed and convulsed my way to the most intense orgasm I'd ever had in my life.

When my tremors stopped, I cracked my eye open. Brody was lying next to me with an intense, turned-on look across his face.

"That didn't take long." I giggled.

"Neither will I." He smirked and stood, shoving his pants down around his ankles, his impressive cock springing free like a catapult from the waistband. He raised an eyebrow and grinned at me when he caught me staring, my cheeks flushing with embarrassment. He crawled across the bed, covering my body with his, and kissed me, his tongue delving deep into my mouth while his warm, hard cock lay against my inner thigh. It had been a long time since I'd had my hands on a man, but I was more than ready. I reached down and wrapped my hand around him, enjoying the hissing sound he made against my mouth as I slowly glided my hand up and down the length of him. I felt a drop of pre-cum form on his tip as I worked him harder and faster.

"Oh God, Kacie . . . wait."

I knew he was ready. I was too. He put his knee in between mine and pushed them apart gently.

Holy shit . . .

"Brody . . ." I panicked.

"Relax, I got ya, babe." He reached over and snatched the condom sitting on top of the nightstand. "Grabbed it when I was brushing my teeth, just in case." He opened the wrapper and slid the latex sleeve over his cock, then positioned himself over me. He licked his two fingers and ran them along my opening one more time. "Jesus, you're so wet." His words were hot as I begged him with my eyes not to wait another second. He read my mind, slowly pushing himself inside me.

Stretching, filling.

Once he was inside me, there was no holding back. I met him thrust for thrust, his fingers entwined with mine as he raised my hands over my head and pinned them to the bed.

"God, you feel so good," he groaned as he closed his eyes tight, pulling his eyebrows together. He was close already. So was I.

"Harder," I pleaded, on the edge of another orgasm.

His hips crashed off mine as he pushed harder into me, our skin slapping with each meeting. The erotic noises and moans that filled the room sent me spiraling into myself, quivering in pure bliss.

"Fuck, Kacie!" he called out, driving himself deep into me, stilling as his cock twitched and he came . . . hard.

He laid his head on my shoulder, trying to regain his composure while I waited for the world to stop spinning.

"You good?" he said against my neck.

"Uh . . . yes. *So* good. You?"

He rolled over, lying flat on his back, spread-eagle next to me. "I've never smoked in my life, but right now, I could go for about twelve cigarettes," he said as he leaned over and kissed my shoulder.

24

BRODY

"Can't you stay one more night?" I begged Kacie.

She was dancing around my kitchen, cooking French toast, and wearing one of my T-shirts. It's so cliché, but there really *is* something crazy hot about your girl wearing one of your shirts with nothing but panties underneath.

"I wish I could." She stuck her pouty bottom lip out at me. "I'm bummed to leave you, but I can't wait to get home to the girls. I really miss them."

Sitting down at the breakfast bar to get a better view of her show, I smiled at her. "You're a good mom."

She looked at me, pleasantly surprised. "Thanks."

"Why did you look shocked by that?" I cocked my head to the side curiously.

She looked down at the stove and shrugged. "I don't know. You're a guy . . . a *single* guy. I just don't expect you to notice stuff like that. You pay close attention and that makes me both happy and nervous."

"First of all, I'm not single. Second, why would that make you nervous?"

She walked over and looped her arms around my neck, covering my face in tiny kisses. "I don't know. I'm just waiting for the rug to be pulled out from under me, ya know? Sometimes you seem too good to be true."

I tucked a stray piece of hair behind her ear and held her face in my hands, forcing her to focus on my eyes. "I'm. Not. Going. Anywhere."

She leaned in and rewarded me with another kiss, which I gladly accepted.

Our moment was interrupted by my phone buzzing on the coffee table. Her gaze flashed over to it, then back to me, obviously still worried about what Blaire had said about Kendall.

Gripping her hand tight, I dragged her over to the couch with me and picked up the phone.

I hit the button and put it on speaker. "Hi, Mom." Kacie's eyes doubled in size, her mouth falling open like we were two teenagers who'd just gotten caught having sex in their parents' basement.

My mom wasted no time laying into me. "*Hi, Mom?* I haven't talked to you in almost two weeks and all I get is, *'Hi, Mom?'* Where have you been? I've left you about two hundred voice mails."

I propped my feet up on my coffee table and sank back into the couch, motioning for Kacie to sit down next to me.

"It's my mom," I said out loud, hoping to calm her nerves a bit.

"Who are you talking to?" my mom asked.

"My girlfriend, Kacie."

Kacie sat next to me on the couch, frozen, shaking her head back and forth as fast as she could.

"Your *girlfriend*?"

"Yes, my girlfriend. Her name is Kacie and she's fantastic. I can't wait for you to meet her."

"Hmm, interesting. Well, I'll let you go since you've got company, but apparently we have a *lot* to talk about." She sighed. "Promise you'll call me later?"

"I promise, Mom, I'll call later. Love you." I disconnected the call and tossed my phone back on the table.

"Oh my God. That was your *mom*? How embarrassing," Kacie said, dropping her head in her hands.

"Why is it embarrassing? We're adults, I'm allowed to have a girl-friend." I reached over and tugged on her wrist, pulling her onto my lap to straddle me. She didn't hesitate; she just flung her leg over the other side of my hip, still rambling on about my mom.

"It's morning, and I'm here. She's going to know we had sex." Her neck was all red and blotchy, undoubtedly flustered.

"Probably. But you know what would be even better?" I paused as she studied my face curiously. "If I can tell her we had sex twice." I gripped the back of her head and attacked her with my mouth.

She returned my kiss willingly, holding my face in her hands, letting me explore her mouth . . . possess it.

"You taste like powdered sugar," I said, breaking free to pull my T-shirt off of her.

"Oh, shit!" She tried to scramble off my lap, but I caught her hips and held her still.

"What?"

"The French toast, it's gonna burn!"

"Fuck it." I waved toward the kitchen. "Let it burn. I'm more inter-ested in something else French right now."

I kissed her again, sucking her bottom lip into my mouth while she continued arguing.

"Brody, your smoke alarm is gonna go off."

The burnt smell of charred bread filled the air and I knew she was right. Not a fucking chance was I letting her go, though.

I cupped her ass and stood up, keeping her legs wrapped around my waist as I carried her to the kitchen. I set her on the counter next to the stove, not taking my lips off hers as she fumbled around for the knob.

She turned the burner off as I grabbed the hem of my shirt and pulled it over her head, tossing it over the counter. The cold air immediately hardened her nipples about the same time I realized she didn't have panties on under my shirt after all.

"Oh my God . . . you had no underwear on."

Biting her lip, she giggled. "I know. There was no time. I was hungry."

This girl exuded sexiness from every pore in her body, even when she didn't know it. She was beautiful and confident . . . and mine.

"I'm hungry too," I mumbled, running my tongue along her neck while I squeezed her breasts and pinched her nipples gently.

She arched her back and pushed her chest into me, clearly enjoying my playing. My cotton pajama pants started feeling annoyingly tight just as she reached in and freed me. Her warm, tiny hand felt unbelievably good encasing my cock, rubbing and stroking from the base to the tip.

"Wanna go in your room?" she purred with a dazed look in her eyes.

"Hell no, I want you right here." Teasing her perfect little mouth with my tongue, I gently ran my hand from her knee all the way up her inner thigh. Her legs instantly coated in goose bumps, and she twitched as I got close to her center.

"Little jumpy, are we?"

"More like needy," she squeaked out, letting her head fall back.

Knowing that she was so anxious to feel my hands on her pussy made it difficult not to fuck her senseless right away, but I was selfish and wanted to bring her close to the edge and back again . . . but not with my fingers. I pushed her knees apart and knelt down in front of her as her head shot up, her body tensing. "Brody, wait . . . no one's ever—"

I watched her eyes roll back in her head as my tongue slowly slid from the bottom of her pussy up to her ready, swollen clit.

"What were you saying?" I teased as she groaned an unintelligible response. Tickling and massaging her tiny sweet spot with my tongue was almost as entertaining as watching her reaction to it.

Almost.

It was hard to concentrate on what I was doing when I was getting lost in her enjoyment.

Biting her lip, she leaned back against the breakfast bar, her hands desperately searching the smooth counter for something to grab on to while I continued my assault on her clit. The closer she got, the wetter she got, making it impossible for me to wait any longer. I stood up and sprinted to my room, grabbing a condom out of my drawer. I think it was the fastest I'd ever run in my whole fucking life.

"Here," I said, handing her the condom.

"You want me to put it on?" she panted, nervously.

No words came out of my mouth. I focused on her eyes and nodded.

With shaky hands, she took the condom out of the package and set it on my tip, upside down. Not wanting to embarrass her, I inconspicuously flipped it over and put my hand over hers, helping her guide it onto me. The need to be inside her was growing by the second and I'd had enough. I grabbed her hips and moved her to the edge of the counter.

"Wrap your legs around me," I growled as I pushed inside of her.

She locked her thighs around my hips, her hands clutching my shoulders as she called out from the force of my thrust.

"You okay?" I paused.

"Yeah, a little sore from earlier, but don't stop," she uttered breathlessly, pulling me tighter. "You feel too good."

I sank my cock in her as deep as I could, then slowly pulled it almost all the way out before plunging back in. Continuing this slow dance was torture on both of us, but it would be worth it in the end. My balls felt heavy, tightening as I grew close, but I knew she wasn't quite there yet.

Fuck . . .

Kitchen towel. Ceiling fan. Dog food. Pumpkins.

Kacie started rolling her hips, grinding on me as she dug her nails into my shoulder blades. "Stop playing around and fuck me," she moaned, and I couldn't help but smile at what a filthy little mouth she could have when she wanted, but I'd tease her about that later. My girl had needs. I put my hands on her ass, holding tight so she wouldn't slip backward as I drove myself hard into her, faster and faster.

"Oh, God," she hissed, biting down gently on my shoulder as her pussy tightened around my cock, the pressure of her contractions pushing me over my own edge. I squeezed her ass so tight I hoped I wasn't hurting her as I thrust through my own climax, grunting and gulping in air as fast as possible.

In no rush to move, she sat curled around me with her head resting on my shoulder, my arms wrapped around her.

"Is that your heart pounding so hard, or mine?" she asked against my skin, sounding winded.

I grinned, taking a deep breath of her scent. "I think it's yours. My heart can't pump right now. All the blood in my body is pooled in a different area."

A couple of hours and a hundred kisses later, I waved bye to Kacie as she pulled out of my parking garage and disappeared around the corner. Diesel and I went for a quick walk, and I headed back upstairs to face my mom.

"Brody Michael . . . what am I gonna do with you?" she said as she answered the phone.

"Now, Mom, is that any way to answer your phone?" I joked.

"It is when your son is in big trouble. What's going on with you?"

"Nothing, Mom. I'm good. I'm *so* good."

My mind started replaying the last day and a half I'd spent with Kacie like a film reel for my soul. Kacie grinning at me over Viper's shoulder as he tackle-hugged her, that blue dress, walking hand in hand as I showed her my favorite places around town, that blue dress, the way she finally opened up this morning and told me a little about her past, that blue dress, making love to her . . . twice.

That. Blue. Dress.

A million different emotions in such a short period of time, but it was one of the best weekends I'd ever had in my whole life.

"So, what's the deal? Who is this girl?" She sounded concerned.

"Remember a couple weeks ago when the storm parked me at that inn for a couple days? Well, she was there. She lives there, actually, with her mom . . . and her daughters." I squeezed my eyes shut, bracing for my mom's reaction.

I wanted everything about Kacie out on the table, nothing held back.

"Her *daughters*?" She sounded calmer than I was expecting.

"Yep, she's got twin girls. They're five."

"Wow." She sighed, processing the heavy load I'd just handed her. "Well . . . tell me about her, and the kids."

Lying back on my bed, I snapped for Diesel, who gladly hopped up and tucked himself into my side.

"She's beautiful, Mom. Tiny, way shorter than me, with wavy auburn hair and the most hypnotic green eyes I've ever seen. Sometimes when she looks at me, I forget to listen to her words because I'm so lost in those eyes. She does this thing when she smiles where she scrunches her nose just a little and I lose my mind every single time. Lucy and Piper are her girls and they're hilarious. The world is so big and new to them, every day is an adventure—it's the most incredible thing to watch them explore and navigate their way through each day. Everything is just bigger and better and simpler to them."

Silence on the other end of the line.

"Mom? Did I lose you?"

She sniffed. "Nope, I'm here."

"Are you *crying*?"

"Maybe."

"Why?"

"Because I've never heard you like this, Brody. Because your dad and I figured you'd be a crazy bachelor forever. Because you sound *so* happy. Because I've never even met this girl . . . and I already love her."

Yeah, Mom, you're not the only one.

25

KACIE

Lauren's wedding was only six weeks away and the list of things that still had to be done was nothing short of a mile long. Add to that my schoolwork, which I was falling miserably behind on, trying to keep the girls from complaining that it was the "most boring summer ever," and watering my budding relationship with Brody, and I was one exhausted mama. There simply weren't enough hours in the day for everything I needed to accomplish, so when Lauren knocked on my door one morning with tears streaming down her face, I knew things were about to get even more hectic.

"What's wrong?" I reached out and grabbed her sleeve, pulling her in out of the rain.

Thick, black streaks of watery mascara ran down her cheeks, and she kept wiping her swollen, red nose with a wadded-up, tear-stained tissue.

"I'm freaking out, Kacie, like totally losing my mind." She sniffed.

"Oh, God, you guys didn't break up, did you?" I asked, completely panicked. "Invitations just went out yesterday . . . I'm sorry, but you guys have to make up."

She reached out and smacked my arm. "We didn't break up, you brat, but he just called and told me that the university he's getting this hotshot scholarship through needs us to come and go to some fancy dinner with elite board members or some shit. He tried like hell to get us out of it, but they were insistent. Apparently it's a huge deal for his program. They're paying to fly us there and everything."

"That's great! A paid-for trip to Italy? Sounds like good news to me," I exclaimed. "I don't get why you're upset."

"It's next week!" She wailed into her snotty tissue again.

Oh, shit.

"If it were anywhere in the US, it wouldn't be such a big deal. I could work on my planning through phone calls and e-mail or whatever, but being all the way across the Atlantic Ocean makes everything a little more difficult," she rambled.

I sighed, looking for a silver lining. "Okay, relax. We can do this. You'll be gone—what, like three days or so?"

"Try nine!" Her words were swallowed up by more sobs.

She laid her head in my lap and howled some more while I stroked her hair, desperately thinking of a solution to her problem. My time was swallowed up whole as it was, but she couldn't afford to put the planning on hold for nine days. She was already trying to do everything in fast motion.

"Sit up," I ordered her.

"No," she refused stubbornly, hugging my legs tighter.

"Okay, you big baby, lay there, just cry quieter for a minute so you can hear me. You are going to have the most amazing wedding ever. Do you understand me? You'll be the most breathtaking bride ever and everything will be absolutely perfect that day. Does this cramp things? Yes, a little, but lucky for you, Alexa and I can multitask really well." She sat up, a glimmer of hope in her eyes. "We'll hurry and get what we can done before you leave, and while you're gone, that cranky bitch and I will step in and be your surrogate brides. Anything you need us to do, consider it done. We got this."

She threw her arms around my shoulders and started crying again. This time, thankfully, they were happy tears.

"Thank you, Kacie. Thank you, thank you, thank you."

"You're so welcome, but please don't snot on my shirt," I teased lovingly, squeezing her back.

After she hugged me for a solid two minutes, she jumped back.

"Oh my God, didn't you go to Brody's last weekend?"

I couldn't help but grin at the memory of being at his house, and in his bed, and on his counter. "Yeah."

Tears flooded her eyes again. "I'm such a bad friend." She wept. "I've been so wrapped up in my life, I haven't even asked about yours."

She hurled her arms around me again and I laughed. "Lauren, when is your period due?"

"I got it today, why?" She sniffed.

"No reason." I giggled. "Come in the kitchen. We'll call Alexa over and fill her in on the wedding stuff, then I'll tell you guys all about Brody's. It was . . . the best kind of good there is."

❖ ❖ ❖

"He fucked you right there on the kitchen counter!" Alexa opened her heavily lined blue eyes so wide they just about fell out of her head.

Lauren leaned forward in her chair, silently hanging on my every word.

"Shhhh!" I hissed, looking around to make sure no one heard her.

My mom was in our apartment, occupying the girls so we could do some planning, but this week's guests were roaming all over.

"Yes."

"Whoa," Lauren uttered.

"Yep, intense. The whole weekend was intense. Brody certainly doesn't do anything half-assed, that's for sure." I sighed happily.

"First of all, I can't believe you've been home for three days and didn't tell me that part." Alexa rolled her eyes. "But I really want to get back to this Blaire thing for a minute. Why didn't you knock her out?"

"Um, maybe because that's totally not me. I surprised myself, though." I looked back and forth between the two of them. "I've never had a problem sticking up for myself before, but with her, I couldn't. I just stood there, frozen, and it only egged her on more. When she went on about Brody and her friend Kendall, it made me sick to my stomach."

"You believe him, though, right?" Lauren asked curiously.

I thought back to the things Brody told me when we were sitting on that bench. They made sense. He had no reason to lie to me, and I couldn't be mad at him for his actions before we even met. If anything, I brought more baggage into this relationship than he did.

"I do believe him. He was very honest about all of it," I told them.

Alexa's gaze slid to Lauren and then back to me. "You know we have to stalk this girl, right?"

"What? No. No way," I argued. "I just want to be blissfully unaware about the whole thing. I don't want to know a thing about her, or her and Brody."

"Oh yeah, blissfully unaware got you real far last time, didn't it?"

Alexa's words stung, but she was right. My relationship with Zach was filled with all shapes and sizes of red flags, but I put my blinders on and pushed through, determined to mold him into the family man I wanted and the dad the girls deserved.

"We just won't tell you what we find, okay?" Lauren smiled at me, pulling her iPad out of her bag as Alexa scooted around to her side of the table with a wicked grin on her face.

"You're probably not going to be able to find anything. I know nothing about her but her first name." I folded my arms on the kitchen table and cradled my head in them. "I'm just going to nap here while you guys waste your time."

"Found her!" Alexa exclaimed.

My head snapped up, and my pulse took off. "You did??"

She peered at me from the corner of her narrowed eye and smirked. "Nope, but nice to know you're really interested."

"Okay, what is Brody's agent's name?" Lauren had her game face on.

"Andy . . . Andy Shaw."

"Let's see if we can find his bitchy wife's Facebook page and go from there." Her eyes lit up as she typed away.

"Boom!" Alexa threw her hands up in the air in celebration. "There she is—at least I think that's her. Fake boobs, fake hair, and a picture of herself in a bikini as her profile pic. Shocker."

"Is this her, Kacie?" Lauren turned the screen just enough for me to see Blaire's obnoxious sneer looking back at me, taunting me. I really wished I had that night to do over again. I would've reacted so differently.

"Yep, that's her."

"Score!" Alexa said proudly, high-fiving Lauren. I just rolled my eyes. "Now let's hope her friends list isn't private . . . crap! It is."

"Wait," Lauren said, "she's too vain to have her profile pics private. Let's see if anyone named Kendall has commented on any of them."

"You two need help, you know that?" I teased, secretly excited that they were on the trail of something. I didn't want to know anything about them being together, but the morbid, overly obsessed girl side of me was *dying* to know what she looked like. Then I would hate myself for looking, and wish that I could unsee it. That's how my world worked.

"Look, look!" Alexa pointed at the screen and jumped up and down happily. "A Kendall liked that pic of her and . . . Andy, I'm assuming. He's *cute* too! Why is he with *her*?"

"Gawk at Andy later. Let's check this chick out." Lauren's tongue ran along her lips as she concentrated, diving deep into her investigation.

"What are you looking up now?" I tried to sound nonchalant.

"I clicked on her page, but it's private. I'm gonna Google her name and see what I come up with," Lauren said. "Kendall Bauer . . . okay, Google, come to mama."

"Whoa," they both said in unison, their eyes fixated on whatever came up.

"What?" Tension rose in my chest.

Please let her have three eyes . . . and green teeth . . . and huge, hairy moles all over her face.

"Nothing, she's, um . . . okay looking," Alexa stuttered while Lauren sat wide-eyed, staring at their find.

We had been best friends for almost a decade. I could tell the very second Alexa was lying about something, and if that wasn't enough, Lauren's face was a dead giveaway. I jumped up from my chair and scrambled up behind them.

"That's *her*?"

On the screen was one of the most beautiful women I'd ever seen in my whole, entire life. She was crawling on the sand, her ultradark brown hair falling down around her face, strands of it plastered to her perfect cheekbones. Her wild eyes were an exotic shade of blue with a purple hue to them, while her pouty lips seduced the camera. A blue bikini swirled around her amazing body, accentuating every asset.

"What is this site?" I asked, scanning the screen for answers. "Oh my God, she's a *swimsuit* model?"

"Wait, just hold on a sec. This is the first link that came up," Lauren said, hitting the "Back" button. "This might not be the Kendall that he was seeing. We need to look more."

Right under her modeling website was a link to a news article. Lauren clicked on it, and within seconds the headline screamed at me.

AMERICA'S NEWEST COUPLE?
Supermodel and hockey sensation seen out for the
second time in a month.

My heart sank when I saw the picture under the headline Kendall and Brody were sitting together at a baseball game, a month ago, exactly two weeks before we met. A hunter-green baseball cap that I'd become very familiar with the last couple of weeks was perched comfortably on top of her head. They were laughing, sharing a soft pretzel. They weren't overly affectionate to each other, but now I would never get the image of her wearing his hat and them having fun together out of my head. This was *exactly* why I didn't want to look her up in the first place.

"Okay, I'm done. Can we please be done now?" I blurted out in frustration, spinning on my heels and marching down the hall to my room. I may have been a twenty-four-year-old mother of two, but that didn't mean I wasn't entitled to a hissy fit every now and then, and now was that time.

26

BRODY

"Hey, it's me."

"Hey, man, I've been meaning to call you," I said into the phone.

Andy and I hadn't talked in over a week since I'd told his wife off and walked out of their house. I definitely didn't want to have this conversation while I walked up and down the aisles of the grocery store, but I didn't want to put it off any longer either.

"I know, I should've called you too. This week is kicking my ass." Andy sighed on the other end of the line. "Listen, Brody, I'm so sorry for Blaire. She clearly had way too much to drink and acted like a total bitch—not that the alcohol was all to blame."

"It's over, no big deal," I said, wanting to put this behind us.

Listening to my best friend apologize and make up lame excuses for his wife's ridiculous behavior made me uncomfortable, but he had to know I was serious about what I said.

"I meant that last part, though, about our relationship. I'm hoping to keep Kacie around for a long time, and if Blaire ever treats her like that again, our contract will take the hit."

Froot Loops or Cap'n Crunch? Fuck it, I'll get both.

"I know. I reamed her ass when you guys left, not about the contract, though, more about being a decent human being. I hope it worked, I don't know."

He sounded defeated, and for a moment, I pitied him, but he had made the choice to marry her. She'd acted the same way in college: better than everyone, no filter, didn't care how she treated people . . . if I were Andy, I would have transferred schools and gotten as far away from her as possible.

"I hope so too."

"Listen, the other reason I'm calling . . . I have to make our reservations for that dinner in two weeks." His tone instantly switched to all business; he was good at that. "You're in for sure, right? You better be."

"What dinner?" I was clueless as to what he was talking about.

"The twelfth annual Wild Kids Charity Dinner."

That's right.

"Uh, I forgot about it, to be honest."

"Well, good thing I reminded you then. You have to be there, Brody, you're the captain of the team." Andy sounded irritated, but he usually was when I blew off things I needed to go to, or forgot to sign important papers, or got arrested for swimming naked in fountains.

"I'll be there, I'll be there."

"How many should I RSVP for? One or two?" he asked cautiously.

I didn't hesitate with my answer. "Two."

A few more minutes of mindless chitchat and Andy and I were right back to normal, like nothing ever happened. We hung up, and I tucked my phone in my back pocket and picked up really cool glow-in-the-dark sidewalk chalk I thought the girls would love. I tossed it in my cart and heard someone snicker from behind me.

"Don't you think you're a little old for sidewalk chalk?" a familiar voice cooed at me.

I spun around and locked eyes with Kendall.

"Hey," I said nervously.

"Hey? All I get is *hey*?" She strolled up to me, planting a kiss on my cheek.

"How . . . how have you been?" I stammered, praying like hell no one around us had a camera. The last thing I needed this weekend while I was up at Kacie's were pictures of Kendall and me in some damn gossip magazine.

"I'm great. I miss you." She pouted, her hands running softly down my forearm. "I've texted a few times, never heard back."

"Yeah, I saw those." A thin layer of sweat formed above my top lip, and my heart was about to pound out of my chest. "Listen, Kendall . . . I should have called to tell you—this certainly wasn't how I planned on talking to you—but I started seeing someone. The casual whatever-this-is thing we were doing . . . that's done."

She cocked her eyebrow and ran her tongue along her teeth, thinking about what I'd just blurted out in the least tactful way possible.

"Wow. Blaire told me you brought some single mom to her house, but I thought it was just a charity case or something. I didn't think you'd actually date her."

Anger coursed through my veins. I was so sick of people who didn't know Kacie making assumptions about her. I had no problem defending her—I would do that every day for the rest of my life—but it was the small-minded, materialistic assholes who knew nothing about her yet felt the need to judge her that pissed me off.

"Yep, I'm dating her. Crazy about her, actually," I sounded off. "I'm supposed to be at her house in an hour, so I'm gonna get going. I'll see you around, okay?" I patted her on the shoulder on my way to the checkout.

"Yeah, probably." She winked at me.

So far I'd only been able to come up to the inn on the weekends, but I was starting to crave the peacefulness and calm that surrounded this place during the week too. Life was better up here with Kacie and the girls. I didn't give a shit about the city, or my condo, or my contracts, or my endorsement offers . . . I barely thought about hockey, for that matter. Relaxing on that wicker couch, under the big covered porch, slyly holding Kacie's hand while the girls rode bikes and drew pictures with their new chalk, was all I needed. This and Diesel, who was sound asleep in the sun at the far end of the porch.

"So . . . do you like cake?" Kacie asked out of the blue.

"Cake?" I laughed. "I'm a guy, I love all food."

"Good." Her smile was up to no good as she turned to face me on the couch. "Next week on Thursday, do you have plans?"

"Do I ever have plans? I do the same thing every day. Eat, work out, shower, eat again, play with Diesel, eat again, and talk to you until late."

"Okay, let me rephrase." She rolled her eyes playfully. "Any chance you could come up here Thursday and go to a cake tasting with me?"

I raised my eyebrows in surprise. "A cake tasting? What the hell is that?"

"Where you taste cake," she said sarcastically, sticking her tongue out at me. "Long story short, Lauren is going to be out of town for a little bit, so Alexa and I are stepping up and doing all her wedding planning while she's away. One of the things I'm in charge of is picking out the cake, but I don't want to go alone because . . . that's a lot of pressure. Plus, then if the cake sucks, I can blame it on you."

"Oh really? You're using me as a shield, huh?" I grinned at her.

"Is that a yes?" she asked, wiggling her eyebrows up and down.

"I'll do it, but . . . it's gonna cost you." I peeked at her out of the corner of my eye.

"Uh-oh," she said skeptically as she relaxed back into the couch, crossing her arms over her chest, staring at me. "Go ahead, tell me."

"I need you to go to another dinner with me."

Her mouth dropped open and she shot up straight, ready to chew me out, but I didn't give her a chance.

"Before you say anything, it's not at Blaire's. It's for the Wild. We have a charity called Wild Kids that helps underprivileged children pay for summer camps, band instruments, and art programs . . . stuff like that. Anyway, I need a date, and I was hoping the most beautiful woman in Minnesota would accompany me." I made sure the girls weren't looking before I reached over and gave Kacie's leg a quick squeeze. I started to pull back when she put her hand on mine, holding it there.

"Leave it a minute," she said, squeezing my hand. Her eyes sparkled as she looked out at Lucy and Piper jumping rope in the yard. She took a deep, cleansing breath, and a small smile danced on her lips. "Yes, I'll go. Of course I have to run it by my mom, but I doubt it'll be a problem."

"Wow. That was easier than I thought." I followed her gaze out to the girls. "I have to warn you, and you're not allowed to change your mind since you already said yes, but Andy represents a bunch of guys on the team, not just me, so most likely he'll be there . . . with her. I meant what I said, though, I won't let her near you."

She shrugged and smiled at me calmly. "You know what? If she is, she is. If it's a charity event, I'm assuming there will be lots of people there. Who knows if I'll even see her? And if she acts like a bitch again, I'll hold my head high like a lady and walk away. Then once I get to the parking lot, I'll ask you to point out her car so I can slash her tires."

This woman blew me away at every turn. Last weekend, Blaire pounced on her like a predator attacking a wounded animal, and instead of hiding in the bushes forever, she was willing to confront her again. All the blows life had dealt Kacie had only made her stronger, and I was in complete admiration of her for that.

27

KACIE

Summer was in full swing and the last few days had been hot, and I mean . . . *hot*. The poor birds were desperately seeking relief by splashing in the various birdbaths Mom had scattered around the yard, and the lake was as full as I'd ever seen it with people boating and swimming.

After the girls covered the driveway with chalk drawings of rainbows and flowers, they were ready for a popsicle break.

"Red, please," Piper called out, hopping onto the stool at the island.

"Pink, please." Lucy followed.

"Coming right up," I said, opening the freezer.

Brody followed us to the kitchen and filled up Diesel's bowl with fresh, cold water before sitting down at the island next to the girls. "Blue for me, please." He grinned at me.

The girls giggled and started shooting questions at Brody, one right after another.

"How fast can you skate?"

"Faster than lightning."

"Why are your hands so big?"

"To match my big feet."

"Does Diesel like popsicles too?"

"Only the blue ones."

He handled his mini-interview like a pro, entertaining them with his animated answers.

"Okay, Twinkies, after popsicles, wanna go swimming?" Brody asked eagerly.

"Yay!" they cheered in unison with juice dripping off their chins.

"While you guys swim, I'm gonna bring my books down and study." I sighed. "I'm so behind."

On a scorching day like today, the cool, shaded grass felt good in between my toes as I walked down to the lake. The girls were ankle deep in the water, squealing as they ran away from Diesel, who was jumping and splashing next to them like a kid on a trampoline. Brody stood a few feet past them. His golden arms were crossed over his broad chest, while he watched them like a hawk, making sure they didn't run past him into the deep water. He looked like their own personal security guard. I liked it; he made me feel safe. Navy-blue board shorts hung off his hips, his toned oblique muscles sliding down into a sexy V as they disappeared into the top of his waistband. My face flushed when I thought about what awaited below that waistband. Knowing that it was inside me just last weekend was enough to make me want to drag him back to my room for a few minutes.

"Excuse me, what are you looking at?" His tone pulled me out of my daydream, with his accusing eyes dialed right into mine.

I looked away, flustered, and tried to find somewhere else to stare, anywhere other than back at him.

He walked up next to me on the shore, his eyes still on the kids as he leaned down and whispered in my ear, "Were you just staring at my body?"

"No," I lied as best I could, but couldn't stop myself from grinning.

"Mm-hmm," he teased. "That's okay, I was staring too. It should be illegal for you to wear a bikini out in public."

My face heated for the third time in ten minutes as I grinned at him and turned toward the tree, seeking relief from the hot sun. I spread the blanket out and lay on my stomach, flipped my book open, and started reading.

The breeze was coming in strong off the lake, blowing my hair in my face and flipping the pages of my book, making it hard to concentrate. I'm sure it also had to do with the fact that I couldn't take my eyes off of Brody in the water, playing with my girls. Their giggles of pure joy melted me more than the hot sun ever could have.

"How's it going?" I followed the feet standing next to me up to my mom's smiling face.

"It's not," I sighed, closing my book. "I can't focus and I need to get moving. My externship at the hospital starts in a few weeks."

"And the externship is what again?"

"Basically, it's job shadowing. The school placed me at Lake County Hospital in the ER. It'll be a little bit of a hike, but not too far."

"Was the ER what you wanted?"

"Yeah, we had to put down our first three choices. My first was ER, second was labor and delivery, and third was anywhere but psych." I laughed. "I'm nervous because I'll be working under a woman named Maureen, and from what I hear, she's tough. I just want to do well."

"You'll be ready." She sat down and patted my rear. "You've always been very responsible about your schoolwork, I have no doubt that you'll excel with this too."

"I hope so. I graduate in less than a year, and it'd be nice if I could land a job right away and get a little place for me and the girls." I peeked at her out of the corner of my eye, nervous about her reaction to that last part of the sentence.

She nodded slowly as a tight smile crossed her lips. "I know. You need your own place. I'd love for you and Lucy and Piper to live with me forever, but that's not healthy for you guys. You need to start your own traditions with them, grow your own family."

"Okay, let's stop talking about this before I cry. Maybe I'll just build a house next door." I laughed.

The thought of leaving my mom's nest did make me sad. She was my security blanket, my protector, my hero. She'd taken care of us for so many years. I just hoped that one day I would be half the woman she was.

"What about him?" she asked, nodding toward the lake.

I looked out at Brody, who had both Lucy and Piper on his shoulders and was marching around in the water.

"What *about* him?"

"Well, you're talking about school and moving out one day. Does he fit in your future?"

"I don't know, Mom. I hope so, but who knows." I took a deep breath. "If you would've asked me years ago if I thought Zach and I had a future, I would have said yes. What do I know?"

"Zach was an immature jerk, Kacie. You deserved way better than him." She looked at me knowingly. "The only good thing he ever did in his whole life was act as a sperm donor for my two precious grandbabies."

"I know, but my point was that clearly I don't always make the best decisions." I watched as the girls innocently tossed handfuls of water up in the air and jumped when it unexpectedly landed on their heads. "But I look at them and think I've already screwed up so bad. There is so much that they are missing out on. I just don't want to make any more mistakes."

"Kacie, snap out of it!"

My head whipped toward my mom, who was looking at me like I was crazy.

"What?" I said defensively.

"Look out at that water again, and tell me what you see."

"I see my daughters, innocently playing and laughing, not realizing how much their mom has already messed up their lives in their five short years."

"Wow . . . pity party, table for one," she scolded. "You need to look at the big picture, my dear. Do you notice that handsome man next to them? He's looking down, smiling at them with all the love he would give his own children. And the best part is . . . he's absolutely crazy about their mama. You need to let your past stay in the past and live in the now—Brody and the girls are your now. Please think about that." She reached over and kissed the top of my head before she stood and walked back up to the house.

Damn mothers and their wisdom.

28

BRODY

"How is this wrong? What does one wear to a . . . cake tasting?" I mocked in my snootiest voice while I stared down at what I was wearing.

Kacie cocked her head to the side, staring at me like I was clueless. "Brody, you're adorable, but you're dressed like you're going to work out at the gym."

"I know, I'm a genius." I grabbed the elastic waistband of my black Nike pants and stretched them out. "Elastic pants, cake tasting. Get it?"

She threw her hands up in the air as she walked her cute little ass down the hall to finish getting ready.

"What's a cake tasting?" Lucy called over from the living room, where she and Piper were playing Mario Kart on the Wii.

"I have no idea, Lucy." I sighed and walked over to the living room, sitting on the couch next to Piper. "Apparently we're gonna try a bunch of different kinds of cake and pick one for Lauren's wedding since she can't do it herself."

"Because she's in Italy?" Lucy asked, not taking her eyes off the screen.

"Exactly," I responded, watching their faces as they continued playing. Their eyes were wide, completely enthralled with their game. Lucy's little tongue darted in and out every time she pressed a button, and Piper leaned her whole body left and right with each turn. "Can I jump in with you guys?" I asked, sitting in the big chair.

"Sure!" Lucy jumped up and ran over to the TV to reset the game, while Piper shoved a controller in my lap. They both came and squeezed in on either side of me.

"Your mouth is hanging open." Kacie laughed.

I hadn't even heard her walk up behind me; I was too busy getting my ass kicked in the go-kart game by two pint-size juice box addicts.

"I was concentrating. These two are really good." Standing up, I dropped the controller on the table and held my hand out to high-five each girl. "Rematch later?"

They slapped my hands and peeked around me, still playing their game.

"You ready?" I smiled at Kacie, my eyes raking up and down her outfit. She had on a pale pink button-down shirt and a black, fitted, knee-length skirt. "Wow, I am underdressed, huh!"

She raised her eyebrows and grinned. "Just a little."

"That's okay, I'm going for comfort. You might regret that tight skirt by the end of the afternoon." I made sure the girls' eyes were still glued to the TV before I reached over and pulled Kacie in for a quick, tight hug behind their backs. I growled in her ear, "I won't mind watching you walk around in it, though."

She giggled and called down the hall, "Mom, we're gonna go, okay?"

Sophia walked into the kitchen with Fred. "Have fun . . . pick something yummy." She walked up and kissed Kacie's cheek, giving my arm a squeeze as she went by.

Fred came over and shook my hand, then scooped the girls up off the couch and carried them into the kitchen, plopping them on the island.

Kacie walked over and wrapped her arms around both of the girls' shoulders, pulling them in for one big hug. "Love you two, so so much. See you later, okay?"

She turned and smiled at me, and I stepped in behind her on the way out of the kitchen.

"Wait, Brody!" Lucy called when we were almost to the doorway. I turned to face her and she opened her arms wide; Piper copied her.

I glanced at Kacie, whose wide eyes made me nervous to push her boundaries, but I also couldn't tell those two no. Walking over, I enveloped their tiny bodies in my arms and squeezed hard, making them giggle and squeal that they couldn't breathe.

"See you later, Twinkies." I waved on our way out the door.

After a quick car ride to the next town over, we pulled up to a tiny yellow house with a white picket fence. "The Great Cakery" was stenciled on the large picture window in front.

"This is it?" I asked, surprised.

"Yep, this is *the* place to go for wedding cakes." She smiled at me as she hopped out of the truck before I could get around to open the door for her.

A bell rang above our heads as we walked through the large, stained-glass blue door and a woman in her mid-fifties came over to greet us. She was a short, chubby woman who radiated as much pleasant energy as anyone I'd ever met. I didn't even know her name yet, and I already liked her. Frosting smudges of every color were smeared across her white apron.

"Hi there. You must be Kacie?" she said as she reached out and took Kacie's hand in both of hers. "I'm Pearl, so nice to meet you."

"Hi, Pearl, nice to meet you too. This is my boyfriend, Brody. I brought him to help me make a decision."

Her eyes met mine as she directed her cheerful grin my way. "Hi, Brody . . . wait. Brody Murphy? Number thirty for the Minnesota Wild? Best goalie in the league? Two-time NHL MVP?"

I smiled politely. "Yes ma'am. It's nice to meet you."

"Oh my God." She giggled nervously. "I'm a huge fan. My husband and I are season ticket holders, have been for years."

"Well, I thank you for that. Once the season starts, you'll have to get in contact with me. I'd love to give you and your husband a special tour around the stadium."

She snorted with excitement. "Oh my, I'd love that. Wow. Thank you." Her eyes darted back and forth between me and Kacie while she wrung her hands, all flustered. "This is such a pleasant surprise. Lauren called last week and explained her situation to me, that you'd be coming in her place, but I had no idea Brody Murphy would be coming with you."

Kacie looked away, smirking at Pearl's excitement.

"I don't think she knew. We're excited, though. I even wore my elastic pants." I grinned at Pearl, and her face flushed.

Kacie's head snapped back to me, her eyes bulging out of her head as her hands flew over her mouth, barely able to contain her laughter.

"Well, come on back and we'll get you all set up." She motioned for us to follow her.

Kacie poked me hard in the side, still chucking. "I can't believe you just said that. Elastic pants, really?"

"It's true," I defended myself. "And I *am* excited—this might be the best day ever."

Pearl led us to a large room through the back door, right next to the kitchen. A table with four chairs sat in the middle, and built-in shelves full of framed pictures of wedding cakes lined the wall to our right.

Kacie and I sat down at the table while Pearl strolled over and took an oversize binder off the bottom shelf. She set it down in front of us and said, "Here, take a look at this while I get the first plate ready.

Lauren already picked the outside, but it just gives you an idea of what we have. I'll be right back." She stopped by the doorway and turned back to us quickly. "What can I get you to drink? Some people like milk, while others prefer water."

"I'll have milk, please." Kacie smiled courteously.

"Two, please."

Kacie cracked open the binder as Pearl disappeared around the corner. I watched her eyes flutter excitedly around the pages filled with pictures of big white cakes that had fake flowers trailing down the sides.

"Are those *diamonds*?" I asked, gawking at a picture that caught my eye.

"Not real ones, they're edible. Amazing, huh?"

I turned up my nose and leaned in close to her, not wanting Pearl to overhear me. "These are all too white. Where's the color? The excitement?"

"These are wedding cakes—they're supposed to be elegant, not exciting."

I walked over to the shelf and grabbed a different binder. "This one looks better." It was full of birthday cakes, retirement cakes, engagement cakes . . . every type of cake you could think of.

"And . . . here we are with your first batch." Pearl set a tray on the table with milk in two fancy-looking glasses that looked way too breakable for me to hold, and a plate with about ten squares of cake on it. "There are two of each kind: our basic chocolate, German chocolate, dark chocolate with a raspberry layer in the middle, crème de menthe, and Oreo."

My head snapped up at Pearl. "You make Oreo wedding cake?" I asked incredulously.

"Yep, and we can put a layer of fruit filling or custard in between too, if you want. Basically, you can completely design your own." She shrugged her shoulders excitedly and grinned at us. "Okay, take your time, sample them, talk about them, and I'll be back in just a bit with your white cake options."

Grabbing a fork off the plate, I dived right into the Oreo cake.

I rolled my eyes back in my head and dropped the fork. "Oh. My. God."

"That good, huh?" Kacie asked, trying it for herself.

"Yes!" I groaned. "I think I'm hard."

"Shhh! Not so loud!" She giggled.

"Seriously, this is the best thing I've ever eaten in my whole life . . . almost." I winked at her.

She gasped and turned a shade of red so dark I was worried her head would explode right there in front of me.

"Do you agree?"

"Yes, I think it's delicious," she said once she regained her composure. "And really moist."

"Oh no, stop right there." I held my hand up. "It's a little late, but it's my turn to implement a condition on our relationship."

Kacie blinked rapidly, frowning at me. "What?"

"The word *moist*, you can't ever say it again."

She threw her head back and laughed at me, covering her mouth so that cake didn't spill out.

"No, no. Stop laughing, I'm serious," I said, but that only made her laugh harder.

She inhaled deeply and coughed, choking on her cake.

"See, that's what you get for making fun of me," I teased in a self-righteous tone. After she was done hacking, she took a big gulp of milk and wiped her mouth with a napkin.

"So why don't you like the word *moist*?"

"Ah-ah-ah. What did I *just* say?" I warned, waving my finger.

"Why don't you like *that word*?" she asked, still chuckling.

"It just sounds gross. Doesn't it?"

"I don't know, I've never really thought about it. It's just a word."

"No, *spoon* is a word. That other *m*-thing is vile. It's like a porn word or something. It needs to be removed from the English language." I shuddered.

"Porn word? Are you innocent all of a sudden? Do I need to remind you about last weekend?"

I didn't speak, I just glared at her.

"Okay, if you feel so strongly about it, I'll be careful not to use it . . ." She smirked. "Unless I'm trying to piss you off."

"How's it going in here?" Pearl interrupted.

"Slow, sorry," I responded. "She doesn't know how to use a fork, so she keeps choking," I joked, pointing to Kacie, whose eyes bulged out of her head.

"Oh dear, do you need a spoon?" Pearl asked, completely serious.

Kacie was laughing so hard, no sound came out—all she could do was shake her head.

"Okay then, no rush. I'll bring the white selections back in a minute; that way you can compare if you want to."

Half an hour and eighteen cake squares later, I was beyond stuffed and extremely thankful for my elastic pants.

We'd tried every piece and had finally decided on the dark chocolate with raspberry filling, even though I pushed really hard for the Oreo. I had to . . . for Tommy. I was killing time flipping through the birthday binder again while we waited for Pearl. One of the cakes showcased in the binder was nothing short of incredible. It was a two-foot-tall exact replica of the castle at Disney World with what I assumed were all the princesses scattered around it. Cinderella, the only one I recognized for sure, was standing on a balcony with Prince Charming.

"Holy shit, Kacie. Look at this!" I turned the book so she could see it.

Her mouth dropped open and her eyes lit up.

"Wow. I mean . . . wow."

"When is the girls' birthday? They need this cake."

"In a couple of months, August thirty-first. I can't get this cake, though, Brody. Did you see the price?"

I spun the book back around and looked at the sticker next to the picture, which I'd totally overlooked.

"Two seventy-five? For cake?"

She nodded slowly. "I told you this place was the best. Lauren is spending a grand on this wedding cake. This place is *way* out of my budget."

We'll see about that.

29

KACIE

Alexa and I impressed ourselves with all that we got checked off our list while Lauren was away.

Cake, band, and flowers . . . done. Centerpieces weren't even on our list, but we found the most beautiful antique vases at a flea market for a steal and couldn't pass them up. Lauren was beyond thrilled with our progress and gushed about how grateful she was. The minute she got back into town, I made her repay the favor by helping me get ready for the charity event with Brody. I wanted to dress to kill; no way was I going to give Blaire any ammunition tonight.

There was no fashion show this time; nor did Mom or I have a say in what I wore. Lauren had a handful of expensive designer dresses that she was saving for a special occasion, and she insisted I wear one of them tonight.

It was a red, fitted Nicole Miller jersey-style dress that gathered down the front and back, showing off the waist Lauren said most women would kill for. Silver, strappy Jimmy Choos that she'd never even worn fit my feet like Cinderella's slippers, nicely showing off the pedicure I had gotten earlier that day with the girls. I never wanted to forget how adorable they looked sitting in those big chairs, grinning from ear to ear with their cute little toes barely reaching the water.

The Wild Kids event was halfway in between my house and Brody's, so it didn't make sense for me to drive all the way to his place. He told me he'd be by at six fifteen to pick me up. As usual, I was ready early and pacing the kitchen like an expectant father.

"Sit down, relax," Mom called from the living room, patting the couch cushion next to her.

"I can't, I'll wrinkle my dress. I want everything to be perfect."

She got up and came into the kitchen, keeping me company while I paced. "Well, you look beautiful and happy. You're glowing. I could cry just thinking about what a change I see in you the last month and a half since you've met Brody. He really is a blessing."

My chest warmed at his name. It'd been almost a week since I had seen him, and I was aching to wrap my arms around him. This long-distance thing was rough, but it made me really appreciate the time we were able to spend together, not to mention the dozens of hours on the phone we spent really getting to know each other. We still never ran out of things to talk about.

"I know, Mom. I'm pretty crazy about him."

"I already knew that—you two don't exactly hide it well. The way you look at each other across the room, the involuntary way you grin when I say his name, the way your heart swells when you see him playing with the girls . . . you two are the real deal." Tears welled up in her eyes.

"Don't make me cry, my makeup will run." I waved at my eyes, hell-bent on keeping them bone-dry. "It's so strange, I went into this bound and determined not to let it get too serious, but I don't think that's what I want anymore. I judged him. I assumed because of what he does for a living, he wasn't capable of being a good guy, a family guy. He's proven me wrong time after time. I like him, Mom. I like him a lot."

"I like the way that sounds." A husky voice behind me set every nerve in my body on fire. As I spun around, my breath caught in my throat.

Wow.

Brody looked like he'd just stepped out of an Armani magazine ad. He was leaning against the wall with one arm behind his back and the other holding on to the lapel of his jacket. The lines of the black tuxedo he wore were tailored perfectly to his body, accentuating every detail from his broad shoulders to his trim waistline. His normally untamed short curls were slicked back just enough, his face silky smooth. Brody was this crazy, macho professional athlete, but tonight, he could easily have passed as a model.

"Wow. You look great, way better than great. So far past great, you can't even see great anymore." I was nervous and rambling. I couldn't even think of a word to justify how amazing he looked.

"You, . . . my girl, are breathtaking." He took a step toward me, revealing that in the hand behind his back were a dozen perfect red roses. When he got to me, he lifted my hand to his mouth, gently brushing his lips across the top. "When we walk into that room, you're going to put every other woman to shame. How lucky am I that you'll be on my arm?"

My mom sniffed again as Piper came barging into the kitchen. "Mom, come look at this car. It's the longest one I've ever seen!"

"What?" I looked from her to Brody, confused. "What is she talking about?"

Brody shrugged nonchalantly and cocked his head to the side. "The limo."

"You rented a limo?"

"I wanted to give all my attention to you tonight, didn't want to worry about driving. Come on." He took my hand in his and pulled me toward the front door.

"Would you mind putting these in water for me?" I handed the roses to Mom on the way out of the kitchen, laughing at the tiny Twisted Petal logo on the plastic wrapper. Knowing Alexa, she went through dozens of roses to handpick the perfect ones for me.

The girls were standing in the front room, their faces fogging up the glass as they stared at the limousine.

"You guys wanna go for a quick ride?"

"Yay!" they squealed and jumped up and down like they would've if he'd bought them each a pony.

He opened the front door and stepped back, waiting for the three of us to go out. Once the girls hit the porch, they were out, sprinting across the yard like Olympians running for the finish line.

"Relax," I said in my mom tone as I walked up behind them. "We're going to sit nice in here and not break or ruin anything. Got it?"

They didn't hear a word I said but nodded anyway as I pulled the limo door open and they climbed inside. Once they were in, I bent down to climb in myself and stopped when I saw the red rose petals sprinkled all over the floor of the limo. I sat down on the bench opposite Lucy and Piper and looked at Brody apologetically when he joined me, knowing this wasn't the way he wanted the night to start out.

He shrugged it off and delivered his smile that could make all my troubles disappear. "I wanted you to feel like a princess tonight." He nodded across at the girls, who were excitedly pushing and spinning every knob and button they could find. "Now I have three princesses." He leaned over to drop a kiss on my forehead, but I was done hiding things from the girls. I wrapped my hand around the back of his neck and redirected his mouth onto mine, meeting in a sweet, wonderful kiss.

No tongue—I wasn't anywhere near ready to teach the girls about all that yet.

Brody asked the chauffeur to drive up and down the main road off our driveway for the next ten minutes. The girls either didn't notice or didn't care that we were driving in a big circle; they were too fascinated with the TV in the car, then the radio in the car, then the fridge in the car, where they discovered bottled water they just *had* to have.

We dropped the girls off with Mom and we were on our way. Brody slid the cover off the built-in cooler in the limo and pulled out a bottle of Cristal. "Glad they didn't find the good stuff," he said, winking at me as he pulled out two champagne flutes and poured us each a glass.

I took the glass from him as he leaned over and kissed me softly.

"Here's to a night we'll never forget."

Truer words were never spoken.

Our limo crawled to a stop at the curb of the Prescott Pavilion, and I was shocked at the chaotic scene of fancy cars, security guards, and photographers.

"*This* is a charity dinner?" I asked, staring incredulously out the window. I don't know what I had expected to see, but this definitely wasn't it.

"Yep, this is it." He squeezed my hand. "You ready?"

An attendant dressed in a crisp white shirt with a black tie and black pants rushed over and opened the door for us. Before I took the young man's hand and got out, I glanced back at Brody to see if he was as nervous as I was. He calmly buttoned his jacket and winked at me.

"Let's go."

I stepped out and moved off to the side so Brody could follow.

"That was a nice view," he whispered into my ear once he was out.

He offered up his arm and I hooked mine through immediately, smiling up at him. We walked up a few steps and heads started to turn; people started to whisper.

"Brody, people are staring," I breathed, leaning in close.

"I know. It's okay. We'll walk the red carpet and go right inside. Just a few more minutes."

"*Red carpet?*" My voice cracked in a panic. "You didn't tell me about that."

"Breathe." He reached up and squeezed my hand reassuringly. "I didn't want you to freak."

"Well, that worked out well, didn't it?"

He stopped walking and pulled me over to the side. "Do you not want to do this? I can walk alone and meet you inside if you'd rather? I want you to walk with me, but I'm not going to force you."

Dread whirled around in my stomach, knocking down everything in its path as it spun and grew like a twister in the summer heat. A month ago, the biggest decision of my life was what shade of pink to paint Lucy and Piper's fingernails; now I had to decide whether or not to walk the red carpet at the charity dinner for my new boyfriend's hockey team. It wasn't the walking that made me nervous; that part was easy—one foot in front of the other. It was the people staring, whispering, and pointing that made me want to crawl out of my own skin.

I looked into Brody's soothing green eyes as he bit his lip, patiently waiting for my answer. I was proud to be his girlfriend and I wanted him to know that. Soon enough, people would figure out who I was anyway. I might as well rip the Band-Aid off fast, right?

"Let's do this," I said, raising up on my tippy-toes and planting a kiss right on his beautiful mouth.

He palmed the back of my head and held me there, elongating our kiss before he rested his forehead on mine.

"You. Amaze. Me."

I didn't have time to tell him he amazed me more before he took my hand in his own and morphed into Sports Superstar Brody, confidently shaking hands and working his way through the crowd.

The red carpet was overwhelming, suffocating. Flashbulbs right in my face, hundreds of them causing me to blink so fast, I'd be surprised if there was one picture with my eyes open. My heart was pounding as hard as ever; the only thing keeping me from sprinting back to the limo and barricading myself inside was Brody's warm hand resting comfortably on the small of my back.

Brody! Brody, over here! Brody!

The reporters were piranhas, all begging for his attention as we walked the line, pausing for pictures every five feet or so.

"Brody Murphy, who's your date?" one yelled out over the others. "Is she your new girlfriend?"

"She's my *only* girlfriend," he yelled back to the feeding frenzy with that charming grin plastered to his face.

"Do we get her name?"

"Soon enough, soon enough. Tonight is about the kids, though, don't you think?" He went over and signed a few autographs, took a few pictures, and the crowd cooled it a bit. He said good night to the masses and led us inside.

After a few more stops to meet people in the foyer, we headed into the ballroom.

Oh my God.

The room was permeated with the soft, unmistakable smell of roses. Every table was decorated with the lushest white and silver linens, and the tabletops were sprinkled with enough candles to give the entire room a romantic glow. Waiters in black tuxedos strolled from person to person, balancing sterling silver trays of foreign-looking food on their fingertips. Bartenders poured pale, bland-looking drinks. Personally, I liked my alcohol in brown glass bottles.

As I stood, completely mesmerized, taking in all of the beautiful scenery in that room, I didn't even notice Andy walk up to us. I turned as he and Brody were doing their weird man hug. I immediately panicked and peeked to see if anyone was behind him.

Not anyone—Blaire.

"She's not with me," Andy said as he turned toward me.

My cheeks flushed with embarrassment that I'd been caught looking for her.

He leaned forward and gently kissed my cheek. "She actually wanted to come over and apologize, but I told her she was to stay away from you the whole night. I don't even want her looking at you. And it has nothing to do with Brody's contract; it's because you're the girl who has made my best friend the happiest I've seen him since he was twenty-one and got signed to play professionally." A tight smile formed on his lips, and I couldn't help but give him a bigger smile back.

"I appreciate that, Andy. Thank you."

"I'm so sorry for the way she acted. You didn't deserve that. It won't happen again, I promise."

Brody stuck his hand out for Andy again and they shook in some sort of show of mutual respect. He turned and walked away, and I let out a breath I didn't even realize I'd been holding.

"You okay?" Brody looked nervous.

A small laugh built up inside me at the irony of *that* interaction making him nervous, but the hordes of people outside calling his name and clawing at him was nothing.

"I'm good." I beamed at him. "I'm so good."

"Let's find our seats, then get a drink, huh?"

I was having the best time . . . dinner was out of this world, the people at our table were wonderful, and Brody couldn't keep his hands, or lips, off me.

I felt like Cinderella.

"I'm gonna use the restroom. I'll be right back, okay?"

Brody stood politely as I got up from the table. Dina, a wife of another hockey player, got up and said she'd go with me. We gabbed about hockey life once the season started, and she actually put my mind at ease. Her life wasn't so different from any other woman who had a husband that traveled for work.

"I'm so glad we talked. You really calmed my nerves."

"Absolutely! You're so sweet. Brody is lucky to have you," she said as she reapplied her lipstick. "You coming?"

"I'll be right behind you . . . I'm going to call my mom and check on the girls."

She smiled and squeezed my hand on the way out.

"Hockey wife? You really think *you're* going to be a hockey wife?" an achingly familiar voice cackled as I started to dial my mom's number.

My stomach flip-flopped as Blaire slithered out of one of the bathroom stalls. "Hi, Kacie. So nice to see you again."

"Hi, Blaire," I said, tucking my phone back in my purse. "I'll see you later."

"Where are you going? I wanted to talk to you some more." Her tone dripped with insincerity as she inspected herself in the mirror. "We never finished our conversation a couple of weeks ago because your douchey boyfriend so rudely interrupted us."

You have got to be kidding me. She doesn't sound very apologetic. What the hell was Andy talking about?

"He's not a douche, Blaire, and I'm not about to stand here—"

"Oh, you're gonna stand there, or you would've been gone already." She turned and looked at me with venom in her eyes. "Admit it, you *want* to know all I know about Brody, because the truth is, you barely know him yourself."

I stood frozen, like an animal in her crosshairs, but I felt stronger this time. Maybe I couldn't get my legs to move, but my mouth certainly could.

"You know what, Blaire? I think it's *you* who doesn't know Brody."

She tossed her head of thick blond hair back and laughed. "Did he tell you all about Kendall?"

I put my hand on my hip and cocked it to the side. "As a matter of fact, he did."

"Oh really?" She straightened up and smirked at me. "Did he tell you he saw her last weekend?"

Bile rose up in my already uneasy stomach. Breathing in through my nose and out through my mouth, I did my best to keep my dinner down, not wanting her to know she was getting to me . . . again.

Is she lying? She has to be lying. He wouldn't have seen her again, right? Not after we . . .

"I don't believe a damn word you say, Blaire."

"Okay," she said, as she whipped her phone out and thumbed something onto the buttons. "I'll prove it to you, Princess."

"I don't have time for your bullshit. My date is waiting for me." I turned to leave the bathroom, but that didn't stop her.

"Go ahead, live it up while you can, it's only a matter of time before he throws you away too," she cooed.

God, this obnoxious woman knows how to push my buttons.

"You don't know what the hell you're talking about," I spat as I turned around.

"Of course I do, Kacie. I've seen it a hundred times with him. He likes a girl and brings her around constantly for a few weeks. As soon as he gets sick of her, he tosses her aside and goes on to the next." She faced the mirror and tousled her hair.

I'd had enough. Nothing I could say would get through her stone exterior; I was just wasting my breath arguing. I stomped toward the bathroom door and almost fell through it when it was pulled open from the other side.

"Sorry," I muttered, trying to regain my balance.

"No problem," the girl with beautiful dark waves and bright bluish-purple eyes said to me.

Bluish. Purple. Eyes.

"You must be Kacie? Blaire has told me so much about you." She smiled with rows and rows of perfect white teeth. "I'm Kendall."

I whipped around to face Blaire, who'd walked up behind me. "What the hell?"

"She texted me and asked me to come meet you," Kendall answered for her. "She said you had some questions about Brody and last weekend."

"I don't have any questions." Anger grew in me and seeped out of my pores as I glared back and forth between the two of them. "You two are insane."

Beth Ehemann

"Calm down, drama queen. I just wanted her to confirm that she did see him last weekend. Didn't you, Kendall?"

"Mm-hmm," she purred. "He was such a sweetie, and a great kisser too."

"Face it, girl. You're nothing but a summer fling," Blaire hissed into my ear. "The only thing he'll ever *really* love is hockey. Once the season starts, you'll be in the rearview mirror crying in your fake designer purse. He'll move on . . . and you can focus all your efforts on making cupcakes with your kids."

I rushed past both of them and headed straight for an emergency exit opposite the ballroom. I needed space. Once outside, I sucked in the cool, crisp air as fast as I could, begging my pulse to slow to a normal rate.

What am I supposed to do now?

I could go flying into the ballroom and start screaming and yelling at Brody like a lunatic, embarrassing both him and myself and making Blaire and Kendall squeal with delight in the process. Or . . . I could tuck my tail between my legs and wait. Wait until we were alone. Wait until I had time to think about the things Blaire had said. Wait until I could distance myself from him enough emotionally so that all of this wouldn't hurt so much.

That's what I would do. Wait.

30

BRODY

"Everything okay?" I stood as Kacie came back to the table. "You were gone a long time."

"I'm . . . fine," she stammered, delivering the fakest smile I'd ever seen on her perfect face.

"What's wrong?"

"Nothing."

"I went looking for you and ran into Blaire. She said you two were chatting in the bathroom. What did she say?"

"Nothing. I just needed air for a minute. I'm fine."

"Okay." I reached for her hand, but the second I touched her she tensed up.

There was that damn word again. Fine.

We limped our way through dessert, barely talking. She seemed to purposely ignore me and chat up Dina, who was sitting on the other side of her, while I talked halfheartedly with my other teammates.

The CEO of the Wild Kids Foundation gave his closing speech and the crowd started to thin out. "You wanna hang around and have another drink?" I asked Kacie, hoping she'd say no so I could get her out of here and rip that dress off her with my teeth.

"Nah, I'm really tired," she answered dryly.

"Okay, well, then you might be happy with the surprise I have for you."

Confusion swept across her face as she just stared at me.

"I talked to your mom earlier about watching the girls overnight tonight and booked us a room in the hotel across the street. A suite, actually."

"Oh." Her face was unreadable. "Would you mind if we didn't stay? I'm really tired and want to sleep in my own bed."

Disappointment weighed on my shoulders. I knew there was something more going on in her head than just being tired.

"Kacie, what's going on? You're acting *so* different."

"Nothing, this night has just been a little overwhelming." She smiled tightly. "It was just another reminder of how glaringly different our lives are, Brody."

"Okay, but why is that a bad thing?"

She swallowed and thought for a minute. "I just have a lot to think about."

"I don't get it. I thought you were okay with the differences and that we were going to slowly work on blending our lives."

Her phone rang and she pulled it out of her purse. "It's my mom, I'll be right back," she said and walked away to hear.

What the hell happened in that bathroom?

"Blaire," I called, walking up behind the blond bimbo.

She turned and glared at me. "Yes, dirtbag?"

"What did you say to Kacie? She's acting weird."

"Nothing. We fixed our makeup and chatted about how yummy dinner was." A sneer crossed her face. "Maybe she finally realized what a loser you are and decided to get out while she still can."

Andy nudged her and shook his head.

"Just remember what I said . . . ," I warned. "If I find out you were a bitch to her again, you're gonna be driving a Kia instead of a Range Rover."

I turned to go find Kacie when Blaire spat from behind me, "Don't threaten me, dick."

Not turning around, I called over my shoulder, "It's a promise."

The limo pulled up to her house, and before I could consider locking her in and forcing her to talk to me again, she hurried out of the limo. Once we got inside, the brush-off continued. She tried to race off to bed right away, but I caught her wrist and pulled her into my arms. She relaxed into my chest immediately, almost like my hug was a relief. I held her tight, hoping that she'd open up and tell me what was really going on, but as long as she wasn't pulling back away, I would just hold her there as long as she wanted.

My chin rested on top of her head and I brushed her hair with my fingers. When she didn't pull back, I ran my hands softly up and down her bare arms, smiling slightly as her soft skin broke out in goose bumps under my fingers. She lifted her head and looked up at me; something was different in her normally sparkly green eyes.

Sad.

In that moment, I had a new goal of taking her sadness away. I hooked my finger under her chin, raising her face higher. I ran the tip of my nose along hers, testing the waters to see if she would push me away.

"I'm gonna go kiss the girls good night and crawl into bed." The words came out of her mouth, but she didn't move. The electricity between us was off the charts. We were playing an emotional game of chicken, waiting to see who would budge first.

"Can I go with you?" I asked quietly.

She inhaled sharply. "Brody, we're at my house. I told you I don't want the girls to know anything."

"Is that really the reason you don't want me to go with you?"

"Yes."

I didn't sleep much, but I doubt it had anything to do with the lumpy couch. I kept replaying the night's events over and over, looking for anything that could have set her off. Had Dina said something about life with a hockey player being hard? Was that why she was thinking twice now?

Diesel woke me early to go outside. After he was done with his business, I was in no hurry to go back to the couch, so I decided to relax on the deck overlooking the lake. As soon as I sat down, Diesel curled up in a ball and went right back to sleep.

"Some companion you are." I glared at him as he peeked one eye at me.

Just as my body relaxed and I finally started to drift off to sleep, the French doors opened, startling me.

Sophia stopped when she saw me jump. "I'm sorry, were you sleeping?"

"No, no, it's okay. Come on out." I sat up and ran my hands through my hair.

Diesel walked over and sniffed her leg as she sat down on the chair next to me, immediately curling up at her feet.

"Kacie is damaged, Brody."

I looked at her but didn't want to derail her train of thought, so I said nothing.

"When her father told me he wanted a divorce, he divorced Kacie too. I don't know if that's what he meant to do or if he was just too embarrassed to look her in the eye afterward. Either way, he moved on with his life and had a couple of other kids with that woman, leaving

Kacie to wonder what she'd done wrong. She took it very personally, blamed herself for their failed relationship."

She took a deep breath, her eyes staring out at the lake. "She tried to contact him a few times, but he never returned her phone calls, and eventually he changed his cell phone number. That was a big blow to her confidence. It took her a while, but eventually she let it go."

My chest hurt. I couldn't imagine the pain of being pushed away by one of your parents, the people who were supposed to love you unconditionally your whole life.

"About the time she got over the abandonment of her father, she met Zach. Has she told you much about him?"

"Not really. I know that he left and she hasn't talked to him since."

"They met in high school and she was drawn to him immediately. They were stupid teenagers and did stupid teenage things. Then, she wound up pregnant."

Hearing about Kacie with Zach sucked to listen to, but this was the most insight I'd ever had into her past.

"I never liked him; something about his arrogant demeanor just bothered me. Call it mother's intuition or whatever, but I knew they wouldn't last. Kacie, on the other hand, was hell-bent on making this family last and giving her girls what she never had. A father. It was the week before the girls' first birthday when she came home from work and the new sitter was at their house with the kids. There was a note on the counter for her from Zach. Basically, he just said *sorry* and took off."

"He left her a letter?"

She scoffed. "It hardly classified as a letter. He scribbled a quick little 'See ya' on the back of a receipt and left. That was it. She hasn't talked to him since."

Her eyes stared into mine, the same shade of green as Kacie's, but Sophia's eyes were older, wiser.

"I shouldn't be telling you this—Kacie would kill me if she knew— but I know that she's feeling things for you she hasn't felt in a long time.

I also know that she panics when she feels like this, and she runs. She's developed this 'Get them before they get me' attitude about men. I like you, Brody, I like you a lot, and I think you're a sincere man. I just wanted you to know this about her, because my guess is she'll never talk about it." She smiled sadly, like she was worried that I was going to bail too.

"I appreciate you telling me all this, Sophia. She's been acting weird with me since last night. I've asked her what was wrong a million times. All she keeps saying is that she has a lot on her mind and Lauren's wedding is stressing her out."

Sophia stood up to go in the house and I followed. "Give her time, Brody. Let her work this out in her head. I promise she's worth it."

I leaned over and kissed her cheek. "I already knew that part, Sophia."

31

KACIE

"You met *Kendall*?" Lauren's mouth hung open, and Alexa's face mirrored hers.

"Yep." I sighed. "Almost fell right onto her feet, literally."

"What the hell was she doing there, anyway?" Alexa scoffed.

"She was a season ticket holder; apparently they get an automatic invite to the dinner." I reached over my kitchen island and grabbed a handful of grapes. "Pearl was there too." I directed my attention to Lauren. "The cake lady, she's so sweet."

Lauren stared in space, processing what I'd just told them about the charity event and running into Blaire . . . again. I hadn't been completely silent like the last time she verbally assaulted me, but I also wasn't as strong as I wish I could have been. My brain was going one hundred miles per hour, too busy thinking about all of the things she was spewing and trying not to puke. Was I really just a summer fling? Brody seemed so much more sincere than that. I'd turned him down in the beginning, but instead of giving up and moving on to another girl, he had come back and made me change my mind. If he wanted Kendall so much, why do all that? Why not just go back to her?

"What are you thinking about, Pooks?" Alexa looked at me sympathetically.

"Nothing." I tried to fake a smile, but it was no use with these two. They knew me better than anyone, as evidenced by the skeptical glares they both gave me in return.

I sighed. "I just can't get what she said out of my head, the summer fling thing." I frowned and shook my head. "I went into this trying to be cautious, but Brody has this way of blasting right through my walls and making me feel things that I was never sure I'd feel again. I always thought one day I'd marry and assumed I'd be happy, but with him it's different—I'm way more than happy. He makes me laugh, he makes me think, he makes me want . . . more out of life. When I'm with him, I'm totally drunk on him and nothing else matters."

Tears escaped Lauren's eyes as she and Alexa gawked at me.

"Oh my God . . . you're in love," Alexa said flatly, while Lauren grinned and nodded like a bobblehead next to her, dabbing her eyes with a tissue.

"I am *not*. I'm just confused." I groaned. "Trying to decide whether to pull the chute now or wait it out."

"What's your gut tell you?" Lauren asked.

"This is Kacie we're talking about. You know she's gonna run," Alexa spat.

"What's that supposed to mean?" I glared at Alexa, not liking her accusatory tone.

"That's what you do, Kacie. Ever since I've known you, you've always waited for the worst to happen in every situation," she said calmly. "It got worse after Zach left. The minute he was out the door, you closed yourself off, and now you run the minute things start to get real."

"That's not true!" My hands started shaking as my tone grew louder.

"Oh really?" She raised her eyebrows as she challenged me. "What has Brody done to make you jump ship?"

I sat silent, looking from Alexa to Lauren, hoping she would step in and defend me, but she was clearly on Alexa's side with this.

"Exactly . . . nothing," she continued. "You're letting those two bitches get into your head about Brody and it's ridiculous. Seems to me that Kendall still wants Brody, but he clearly has no interest in her. Why on earth would you believe those skanky hos over him?"

Lauren's gaze whipped toward Alexa. "Did you just say 'skanky hos'?"

"I don't know." I ignored Lauren, fingering my silver necklace.

"You do know but you don't want to say it, so I'll say it. You're scared." She tilted her head to the side and waited for me to argue, but I couldn't. "I'll continue . . . you're scared because while you didn't plan for it, you've fallen for this guy, head over heels. You're in love with him and that's a *good* thing, Kacie, but you don't see it like that."

"She's right." Lauren finally spoke up. "It *is* a good thing. Brody seems like a great guy, and more than that, he seems just as crazy about you. Why would you end that?"

"Because she thinks she's not worthy of him."

My head snapped up at Alexa, tears stinging the corners of my eyes.

"You think that because your dad left, and Zach left, that Brody will too, and that's not necessarily true." Alexa came around the island and pulled my hands in hers, looking straight into my eyes. "Are you gonna marry the guy? Who knows? But you can't keep pushing people away because you're too scared to get hurt again."

"Zach was a dick, Kacie." Lauren's blue eyes were glossy but loving. "His reasons for leaving were his issue, not yours. You did nothing wrong. Same with your dad. Stop thinking it's you."

My stomach rolled; this conversation was too much. I needed air.

I pulled my hands free from Alexa's and rushed to the French doors at the back of the house.

"You running again?" Alexa called after me, freezing me in my tracks. "You don't like what you're hearing, so you're gonna go? I'm not at all surprised. This is exactly what we're talking about, Kacie. Stop running!"

My knees buckled as I dropped down on the couch, pulling my hands over my face and crying. Hard.

Lauren rushed to my side, pulling me in for a tight hug. "That's enough, Lex, she gets it."

"I don't think she does, Lauren. She's gonna blow the first good thing that has come into her life in a really long time—and for what? For Blaire? For her dad? For *Zach*?"

I barely heard Alexa's words over my sobs.

"It was so hard, Lauren," I wailed in her arms. "I don't know why he left; I don't know what I did. I fought like hell, but I couldn't keep my family together. It gutted me. I can't do it again, not with Brody."

I sat up and wiped my hand on the sleeve of my hoodie, not caring one bit that I looked like a feral animal.

"Here." Alexa walked up and handed me tissues.

"I know you're right, Lex," I muttered once I calmed down. "I know I run, I don't know what else to do." Tears continued to stream down my cheeks as I desperately searched both of their faces for answers.

"What if you stayed?" Lauren asked sweetly as she reached over and brushed my messy hair out of my face.

"What if he leaves me?" I asked out loud, even though it hurt like hell to say those words.

Alexa sat on the other side of me and put her arm around my waist. "Then we egg his house."

A tiny laugh simmered in my stomach, building slowly until I couldn't hold it in any longer. "He lives in a condo, with security." I sniffed.

"There are ways around security. You just leave that to me." Alexa batted her eyelashes at me and flashed an exaggerated smile. "But . . . why are you worrying about what hasn't happened yet?"

"Because she lives on the catastrophe cliff," Lauren said nonchalantly. Alexa and I both spun toward her. "The what?" Lex asked.

"Catastrophe cliff," she repeated. "Tommy and I learned about it in counseling. Basically, it just means that you are always on edge, waiting for the worst that can possibly happen to actually happen, though more than likely it never does."

"Oh my God . . . she hit the nail on the head, Kacie. That's *exactly* you!" Alexa's eyes were wide. "Except you don't just hang out on the edge of the cliff, you built a fucking house there!"

"Wait . . ." I turned my attention back toward Lauren. "Why are you and Tommy in counseling? You two are the most normal couple I know . . . no offense, Lex."

"None taken, it's true." Alexa smirked.

"Premarital counseling. We like going there to talk our stuff out, so we're gonna continue even after the wedding."

"Okay, can we talk about the wedding for a while, please?" I sat up straight and cleared my throat. "We only have a few days left; enough about my issues for now. Let's figure out what we still need to get done."

The rest of the evening was full of pizza, nachos, and gabbing . . . the best impromptu bachelorette party *ever*.

32

BRODY

Today was the big day.

Not mine, but Lauren and Tommy's. I was up early, running around my condo like an idiot trying to get all my stuff together. Last night, I was supposed to stay at Kacie's, but she called last minute and said she had decided to spend the night at a hotel with Lauren and Alexa. I couldn't fault her for that, and normally it wouldn't bother me, but she'd been so distant since the Wild Kids dinner, it just seemed like another excuse not to see me. She blamed it on the wedding and trying to get caught up with school before the new semester started, but something just didn't feel right. Regardless, I was excited to see her tonight, and she *did* say that she was looking forward to having me stay at her place after the wedding. Maybe I was reading too far into things.

A few hours later as I pulled into the driveway at the inn, my phone chirped. I looked at the text: it was from Kendall.

K: Hey, stranger, I'd like to talk to you. Dinner next week?

I deleted the message without a second thought and gathered up my things from the truck. I walked up on the front porch, surprised to see Lucy sitting on the wicker couch with her hands folded in her lap.

"Hey, kiddo. What's going on?" I went over and sat down next to her. She had on a pale yellow dress and her normally straight blond hair was half pulled up in loose curls.

"I told Mom I wanted to go outside so she said I had to sit here and not move."

"Well, you look very pretty."

"Are you coming to the wedding?"

"Yep."

"Are you gonna dance with my mom?"

"Um, maybe. Would that be okay with you?"

She furrowed her little blond brow and thought about that for a minute.

"Yeah. My mom smiles a lot when she talks about you. I think she would be happy to dance with you."

I grinned like a fifteen-year-old kid who just got told in the lunchroom by a friend of a friend that his crush liked him back.

"Hey, Lucy?"

Her innocent, deep brown eyes looked up at me, and I was suddenly overcome with the urge to protect Lucy and Piper, and their mom. Call it being macho, call it possessive, but these three were mine, and I would tear apart anyone who messed with them.

"Do you think I can dance with you too?" I asked her.

A giant grin lit up her entire face. It was her mom's grin, crinkled nose and all.

She didn't say yes, but she laid her head on my arm and giggled, so I was pretty sure that was the equivalent of a smiley face on a text from her mom.

"Lucyyyy! Come in here, please," we heard Kacie call a few minutes later.

We stood up together and she charged ahead of me through the front door. I rounded the corner and stopped.

Kacie was sitting at the kitchen table with her back to me, curling Piper's hair. She had on a yellow dress, a little darker than the girls', and strapless. She was mesmerizing; the silhouette of her sitting at the table taking care of her children was visually overwhelming.

"Quit moving, goofball," Kacie said to Piper.

"This dress is itchy."

"Well, you look adorable in it. I'm the luckiest mommy in the world to have the two of you," she said as Lucy parked it in the chair next to her.

"Brody said I looked pretty," Lucy announced.

"Brody?" Kacie looked at Lucy. "He's here?" She followed Lucy's little finger that pointed in my direction.

She spun around and our eyes locked. It was there, whatever it was. God, she was stunning. She had on a little more makeup than usual, and while I normally loved her natural look, she was nothing short of magnificent.

"Hi." I grinned at her.

"Hi," she repeated quietly.

"You . . . look fantastic," I said, as she bit her lip shyly and looked down at herself.

"Thanks. I wasn't sure what I thought of the color at first, but I guess it's okay, huh?"

My eyes inspected the length of her whole body before returning her gaze. "Way better than okay."

I strolled over and wrapped my arms around her, knowing damn well that the girls were sitting right there and most likely staring at us. I didn't care, though; things between us were strained for some reason, and right then, I needed to hold her against me. When she didn't resist my hug, I wanted to do a backflip, though someone would have to teach me how first.

After a minute of us just breathing together, she pulled back and gazed at me from under her long lashes.

"Why do you have to be so damn irresistible?" She sighed.

"Why are you trying to resist me?"

"Why are you answering my question with a question?"

I grinned down at her, and the urge to kiss those sassy lips was almost unbearable.

"You guys just about ready?" Sophia called out as she came into the kitchen. "Oh, hi, Brody, don't you look handsome."

"What about me, Gigi?" Lucy said, jumping up from the table proudly.

"Oh, my precious babies!" Sophia's voice cracked as she clapped her hands together.

Kacie grabbed her camera off the counter and handed it to her mom. "Would you mind taking a picture of the four of us?"

"It would be my pleasure."

The four of us? Score.

She called the girls over and positioned them in front of us. I put my arm around her waist and pulled her in closer as she rested her hand on my chest.

This picture, this moment . . . felt right.

"Everybody ready?" Sophia said from behind the lens. "One . . . two . . . three."

"Okay," Kacie called out. "Everyone ready to go?"

I looked at my watch. "Yep, it's about that time."

"So the plan is still the same, right?" Kacie turned toward her mom. "You're going to take the girls from the church to the reception hall, stay for dinner, then bring them home?"

"You got it," Sophia responded before yelling toward the back of the house, "C'mon, you old fart."

Fred walked out of the powder room dressed like a pimp in a dark gray suit and yellow tie. Kacie let out a catcall that made everyone giggle.

"I cleaned up nice, huh?" Fred struck a pose, opening his suit jacket.

"We're gonna have to beat the ladies off you with a stick tonight, Fred. Okay, I think that's everyone, right?" I opened the front door and watched for the girls' reaction.

Their little faces lit up; their mouths dropped open when they saw the car sitting in the driveway. "A limo!!!" they squealed as they hugged each other.

"Do you like it?" I asked.

"What is this?" Kacie looked as shocked as they did.

"Why are you answering my question with a question?" I grinned and cocked an eyebrow at her.

Her eyes laughed but all her mouth did was stutter, "I don't understand . . . how . . ."

"Easy. I had a car brought to the reception hall for Fred, Sophia, and the girls for when they're ready to leave. I also had a car brought there for us." I glanced at the girls, who were struggling to put their shoes on and peek at the limo at the same time. "I just thought they were so thrilled with it last week, it'd be nice if they could actually go somewhere in it, not just around in circles."

Kacie looked at me adoringly. "You're something else, you know that?"

The church looked great. Alexa and Kacie had done a fabulous job of decorating it with flowers and yellow accents earlier that morning. Lauren looked beautiful, and Tommy wept like a big baby through their vows. The whole ceremony went as smooth as could be, and then . . . it was time to party.

The reception was at a swanky hall with more yellow accents. I was seated at a table with Derek, the girls, Sophia, and Fred. During dinner, I kept the girls entertained with my artillery of amazing knock-knock jokes and chatted with Derek, who I'd never really talked to before but ended up liking a lot. Kacie and I kept exchanging glances, holding on to each other's eyes just long enough for the tension between us to boil at the surface. Whatever had been bothering her the last few days was nowhere in sight now. Maybe it *was* wedding stress, like she said. The food was amazing, but I wanted dinner to be over so I could boogie with the hot bridesmaid.

Finally, the waiters came around and started clearing the tables.

Lauren and Tommy had their first dance as husband and wife. Tommy cried . . . again. Who would've thought that the big, dumb jock I'd met that day before the fair was turning out to be such an emotional basket case on his wedding day? Good for him, though; good for both of them.

After the usual dances were done and people started buzzing around the outskirts of the dance floor, I noticed Sophia starting to pack up the girls' things.

"Could you wait one minute?" I asked her.

She looked confused, but nodded as I turned and hurried to the DJ booth. He leaned over to me, covering his other ear with his hand, then smiled and gave me a thumbs-up.

"Attention, party guests, I have a request to fulfill a little earlier than I normally would, but two little princesses have to get going and they were promised a special dance. This song is for . . . the Twinkies."

I took the girls' hands and led them out onto the dance floor as "Isn't She Lovely" by Stevie Wonder started playing. I motioned for each of them to hop on one of my feet as I spun and bounced them around the dance floor, doing my best to keep to the actual beat of the music. I was dying to look over at Kacie's face, but I didn't want her to think this was about me impressing her. It wasn't; it was about my moment with the girls who I'd really grown to love. Our moment. One of hopefully many to come.

Once the song ended, the crowd cheered and I thought my legs were going to fall off, but the huge grins on their faces made it absolutely worth it. Kacie was waiting at our table for us when we got back.

"Mommy, did you see us?" Piper asked excitedly.

"I did, you guys looked beautiful. And what great dancers you are!"

"We didn't dance." Lucy giggled. "We stood on Brody's feet the *whole* time."

"Wow!" Kacie slapped her cheeks with her hands, pretending to be surprised. "I think you fooled everyone."

I offered to go with Kacie to walk everyone out, but she said she needed a minute with her mom, so I took the opportunity to get myself a beer. Derek walked up behind me and clapped his hands on my shoulders.

"Make that two, please," he said to the server, leaning against the wood bar with me. "What a night, huh?"

"Absolutely." I nodded toward Tommy and Lauren, who were kissing on the dance floor. "Those two seem pretty damn happy."

"Yeah, they do. So does Kacie." Derek eyed me curiously.

"Does she? Good." I sighed. "We've had a weird week or so. I thought I'd done something wrong, but all she says is she's fine."

Derek cringed. "Fine is *never* good."

"I know!" I handed Derek his beer and we started back to the table together.

"Kacie had a rough time after Zach ditched her; she's been a little skeptical ever since. Like she's waiting for a bomb to drop or whatever." He shook his head, staring off at the dance floor. "I don't know, women are weird."

"I'll drink to that," I said, clinking my beer with his.

"What are you two toasting?" Alexa stood behind us with her hip cocked to the side, arms folded defensively across her chest. Kacie was just behind her with one raised eyebrow, and her lips puckered as she chewed the inside of her cheek. She looked sexy and confident . . . and sexy.

Derek spun around and scooped Alexa up in his arms, kissing her neck. "How fucking hot our women are."

"True story." I pulled Kacie into my arms and started dancing at the table with her.

"No way." She pulled back, shaking her head. "If I'm gonna dance, I need to have a whole lot of liquor."

"Coming right up." I grinned, dragging her to the bar.

"These are so gooooood," Kacie slurred after her fourth green apple martini. Her eyes were relaxed and happy; her movements were as loose as I'd ever seen.

"How are you feeling? Think you should slow down?" I asked cautiously.

"Hell no!" She tossed her arms around my neck and slithered herself up and down my body in a way that men usually pay for. "I'm just getting started, baby."

"Baby?" I laughed.

"Yeah, baby." She licked her lips and grinned up at me, wobbling from side to side. "You're *my* baby."

I grabbed her hips to keep her from falling over. "You got that right . . . baby." I reached down and covered her mouth with mine. Her cold, sweet-tasting tongue darted into my mouth, kissing me deep.

"You ready to go? I'm worried you're gonna be sick tomorrow."

"I'm fine," she said in a garbled tone.

"You are?"

"Sharp as a tack!" She giggled.

"Alexa and Derek are taking off, and most of the other people have left too. You sure you don't want to go?"

Kacie straightened up with a surprised look on her face. "That Alexa is one smart bitch, huh?"

"Um . . . okay?"

"No, Brody. Really, think about it. She helped design all this." She threw her hands up in the air as she spun in a drunken circle. "And, she knows when I'm bullshitting her. She's *really* good at that."

"Bullshitting her?" I asked, reaching out every so often to reel her back in.

"Yeah, she said I loved you. I said no. She was right."

I stood, frozen on the dance floor in shock while she wiggled her way around me.

"You love me?" I asked after the shock wore off.

"Holy shit, yes." She giggled, opening her arms wide. "A *lot*!"

No words came out of my mouth; oxygen barely made its way to my brain. I didn't know how to react. No woman had ever told me she loved me before, and definitely not one I was certain I loved back like Kacie.

"Okay, I think maybe it's time to go, huh?"

"You want to get me home and take advantage of me, don't you?" she whispered in my ear. "I accept."

She wrapped her arms around my waist and held on tight as I led us out to my car, waving at a beaming Lauren and Tommy as we left.

I gently set Kacie down in the passenger seat, and before I could scoot around to my side, she grabbed my face and pulled it down to hers, kissing me again.

I tore myself away from her before I lost all control and peeled her dress off right there in the parking lot. Odds were, there were security cameras, and there was no doubt in my mind that footage would be in the news by morning.

"You're so hot, Brody."

I couldn't help but laugh at her a little. I'd never seen her like this, and oddly enough, it was adorable, just like everything else she did. This woman normally controlled every aspect of her life; it was nice to see her let loose for once.

She reached over and grazed her fingernails along the back of my neck while I drove us home. It was driving me crazy and making me hard.

"I meant what I said tonight . . . I love you, Brody." Her head lay against the back of the seat angled toward me; her shimmering green eyes barely cracked open.

"I love you, Kacie." I reached over and brushed her cheek with the back of my hand.

I sat at the stoplight long after it'd already turned green, just so I could watch her fall asleep.

33

KACIE

I tried to roll over but I couldn't move. It felt like someone had replaced my limbs with sandbags. And my head . . . holy crap, my head. Every time I moved it, I thought it was going to break free and roll right off the end of my bed.

How the hell did I get into my bed?

The harder I tried to remember last night, the louder the blood rushed in my ears. My head felt like it was being squeezed in a lion's mouth, a very angry lion who was being stabbed with a scalding-hot fireplace poker.

Groaning as I rolled over, I peeked one eye open to see the clock, but a piece of paper covered it. I lifted my seven-hundred-pound arm and snatched the piece of paper off my nightstand, blinking rapidly until the words came into focus.

We're in the family room. Take your time, and the aspirin.

Brody

As painful as it was, I lifted my head and saw two aspirin and a glass of water next to my clock. I sat up in bed and concentrated on nothing but breathing for a few minutes.

In and out. In and out.

The waves of nausea finally calmed into ripples, allowing me to reach over and scoop up the pills. I popped them into my mouth and took a sip of water. The sip turned into a giant gulp as I chugged mouthful after mouthful of the cold, refreshing liquid. I set the empty glass down and looked at my outfit.

Brody must have put pajamas on me too.

I wanted nothing more than to burrow myself deep into my bed for the next twelve hours, but my bladder wasn't having it. Dragging myself upright, I silently wondered if I was still drunk. Everything hurt. Holy crap, did I drink too much last night or run a marathon?

I lumbered to the bathroom and then made my way out to the family room to see what my girls were up to, praying someone was watching them.

I turned the corner to the family room and stopped dead in my tracks.

"What the . . . ," I mumbled, trying to force my brain to process what I was seeing.

Lucy and Piper had a salon set up in the living room. Brody was propped up on the couch with cotton balls stuffed in between his toes, a mess of pink polish on his toenails, and his hair was pulled up into ten different short ponytails and dotted with barrettes.

He cocked his head to the side and narrowed his eyes at me. "You tell *anyone* about this, I'll tell the world you drool in your sleep, a lot."

A laugh escaped my lips, causing the pressure in my head to accelerate to an excruciating level. "Ow, ow, ow," I whined, holding the sides of my head as I backed into the kitchen and fell onto a chair.

"See? That's what you get," Brody teased. "Hey, guys, I'm gonna take a break. I'll be right back, okay?"

"My turn!" Lucy called, offering to take Brody's place.

He walked over and bent down, placing a gentle kiss on the top of my head.

"Ow. Even my hair hurts."

"Serves you right, Martini Queen." He laughed.

"Shhh, not so loud. Maybe a whisper for today?" I rested my head on my hands and prayed for death.

"You hungry?" His words made my stomach turn. "Maybe you'd like a . . . *green apple*?"

"Are you trying to make me sick?" I mumbled against the wood table.

"Not really, but this is kinda fun. How about some coffee?" He stood and turned the coffeepot on.

"Yes, please," I growled.

Brody didn't talk through my whole first cup of coffee and half of my second. He told the girls Mommy had a headache and promised them that if they played quietly, he'd let them paint his fingernails later.

"Do you remember anything about last night?" he finally asked.

I thought hard, but nothing came back. "The last thing I really remember is walking my mom and Fred to the car. Where is Mom, anyway?"

"She said she had breakfast plans with a friend but didn't want to go because of your . . . condition." He chuckled. "I told her I'd watch the girls and take care of you."

"You handled the girls all right," I teased as I filled my coffee cup for the third time. I might not sleep for the next two days because of all the caffeine, but as long as the headache was gone, that was just fine by me.

"Last night was interesting." Brody had a funny look on his face.

"Did I do anything stupid?"

"Nope, not at all." He cocked an eyebrow at me. "But you're one hell of a dancer."

I groaned and dropped my head back onto my hands, harder than I intended to. "Ow. Did you put me in bed?"

"Mm-hmm."

"Did you change me?"

"Mm-hmm."

"Did we . . ." My eyes darted over to make sure the girls couldn't hear us.

He laughed. "No. I'm not exactly into necrophilia—you were passed out before the first stoplight. You did say one interesting thing, though."

"What was that?" I asked, without lifting my head to look at him.

"You said you loved me."

I stopped breathing, as panic filled my chest and made my head pound harder. Slowly, I lifted my head and looked at Brody, who was smiling contentedly, blowing on his own mug of coffee.

"I did?"

He nodded slowly, his eyes searching my face.

"Sorry about that." I cringed.

He pulled his brows together and frowned at me. "Sorry? Why would you apologize?"

"I was drunk, I shouldn't have said that."

"Do you?"

"Do I what?"

"Do you love me?"

Oh God, oh God. I wanted to puke and it didn't have anything to do with my hangover. My head hurt, and now my heart hurt. Looking at Brody's soulful eyes, knowing he was waiting for an answer I couldn't give him was hard. Too hard.

I did love him. I loved him so much I sometimes couldn't breathe around him, but I couldn't tell him that. I would never let those words leave my mouth; that would make all of this too real. It would give him all the power.

I wanted to get up and leave the room, but Alexa's voice nagging me to stop running kept ringing through my head. Her voice wasn't the only one in my head. Blaire's was there too, cackling and warning me that I was nothing but a summer fling. If he was just going to throw me away, there was no way I was going to tell him the truth.

"Kacie." Brody's voice pulled me out of my thoughts.

My eyes traveled around his face . . . the face of the man I loved, the face I had to lie to in order to protect myself.

I took a deep breath.

"No."

34

BRODY

"You have ten new voice messages. To play these—" I shut off my phone and tossed it, not giving a shit when it tumbled off the bed and hit the floor with a cracking sound. None of those messages were from Kacie, and that pissed me off.

Lauren and Tommy's wedding was two weeks ago, and Kacie and I hadn't talked since the morning after, when she told me she didn't love me. Hell, I'd barely left my condo in that time. Gym and back. That's about it. I talked to my mom every few days so that she didn't call in a missing-person report, but I still hadn't told her about Kacie. I didn't want to say it out loud; it just made me angry.

After she said no, we sat at that kitchen table for a long time, not saying a word. She didn't know what else to say, and I only wanted to call her a liar. I'm one of those people who believe when we're drunk, we say what we really mean. I think that liquid courage helps us get out what we really *do* want to say, when we don't know how to just *say* it. There's nothing I could do, though; whether she loved me or she didn't, I had to take her for her word.

That left me here, wallowing in self-pity, dirty bedsheets, and the Classic College Football Network for two weeks, not giving a shit about the world outside of my house. I reached over and opened the canister on my nightstand, pulled out another Slim Jim, and shoved it in my mouth before throwing the wrapper on the floor.

Fuck it.

Just then I heard my condo door open. For a fleeting second, my head went somewhere it shouldn't have gone, but reality set in when Andy called my name.

"In here," I yelled back.

He appeared in my bedroom doorway with a disgusted look on his face. "Dude, what the fuck?"

"What?" I glared at him defensively.

"I've been calling you for a week and haven't heard back. What's going on with you?"

"Nothing, I'm just chillin'."

"Chillin'?"

"What do you want, Andy? I have things to do."

"Oh, what—like call a heart surgeon and schedule your bypass appointment now because of all these?" He walked over and picked up my Slim Jim canister. "I talked to Viper; he told me what happened."

"It's not a big deal. Whatever." I waved him off.

"If it's not a big deal, why are you drowning your sorrows in sodium and reality television?"

"Don't forget beer," I joked.

"Listen, why don't you come over this weekend?" he asked.

"Fuck. That."

"Let me finish, asswipe. Blaire and all her obnoxious friends are headed to a weekend getaway in Napa Valley. It's just me and the kids. I'll invite Viper and a few of the guys over. We'll smoke expensive Cuban cigars and drink too much, so plan on crashing at my place."

"No."

"Come on, if worse comes to worst, you can go up and play with Logan and Becca."

"If I say yes, will you leave?"

"Absolutely," he said.

"Fine." I sighed as I rolled over. "Now get out. And leave the Slim Jims!"

Andy laughed as he walked toward my bedroom door. "I'm holding them for ransom."

I pulled up to Andy's house and sat in my truck, contemplating turning around and going home. I just wasn't feeling this. As I had just about talked myself into driving home, Logan appeared on Andy's porch, waving at me to come in.

Crap.

"What's up, buddy?" I scooped up Logan as I made my way up to the porch.

"I got a new PS3 Lego game, wanna come see?" he asked excitedly.

"You know what? Let me say hi to your dad and I'll be right there, okay?"

Andy was in the kitchen, taking pizza out of the oven when I walked in. "Hey, glad you made it."

"Me too, I guess."

"Have you talked to her?"

I glared at him. "No, and I'm not talking about it tonight."

"Okay, okay." He put his hands up in front of him. "I won't ask anymore."

"Where should I put this?" I held up the bottles of tequila and rum I'd bought on my way over.

"Uh-oh, tequila? Someone means business tonight, huh?" Andy raised an eyebrow at me and sighed. "Why don't you put them in the blast chiller down in the basement?"

By the time I came back upstairs, the unmistakable sound of Viper's bellow sounded throughout the house. "The party can now begin, the king is here!" He went through the kitchen with one arm up in the air, a case of beer tucked under the other.

"The king?" I teased, coming up behind him. "You sure do like yourself, huh, V?"

"I do, I do." We shook hands and he set his beer on the table.

"Big Mike, how are ya?" I went over and shook the giant paw of one of our defensemen. Andy represented both Viper and Big Mike, so it came as no surprise that they came over too.

"I'm awesome," he said with a big, goofy grin on his face. "Guess what? Michelle is pregnant."

"That's excellent. Congratulations!" I said as sincerely as I could, though right then I didn't think I could truly be happy for anyone about anything. Selfish, yes, but it was the truth.

Before we even got the night started, there was more commotion at the front door, except this time it was the devil's voice I heard.

"What are you guys doing back here?" Andy's mouth hung open, his face frozen in shock at Blaire and her friends standing in the doorway.

"Our flight was canceled because of storms over the Valley, so we're all gonna have a giant sleepover here. The limo is coming back super early in the morning and we'll be on the first flight out." She looked around the room, turning up her nose as she went. "What's going on here, Andrew?"

If there was one person in this world Blaire hated more than me, it was Viper.

"What does it look like? I had the guys over for dinner and drinks," Andy responded defensively.

"Hi, Brody."

A head peeked out from behind Blaire.

Shit, Kendall.

"Hey, Kendall," I said dryly, suddenly wishing I were a tiny girl in a blue dress from Kansas and I could just click my heels together and be home. Actually, anywhere other than this kitchen would be just fine with me.

There we stood, Blaire's group and ours, the East and the West, the Crips and the Bloods, staring each other down to see who was going to head where.

Andy finally broke the silence. "We're gonna head to the basement and watch some baseball. You guys do whatever you want."

"Okay, Andrew." She slid over and kissed him on the cheek, almost making me hurl in the process.

Kendall walked over and wrapped her arms around me, pulling me into a hug. I leaned down and embraced her back as loosely as I could. She smelled good. Pulling back, she looked up at me from under long, fake lashes, a suggestive little grin playing on her lips. For a moment I wondered if I could lose myself in her, at least for one night. Lord knows I needed a distraction.

"I need to talk to you, but I want us to be alone. Too many people here," she purred.

"Come on, Murphy," Viper called as they headed out of the kitchen.

"I'll catch you later, okay?" I pulled away as Kendall pouted.

"Thanks, bro." I patted his back as I caught up to the rest of them.

"Dude, she almost had you. The claws were out, she just hadn't implanted them yet," he joked.

We migrated downstairs to Andy's theater room and claimed our couches for the evening while Andy put the Twins/Cubs game on the big screen and passed cigars out to everyone. Before I got too comfortable, I wanted a drink. A strong one.

"I'll be right back; anyone want anything?"

Viper and Big Mike didn't turn around, they just held their beers up. Andy shook his head.

I walked across the basement to the bar and grabbed a glass out of the cabinet before heading into their enormous wine room with the blast chiller inside. If I was gonna drink tonight, might as well go big, right? I grabbed the tequila out of the fridge and turned to leave, freezing when I heard Kendall's voice in the hall. I backed up against the wine rack, not wanting to be seen.

"You didn't tell me Brody was gonna be here," she whispered.

"I had no idea. I didn't even know Andrew was having people over," Blaire defended herself. "We were supposed to be on a plane right now, remember?"

"He looks sad."

"Yeah, Andrew said he's been sulking for a couple of weeks."

"About that girl?"

I caught Blaire's reflection in the glass. She was leaned up against the wall, her arms folded over her chest.

Shit, they aren't moving. I'm trapped.

"Kacie."

Hearing Kacie's name come out of Blaire's mouth annoyed me, but I didn't want to go out there and get stuck talking to Kendall again.

"He liked her that much?" Kendall asked.

"Who the fuck cares?" Blaire laughed.

"Shhh."

"Oh, they can't hear us, they're in the theater room with the door shut. Really, though, I could care less who the fuck he likes or how much. That boy needs to be concentrating on hockey and nothing else. I know that makes me a bitch, but so be it. The minute Andrew told me how crazy he was getting about her, I had to do something." She laughed softly. "She was already so insecure, it wasn't even hard to chase her off. I knew the minute I said *summer fling*, that was it, the seed was planted. Fucking priceless."

I can't fucking believe what I'm hearing. When did Blaire talk to her again? Oh my God . . . the charity dinner. That's why Kacie has been so weird with me ever since. Fuck, how could I have been so stupid not to figure this out sooner?

My blood was boiling, but I didn't move an inch. I had to hear what else was said in that bathroom.

"You were behind her, did you see her face when I walked in?" Kendall giggled. "Classic."

Holy shit, Kendall was in that bathroom too?

"No, but I wish I could have. I bet she almost shit her pants." Blaire could hardly talk because she was laughing so hard. "Tough shit. Little Mommy can go find a meal ticket somewhere else. Maybe she'll scoop up a nice baseball boy this time."

"Maybe I'll snag him while he's on the rebound," Kendall snickered.

"Yuck. I don't know why the hell you want him, Kendall, seriously. You can do so much better." Blaire sounded annoyed. "You two did your disgusting thing; he wasn't exactly beating down your door. Move on. Besides, didn't you just hear me? He needs to worry about blocking goals, nothing else."

I'd heard enough.

I stomped out of the wine cellar, and both of their mouths hit the floor when they saw me.

I glared at Blaire, my chest heaving in anger. "*You* chased her away! It wasn't me, it was *you*, you fucking cunt!"

Blaire didn't argue; she stood there, shell-shocked. She knew she was busted.

"Brody . . ."

"Shut it, Kendall . . . ," I snapped at her. "I expected this behavior out of Blaire, but you too?"

She said nothing, just looked at the ground while I turned my attention back to Blaire.

"What the fuck is your problem? You feel so goddamn wretched living in your own skin that you have to make others feel like shit so that you feel better?" My blood boiled as I stood over her, not caring how loud I yelled anymore. "She did *nothing* to you, Blaire, *nothing*! You use everyone. People are things to you, and if they can't do something for you, you shit on them. Congratulations on being a terrible fucking human being."

Blaire's lip quivered as Andy and the other guys came to see what the yelling was about.

"What's going on?" Andy asked nervously.

"Andy, I love you like a brother, but you're fired," I said to him as calmly as possible before I turned to Blaire one more time. "I warned you, you bitch. You fuck with me, I'll fuck you ten times harder. I just hit you where it really matters to you . . . your bank account."

35

KACIE

A few weeks ago, before Brody's and my . . . falling out, he asked me about going to a second charity dinner. Of course, I said yes. That dinner was last night and I'd be lying if I didn't admit that I was silently staring at my phone all day yesterday, hoping that Brody was going to call and tell me he was on his way to come and get me. Unfortunately, my phone was silent all day.

Today, I didn't want to get out of bed. I wanted to lie there and sulk and feel bad for myself even though I knew I'd caused my own pain. Every single day over the last three weeks I had at least one moment, or twenty, when I wanted to pick up the phone and tell him I was stupid and I was sorry and to please forgive me, but I never did. Pride is an evil bitch.

My phone rang on my nightstand.

"Hey, how are you today?" Alexa asked after I answered it.

"I'm fine. Feeling sorry for myself, but fine." I yawned.

"Did you sleep at all last night?"

"Yeah, that's all I did, actually. I went to bed early so I couldn't think about it."

"Have you been up today yet?" she asked slowly, cautiously.

"No, I'm still in bed. Why?"

"Just curious."

"Liar. What?"

"Nothing, really. Call me after you're up and moving."

"Alexa Renee . . . I listened to you lie to your parents daily growing up. Don't pull that 'nothing' shit with me."

She was quiet for a minute before she let out a heavy sigh. "He went."

"He went where?"

"To the dinner."

I laughed. "I knew he would, Alexa, it was for one of the charities he sponsors."

"He . . . didn't go alone."

"Oh."

A bomb went off inside my stomach, the tremors reaching all the way out to my fingertips. The thought of him taking another woman to the dinner I was supposed to go to, walking the red carpet with her, holding her hand . . . made me ill. I got off the phone with Alexa and grabbed my laptop, trying to talk myself out of looking the whole time I typed "Brody Murphy" into the search bar.

The most recent link was from late last night. Because I'm a glutton for punishment, I clicked on it.

My heart sank.

Brody looked delicious all the time, whether he was in workout clothes, blue striped pajama pants, or in a black tuxedo, like in this picture. His hair was shorter, making his smile look bigger, more defined. He grinned at the cameras, and I could tell from this picture that he was "on." He was in superstar mode.

A gorgeous redhead was beside him, beaming like she'd just won the lottery. She was with Brody, so I suppose she had. She wore a long, hunter-green dress and had boobs to die for. Her lips were painted fire engine red to match her nails. His fingers were intertwined with hers and they both flirted with the cameras like a couple of models. She certainly rocked that red carpet way better than I did. She was beautiful, and I hated her.

I didn't want to see any more of them together, but what did I do? I clicked on the next picture, and that's when my heart stopped beating.

Her head was thrown back slightly, laughing at whatever Brody was whispering in her ear. His arm was around her waist, pulling her in close. They definitely knew each other; they were comfortable with each other. Very comfortable. I couldn't take any more; I shut the laptop and stomped out of my room.

"Good morning." Mom smiled as I entered the kitchen.

"Hi."

She stared at me, her eyes wide. "What's wrong?"

"Nothing. Are we out of oatmeal?"

"I think so. I'll get some on my next trip into town."

I slammed the cabinet loudly, not saying a word.

"Are you okay?"

"I'm fine. Where are the girls?"

"They went out back to play while Fred mows the yard."

The sentence wasn't even out of her mouth yet when the girls came running into the house. "Mom, can we go swimming?"

"Sure." I sighed. "Let's get dressed and put sunscreen on."

I really just wanted to crawl back in bed, but it wasn't fair of me to deprive the girls of a good day because of my bad mood.

We marched down to the lake, the girls complaining the whole way that they had to wear their floaties.

"I'm sorry, but I don't feel like swimming right now. I'm going to sit on the shore and read, so you *have* to wear your floaties."

They looked disappointed, but I was the mom and got the final call on that one, though I suppose I could have said it nicer.

As I parked my rear on an old tree that had fallen over years ago, the girls set out for the water, leaving me alone with my thoughts. My emotions were out of control today, going one hundred different directions. I was jealous, for obvious reasons. I was angry, mostly at myself for lying to Brody about how I felt. I was upset that I had been stupid enough to torture myself and look at those pictures even though I knew it was going to hurt me. A small part of me was angry at Brody for taking that girl to the event—he could have fought harder for me. When was someone going to fight for me? Why was it so easy for people to let me go?

Bringing my book out here was completely pointless; I couldn't take my eyes off of Lucy and Piper when they were in the water. Plus there were a group of idiots out on the water this morning, driving their WaveRunners around like lunatics. Twice now they had come in too close for my liking. On the third trip around the lake, I stood up and screamed at them at the top of my lungs.

"Don't come in this far again, you jerk, there are kids playing!"

The guy looked back at me, waved, and took off.

"What was that about?" Mom asked, walking up behind me.

"Those guys are driving around like they own the place!" I glared at her.

"Okay, calm down." She held her hands up defensively. "I agree with you yelling at them, but you're yelling about everything this morning."

She walked over and sat down on the stump next to me.

"Sorry," I snapped, not very apologetically. "I'm just . . . in a mood."

"I can see that. Care to talk about it?"

"No."

"Would you rather talk to Brody about it?"

"What?" I swung around to face her. "Why would you ask me that?"

"He's here."

"He's *here*?"

"Yep, just walked in. Want me to watch the girls for you while you talk to him?"

I didn't even verbalize an answer, I just grunted and stalked up the hill toward the house. I got to the back door and paused, taking a deep breath before I went in. He was sitting at the kitchen island with his chin resting on his hands, looking straight ahead, smiling . . . at her.

She was here.

The redhead.

From last night.

In my house.

"Hey!" he said cheerfully when I walked in.

"Hi," I replied flatly, trying to get my blood pressure under control so I didn't kill him with my own bare hands.

She stood up and beamed at me as I walked into the kitchen, holding her hand out. "You must be Kacie. I've heard so much about you. Nice to meet you."

"Kacie, I'm glad you're here. I really wanted you to meet Shae."

"Hi, Shae." I reached out and halfheartedly shook her hand.

"I'm sorry to run off so fast, but Brody, I have to use the restroom bad. Where is it?"

He pointed up the guest stairs. "Up there, third door on the right, across from our room."

A lump formed in my throat the size of Texas as rage, not oxygen, fueled my bloodstream. She scurried up the stairs, barely out of earshot before I turned and lost it on Brody.

"Your *room*? You're staying here? Both of you?" I spat with my fists clenched at my sides.

"Yep." He smiled at me, looking me up and down. "You look great."

Completely ignoring his compliment, I continued, "What the hell are you thinking?"

"What?" He sounded clueless.

"This. Her. Here." I couldn't even form a sentence anymore. The logical part of my brain was dead, filled instead with seething anger.

"Shae is great, really sweet. I wanted you to meet her; I think you'll get along."

I swear I heard my heart shatter like glass as sadness replaced the seething anger. "How could you bring her here? Why would I want to meet her? My replacement. Why are you throwing this in my face?"

"I'm not throwing anything in your face. You made your decision. You said you didn't love me," he accused.

Tears burned my eyes. Angry tears, hurt tears, devastated tears. No way were they ever spilling out, though. I pinched my arm hard to distract myself from the emotional pain and make them go away.

"Yes, I said it, but that . . ." I waved my hand toward the stairs she'd just run up. "That is just cruel. To bring her here, to make me stare at the two of you all weekend. Why? To torment me, teach me a lesson?"

He stood up from the island and walked over in front of me, staring straight past my eyes and into my soul.

"Do you love me?" he asked.

"What? Why now? Why would you ask me that now?"

The bathroom door opened upstairs and I startled, taking an automatic step away from Brody. Shae skipped down the stairs and looked out the back door, her bright red hair flowing down her back. "This property is beautiful. I'm gonna step out on the deck and look at the lake. You coming?" she asked, turning toward Brody.

He grinned at her, driving the knife further into my heart in the process. "I'll come out in a minute."

"Okay. It was nice to meet you, Kacie. I'm sure we'll talk later." She smiled sweetly at me as she opened the door. "Oh, and you were right, Brody, Mom and Dad would *love* this place. We need to bring them here."

My eyes were glued to where Shae was standing, my brain trying to process if I'd just heard her correctly.

I whipped my head back to Brody, who had backed up and was sitting on a stool, facing me with a shit-eating grin on his face.

"*Mom and Dad?* As in, you two have the same mom and dad?" I asked, feeling like a complete idiot.

"That would be correct. That's my baby sister, Shae Murphy."

"Were you *testing* me?"

"That would also be correct." He could barely contain his happiness at my complete meltdown at the thought of him with another woman.

"Why?"

"I had to see your reaction. Someone who doesn't love someone doesn't get that mad when that someone is with someone else."

"Oh my God . . . I'm going to kill you. I feel so stupid, and your sister probably thinks I'm a total bitch." I put my hands over my eyes, wanting to die of pure embarrassment.

He tilted his head back and forth and looked up at the ceiling, thinking about it. "Probably, but lucky for you, she grew up with me. She's learned to forgive."

He reached out and grabbed my hips, pulling them close to him. I didn't fight. I missed him, everything about him. His smell, his smile, his expressive eyes, the way he made my problems melt away with one hug. I'd never missed a person the way I'd missed Brody the last few weeks.

"So, I'm gonna ask you again . . . do you love me?"

Before I could answer yes, the back door flew open and Shae stood in the doorway, trembling and white as a ghost.

"Call nine-one-one, a little girl in the lake just got hit by a guy on a WaveRunner!"

36

BRODY

Everything around me went into hyperspeed. As soon as Shae came to the back door and yelled that one of the girls had gotten hit, before I could even take my phone out of my pocket, Kacie was out of my arms and sprinting toward the lake as fast as she could. I dialed 911 and rushed out of the house past Shae, who stood frozen in the doorway.

"Was it one of Kacie's daughters?" she called out in a panic.

"Think so!" I yelled as I gave the operator Kacie's address.

When I got to the bottom of the hill, Piper's little body was on the shore with a huge gash in her head. Just the sight of her lying there like that made me light-headed. Kacie was kneeling over her, trying to keep her awake. "Piper! Piper! Stay with me, baby. Talk to Mommy. Piper!" Her voice cracked as she slapped Piper's face, trying to keep her awake.

There was nothing she could do. Piper's eyes closed as Kacie kept hitting her little cheek, trying to wake her up.

"Does she have a pulse?" the operator asked me. I relayed the question to Kacie.

"Yes," Kacie responded.

"Okay, keep her still, do not move her. The ambulance is on the way. I'll stay on the phone with you until they get there," the operator said.

I'd never shaken that bad in my life; I could barely hold on to the phone. "Here, hold this, listen to whatever she says," I said to Shae as I gave her my cell phone.

I went over and bent down next to Piper across from Kacie. I knew Kacie was almost finished with nursing school, so the panic on her face was making me panic too.

She quickly looked around. "Can someone run and get a towel? Fast!"

The small crowd that had gathered looked from person to person while I reached back and pulled my T-shirt off. "Use this."

She balled it up and put it on Piper's head wound, which looked really bad. My heart broke at the pool of blood under her little head.

"Hold that firm against her head," she ordered me.

Once I put my hand on the shirt, she opened each of Piper's eyes, one at a time, and cringed.

"What?" I asked.

"Her pupils, they're different sizes."

I shook my head. "What does that mean?"

"It's a sign of a brain injury."

My mind raced in a thousand different directions at the sound of that. Brain injury—what did that mean? It sounded horrendous. Kacie's face was contorted into such despair as she looked down at her daughter, constantly checking for a pulse. It nearly killed me.

The paramedics rushed around the side of the house and down to the lake with a stretcher. After examining Piper quickly, they rolled her off the ground just enough to slip the wooden backboard underneath. After they strapped her securely onto the stretcher, they whisked her and Kacie off.

"Wait!" Sophia called out in a panic.

"Here, I'll take her. Go." I reached out and took Lucy out of Sophia's arms, and she turned and sprinted up the hill.

One police officer was talking to Fred and other witnesses while another officer was putting handcuffs on the guy I assumed had been driving the WaveRunner. I glared at him while I momentarily debated whether or not it would be worth the arrest to go over and rip his arms from his body. Just as I'd decided it would be worth any time I would get, Lucy laid her head on my shoulder and sniffled.

"Hey, you okay?" I asked, desperately trying to crane my neck so I could see her face.

She didn't reply, she just cried softly. I hugged her as tight as I could without hurting her. In that moment, I would do anything, and I mean *anything* in my power to take away her pain. I would do anything to take away Kacie's pain, and I would sell my soul to the devil himself to trade places with Piper.

Holy shit, did this all just really happen? I felt like I was watching a bad movie.

"You okay?" Shae came up and rubbed my shoulder. Her eyes were red-rimmed, and she was sniffing too.

"Yes. No. I don't know. Right now all I'm worried about are these girls, all three of them." I smiled at her and walked away from the crowd, the police, and the bloodstained grass. I sat on a stump and rocked Lucy back and forth. She was shaking like a leaf in my arms.

"Honey, it's okay. Piper's gonna be just fine. Okay?" I prayed I wasn't lying to her, but I didn't know what else to say.

"Her head was bleeding a lot," she said softly.

I held her tiny head in my hands, tight against my chest, and rocked back and forth. "I know it was, baby, I know."

I wasn't a dad—I wasn't anywhere near close to being a dad—but in that moment, my heart hurt so bad I wanted to crawl out of my skin. And if *I* felt this way, I couldn't imagine how Kacie was feeling.

"Hey, I'm gonna head to the hospital; you wanna go?" Fred asked as he walked up to us.

I stood up, still not setting Lucy down. "Yeah."

Lucy's head popped up and she looked at me with fear in her eyes. "Can I stay with you?"

"Of course," I said as I tucked her hair behind her ears. "How about we all ride together, after we both put some clothes on?"

She mumbled in agreement and laid her head back on my shoulder.

"You should come too." I turned to Shae, who nodded through tears.

When we got to the hospital, Fred went up to the desk and inquired about Piper's condition.

"Are you all family?" I heard her ask.

Fred looked back at each of us. "Uh. Yes."

"I'll call a nurse to take you to where you can wait for them." She smiled politely.

Before Fred walked back to us, a big white door swung open and a nurse called out, "Piper Jensen." We all got up and somberly followed her around a couple of corners and into a waiting room where Sophia was sitting. As soon as she saw us, she jumped up, ran straight toward me, and took Lucy out of my arms. Her lips quivered as she tried not to break down in front of her.

"How is she?" Fred asked.

"I don't know anything yet; I've been sitting here. Kacie went back with them. They tried to tell her it was best that she stay out here but she dug her heels in and refused to budge."

That's my girl.

"I'm gonna run and grab something to drink. Anyone want anything?" Shae asked.

We all shook our heads as she smiled and left the room. Within five minutes of us sitting and getting comfortable, Lucy was sound asleep on Sophia's lap.

"Poor kid." Fred looked down at her sympathetically. "I don't know how she can sleep with all this going on."

"I think she's so wiped out from all the trauma, she needs this rest."

"So . . ." I hesitated, but needed to know. "What happened?"

"It all happened so fast, Brody. Earlier Kacie yelled at the guy for coming in too close—that was right after you got here. I went down there to tell her you were here, she came back in, and within just a few minutes, he'd circled around again and tried to cut the turn and missed. Slid right into her. At first I thought it hit both of them . . ." Her voice cracked, tears streaming down her face. "But then Lucy stood up and started crying. I ran into the water and Piper was floating; the water around her was dark red. I screamed and that girl on the deck, your friend, must have told you guys, because within seconds, Kacie was flying down the hill."

"That's my sister, Shae," I said, not wanting Sophia to think I was shallow enough to bring another woman there.

"Oh, okay." She sniffed. "Anyway, Kacie came running, Fred came running, and then everything started moving so fast."

The doors leading to the pediatric intensive care unit swung open and Kacie walked through them, her face as white as I'd ever seen it. Her T-shirt was splattered with the blood of her daughter, and she was barefoot. I didn't even realize she'd left with no shoes on; I wish I'd thought to grab some for her.

She walked a straight path right into my arms, crashing hard against my chest as her knees buckled.

"Kacie, talk to me; what's going on?" I rushed out as Fred stood and came next to me to help balance her.

She didn't talk, she just sobbed, scrunching my T-shirt in her fist as she buried her face and wailed. My heart dropped.

Why is she not saying anything? Jesus, please say something.

I didn't know what to do so I just stood there and let her cry on me, gently rubbing her back and kissing the top of her head.

"Honey, what's going on?" Sophia begged in a loud whisper, trying not to wake Lucy. "Please . . . talk to us."

Kacie pulled back as Fred handed her a box of tissues. "Thanks," she muttered quietly. "Um, I don't really know yet. They closed her head . . . it took twenty-three staples. She's going in for a CT scan now so they can see how severe the swelling in her brain is."

"Was she conscious?" Fred asked.

Kacie shook her head. "They gave her medicine to keep her asleep for now."

"Oh my God," Sophia cried as she covered her face with her free hand.

Fred rushed over and put his arm around her, tears falling from his face.

"How are *you*? Can I get you anything?" I asked, desperate for her to need me.

"I'm . . . awful, I'm overwhelmed, I'm freaking out. I just want her to be okay." Her voice trailed off as the tears came back.

"She will be." I pulled her against me. "She's got a strong mama who taught her to fight like hell. She'll be okay." My words only made her cry harder.

"I need to sit," she said after a few more minutes of tears. She limped exhaustedly over to the chair next to her mom, leaning over and kissing Lucy's cheek. "How has she been?"

"She was pretty upset, not talking much, just crying." Sophia smiled at me. "She's actually been with Brody almost the whole time."

Kacie looked at me and smiled, exhaustion covering her face.

"Kacie Jensen?" a nurse said from the doorway.

"Yes." Kacie stood up and leaned against me.

"She's out of CT; you can sit with her again if you'd like."

"Okay, thank you." Kacie hugged her mom, kissed Fred's cheek, and walked by me. Before she got all the way to the doors, she turned and rushed back to me, rose up on her tippy-toes, and kissed my lips. It wasn't a sexual kiss by any means; she just pressed her warm lips against mine and sighed, seemingly happy that I was there.

"Thank you," she said softly against my mouth before she disappeared through the doors. I didn't exactly know what for, but she was so welcome.

Shae came back a few minutes later with water bottles and juice boxes for everyone, and the waiting began.

After an hour or so of torture, the door swung open again, startling all of us as the nurse ushered another group in. My mouth fell open when I saw my parents.

"What are you guys doing here?" I asked incredulously, hugging them both at the same time.

"Shae called and told us what happened. We felt helpless, we didn't know what to do." My mom had tears in her eyes. "So we got in the car and came."

"Thanks," I sighed. "I don't know what to do either."

I felt bad that they had driven all this way, especially since I hadn't exactly been honest with my mom and told her about what was going on, or *not* going on, between Kacie and me. A little hand wrapped around my fingers and I looked down at Lucy standing next to me. "Hey," I said, squatting down to her level. "You okay?"

She nodded and held her arms up. I scooped her up in my arms and faced my mom. "Lucy, this is my mom and dad. Can you say hi?"

"Hi," Lucy said quietly, laying her head on my shoulder.

"Hi, Lucy, it's so nice to meet you." My mom's voice shook, clearly overwhelmed.

Lucy peeked at her and smiled, then she cupped her hands around my ear and whispered, "Brody, I'm hungry."

"You are? Okay, want me to go get you something?"

She nodded and squirmed to get down.

I finished introductions with my parents and Fred and Sophia, waited patiently as Sophia and my mom hugged and cried together, and then excused myself to go find something for Lucy to munch on.

"Brody? Hang on." My mom peeked her head out of the waiting room. I stopped so she could catch up, hooking her arm through mine.

"So there aren't any updates?"

"Not since the last time Kacie came out. Apparently Piper got a CT scan to check on her brain, but that was the last we heard."

"What about the guy on the WaveRunner? Did they catch him?"

"Yeah, they took him away. I was so pumped right after it happened that had he even thought about running, I think I would've swam after that fucking WaveRunner and caught him myself." I looked down at her, smiling apologetically. "Sorry."

She let out a quick laugh. "It's okay. After the day you've had, I would say the f-bomb is in order. So . . . how are *you*?"

I sighed. "Pretty shitty. There is absolutely nothing I can do to make this situation better. I feel so helpless."

"Welcome to parenthood." She smiled up at me, the crow's feet around her eyes looking more prominent today.

"I'm not a parent, Mom. I feel bad for Kacie."

"Seriously? Here, sit a minute." She walked over into a private seating area off to the side and sat down, motioning for me to follow her.

"I know you and Kacie have only been seeing each other a couple of months, and you aren't the girls' biological father, but you love them like a parent. This is it; this is being a parent." She laid her hands on mine, her gentle eyes searching my face. "It's precious agony, Brody."

The culmination of the last couple of weeks of strain between Kacie and me, what happened to Piper, and my mom's words all joined together and made my emotions boil at the surface. She sensed it and opened her arms, pulling me in and squeezing me tight while I lost my mind and silently sobbed into her shoulder for a few minutes. When I came up for air, she rubbed my cheek with the back of her hand. "You feel better?"

"Kinda. Thanks, Mom, but I'll feel much better once Piper is out of the woods and home."

She squeezed my hand. "Say a little prayer, she'll get there."

"Let's go get Lucy something to eat, everyone else too. Looks like it's gonna be a long night," I said as we stood and walked toward the cafeteria. A gift shop off to my right caught my eye. "Hang on, I want to run in and see if they have flip-flops."

"Flip-flops?" She looked at me, confused.

I laughed. "I'll explain later."

37

KACIE

Piper's body looked tiny and fragile lying so still in that big hospital bed. Her head was wrapped in white gauze to keep her wound sterile, an oxygen mask covered her nose and mouth, and her little arm had an IV sticking out of it. Purple bruises were already forming on the right side of her face, sprinkled with a few scrapes. It gutted me to see her like that; I wished more than anything it had been me in that lake instead of her.

Someone knocked softly on the door.

"Can I come in?" my mom whispered as she peeked her head in the room.

"Yeah, come on in," I said, relieved she was here. "She's still out."

My mom gasped and froze when she walked through the door and saw Piper. "Oh my God" was all she muttered, her eyes watering as she pulled her hands up over her mouth.

"She's okay, Mom." I smiled reassuringly.

"It's hard to see her like that." Her voice was shaky.

"I know."

She walked over and pulled up the other chair next to me, not taking her eyes off Piper. "What did the doctors say?"

"They did the CT scan. She has a bad concussion, plus the gash on her head." I sighed, thinking about how yesterday at this time we were Hula-Hooping in the backyard without a care in the world. Crazy how fast life can change. "The doctor said he doesn't think she got hit head-on, that maybe she was under the water when it happened."

Mom's head whipped around to face me. "What do you mean?"

"He thinks she happened to go under the water seconds before she was hit—the bruising on her shoulder is even worse. Had she been all the way above water, it could have been . . . really bad."

Mom looked back at Piper and closed her eyes. Her lips moved but no sound came out; I knew she was praying.

"Anyway, they are definitely keeping her overnight, maybe for a couple of nights. It all depends on the swelling in her brain. They'll do another scan tomorrow."

"Will there be any permanent damage?" she asked hesitantly.

"They don't think so, but we won't know for sure until she's awake. The doctor thinks she'll be just fine in a few weeks."

She reached over and put her hand on mine, squeezing it. "Thank God."

Indeed.

"How is Lucy?" I asked.

"She's okay." Mom smiled at me and tried her best to sound normal. "Brody got her a grilled cheese sandwich and some apple juice. Honestly, she's loving all the attention out there. Everyone is falling all over her."

"Who's everyone?"

"Oh . . . Fred, Shae, Brody, and his parents."

"Brody's *parents?*"

"Yep, they got here a little while ago, and they're wonderful. I'm not surprised by that, though; Brody is pretty wonderful too." She smiled at me.

"Yeah, he is." I sighed. Blaire's voice rang loud in my head, reminding me that he'd never actually be mine.

What was I thinking, kissing him in the waiting room? Clearly my emotions are clouding my judgment.

Another knock on the door.

"Come in," I called out.

The door slowly opened and a petite woman in her mid-fifties stood in the doorway, wringing her hands. I knew exactly who she was by her expressive eyes. Mom and I stood up as I reached down and smoothed out my T-shirt, suddenly panicked. I didn't want to meet her like this. I had on sweats, a bloodstained T-shirt, ugly hospital booties with rubber bottoms, and no makeup. I'm sure my face looked red and puffy, like the Kool-Aid Man, from crying all day.

"You must be Kacie." Emotion overcame her as she fought back tears. "I'm JoAnn Murphy." She unexpectedly pulled me into a hug, which felt amazing. I gladly returned the embrace.

"It's so nice to meet you. Brody has talked about you so much, I feel like I already know you."

"I'm gonna step out so you guys can chat for a bit." Mom smiled as she stood up and quickly made her way to the door.

"Here, sit down." I turned and sat on the couch while she pulled up the chair across from me. "I'm sorry about how I look. Probably not a very good first impression."

Reaching out, she grabbed my hand in her own. "Kacie, you have been through more today than I've been through in twenty-seven years of being a parent. Trust me, I'm not judging your appearance."

I liked her a *lot*. She was warm and friendly and immediately felt like a friend. "I feel bad that we're meeting like this at all. I assumed our first meeting would be over lunch or dinner." She paused for a minute and looked over at Piper. She swallowed, taking it all in. "How's she doing?"

"Okay; they still have her sedated. Trying to let her brain heal a little before they bring her out."

"Being a mom is tough, isn't it?"

"Very."

"There's a saying . . . I don't remember it exactly, but something about how having kids is like allowing your heart to walk around outside of your body. It's so true." She shook her head in amazement.

"Absolutely," I said, staring at Piper, looking for any small movement. "Except right now, I don't feel like my heart is beating at all, it's inactive. It won't beat again until she's awake and smiling at me."

She reached over and squeezed my hand.

"Oh, I almost forgot—" She paused and dug for something in her purse. She pulled out a plastic bag and handed it to me.

"Thanks," I said, confused.

"Brody got them in the gift shop, asked me to give them to you."

I peeked into the bag, breaking out into a huge grin when I saw the light blue fluffy hospital slippers.

"He tried to find you flip-flops, but this is all they had."

Brody's constant fuss to take care of me made me feel something I'd never really felt before . . . special. Most girls swooned over things like diamonds and fancy cars. For me, all it took was shampoo and hospital slippers.

"He's very sweet. You've raised a great man." I smiled at her.

"He *is* a great guy, I agree, but this new side of him, this attentive side, is something I think was brought on entirely by you."

My head snapped up at her. "Me?"

"Kacie, he talks about you and the girls constantly. I know I just met you, but I feel like I already know you. You've made such an impact on him in such a short period of time. It's remarkable. You've changed his life."

I'd cried so much today that I didn't think my body was capable of making more tears, but there they were, threatening to fall again. "He's changed mine too," I said, staring down at the slippers through my blurred vision.

"Knock, knock." Brody pushed the door open slightly. "Can I come in?"

JoAnn smiled at her son and waved him in. "Of course, honey."

He walked across the room and sat down on the couch next to me, resting his arm along the top. I could tell he was giving me space and waiting for me to give him the okay, but that wasn't gonna happen.

He stared straight at Piper, clenching his jaw. "How is she?"

"She's okay, still sedated."

His head turned and his eyes bored into mine. "They still have her sedated?"

"Yeah." I nodded slowly. "It's normal, though, don't worry. They're just giving her brain a break."

"How about you? Do you need a break?"

"Me?" My eyebrows shot up. "I'm not going anywhere."

"Kacie, you've barely left the room since we got here this morning, and it's almost dinnertime. When was the last time you ate, got some fresh air?"

I stared at Piper; the thought of leaving her like this was too painful. "I can't leave her, not yet."

"Kacie? If I may, honey, you said yourself, they have her sedated . . . why don't you go get something to eat and step out for a bit? Might do you some good. I'll stay here with her until you guys get back." JoAnn's lips curled slightly into a tight, reassuring smile.

Brody stood and held his hand out to me.

I was too tired to argue.

"I'll just be gone a few minutes," I said to JoAnn, who stood to hug me again on our way out.

"No problem, honey. Take your time."

Brody and I started toward the waiting room when I froze.

"Wait." I looked down at my bloodstained T-shirt. "Is there another way down to the gift shop? I don't want Lucy to see me like this."

"We'll find one." He pulled me the other direction.

We weaved our way left and right through empty, white hallways until we finally found the lobby.

"Thanks." I smiled up at him and gently tried to pull my hand back.

"Don't," he said firmly, squeezing my hand tighter.

I wanted more than anything to wrap my arms around him and just be, but he wasn't mine, he never would be, and holding his hand just made things harder.

I sighed. "Brody—"

"Not today," he cut me off. "We're going to talk soon, but not today. Today I need to hold your hand as bad as you need to hold mine, so just don't."

A few minutes later, we walked out of the gift shop and headed toward the cafeteria. I was sporting a brand-new light pink "World's Greatest Aunt" T-shirt.

We didn't talk, just shuffled hand in hand through the hallway. At that moment I was so drawn into myself, deep in thought about everything that had happened, Brody was my lifeline to the outside world. He apologized when I bumped into people as he led me to a table in the back of the cafeteria.

"Sit down. I'll be right back," he ordered gently.

I sat and quietly looked down at the wood laminate table, fully aware that people were staring—either at Brody or the depressed girl he walked in with—and I was in no mood to return fake smiles.

He returned a short time later and sat across from me, setting down a turkey sandwich, a salad, a banana, chocolate pudding, a bag of Cheetos, a bottle of water, and chocolate milk.

I frowned and looked up at him. "How hungry do you think I am?"

"I don't know." He shook his head, smiling slightly. "I just wanted to make sure you ate something."

We were quiet while I ate, but it felt like a big, white elephant was sitting at the table with us. He said we weren't going to talk today and I appreciated that. I didn't think I could form a sentence that made sense, nor did I have the will to push him away again. I felt so weak that had he said one sweet thing to me, I would've caved and lost myself in his arms.

I nibbled at the turkey sandwich and ate half the banana while he devoured everything else. We threw away the garbage and walked back up to the waiting room in silence. I was so anxious to wrap my arms around Lucy, I was almost jogging. As soon as I saw her, I dropped to my knees as she threw her arms around my neck, knocking me back.

Trying hard to remain strong and upbeat, I couldn't help the few tears that escaped. I sat cross-legged on the hospital waiting room floor with Lucy curled up in my lap for several minutes, just feeling her breathe and smelling her hair. I wanted to run into that room, scoop Piper up, and hold her just like this.

"Mommy, when does Piper get to come home?"

The knot in my stomach grew. "I'm not sure, baby. We have to wait and see what the doctors say, okay?"

"Can I go see her?" she asked.

I looked up at Brody, whose eyes went wide as he shook his head back and forth slightly.

"Oh, baby. She's resting right now; she can't talk back to you."

Her head snapped up to look at me. "I know, Mom, but I want to talk to *her*. Please?"

I never had a sibling, so I would never understand that bond they had, and being twins only made that bond stronger.

"Okay," I sighed. "Come on."

"Is that really a good idea?" Brody asked nervously.

I shrugged. "I have no idea."

We walked through the automatic doors as I silently prayed for a nurse to stop us and say that Lucy wasn't allowed in. No one did; they just gave us sympathetic smiles as we walked by. We got to Piper's room, and Lucy reached up and held my hand, squeezing it tightly.

"You're sure you want to go in here?"

She nodded and Brody put his hand on her shoulder.

I pushed the door open and watched Lucy's face closely as she took in her surroundings. Her brown eyes were wide as they darted around the room, finally settling on her sister. My mom and JoAnn stopped talking and stared at Lucy.

Lucy looked up at me. "Can she hear me?"

"Yep, but she can't answer you. Wanna sit next to her?"

She nodded again as I lifted her up onto the foot of the bed next to Piper. Her eyes inspected every inch of her sister, from the IV to the dried blood in her hair.

"Does that hurt?" She pointed to the IV.

"Nope." I tucked a piece of her blond hair behind her tiny ear.

This time she pointed to the oxygen mask on Piper's face. "Does that hurt?"

"Not at all."

"I bet *those* hurt." She stretched, trying to see the staples in Piper's head.

"Those probably would have hurt, but she was asleep when they put them in, so she didn't feel it. Her head will probably be sore when she wakes up, though."

Lucy paused. "Is she gonna wake up?"

Her question sent me into a tailspin. My chest grew tight and I couldn't breathe. The room felt like it was spinning so fast I couldn't focus my eyes on any one thing.

"Whoa, whoa. You okay?" Brody reached out and grasped my shoulders.

"Yeah, I just feel a little woozy," I panted.

"Come sit here, by the window," my mom said, jumping up as JoAnn reached behind them and cranked the window open slightly.

I leaned my arm on the windowsill and rested my head on it, taking slow, deep breaths of the fresh air that blew inside. The conversation behind me turned into mumbles as I blocked it out, concentrating on nothing but breathing.

"You okay?" JoAnn gently rubbed my shoulders.

I looked up at her and cracked a small smile. "I think so. This day has just been . . . overwhelming."

"I'm sure it has." She sat down next to me. "I think we're gonna get going—if you don't need anything else?"

"No, I'm good." I pulled her in for a hug. "Thank you for coming. It means so much to me."

She squeezed back, tight. "Oh, honey. No problem; I wish there were more we could do."

"I think we're gonna go too." Mom walked up. "I need to get Lucy home to bed, it's been a long day for her."

I hugged my mom and scooped Lucy up in my arms, covering her face with kisses. "I'll see you tomorrow, okay?"

"Okay, Mommy. If Piper wakes up, tell her I'm not mad at her for getting her blood on my floaties."

I chuckled. "Okay, baby. I'll tell her."

Mom, Lucy, and JoAnn made their way to the door, Brody walking behind them. "Thanks for all your help today," I said as I softly rubbed his arm.

He looked surprised. "I'm not going anywhere, I'm just walking them out."

"Oh." My eyebrows shot up. "You're staying for a while?"

"Or for the night." He laughed. "I'm not leaving you here alone."

I didn't argue. I was glad he was staying with me.

The next morning my back was screaming at me and my neck was sore. Sleeping on a hospital couch was never comfortable. Ever. I cracked my eyes open as soon as the sun filled the room and peeked at Piper, who looked the same. I sat up and stretched, a white blanket slipping off my lap. I didn't even have to think hard about who had covered me.

I looked over at Brody, sleeping on a chair with his feet propped up on the end of Piper's bed. His hands were locked and resting on his stomach, while his mouth hung open. I didn't even remember falling asleep last night; the last thing I remembered was him asking me if I needed anything to drink.

Slipping quietly into the bathroom, I washed my pale face and pulled a new toothbrush out of the package that was sitting on the counter. I knew who put that there also.

"How's our girl this morning?"

I hurried out of the room and saw Dr. Wagner standing next to Piper's bed. Brody was sitting up, rubbing his eyes with his palms.

"Good morning." I walked up next to them.

"We're gonna take our all-star patient for another CT scan, and we'll make our further decisions based on that, okay?"

I nodded, still in a daze as a nurse came in and swiftly unhooked Piper from her machines before wheeling her out the door.

"That was fast." Brody yawned.

"Yeah, we need good news on this scan." I hugged myself, suddenly cold from nerves.

He tilted his head and brushed my cheek with the back of his hand. "Think positive. I have a good feeling about this one."

I closed my eyes and leaned into his hand slightly.

"You wanna take a shower?" I snapped my head up, trying to keep from making physical contact with him.

He sighed. "Yeah, I'll go quick."

I paced the room nervously while Brody showered, praying over and over for Piper's body to have begun healing itself already.

The door opened a little while later, Piper's bed rolling through it.

The nurse smiled as she pushed her into the room and hooked her back up to her machines.

"It'll be just a few minutes," she offered on her way out the door.

I already knew that, but didn't bother responding.

Brody came out of the bathroom, freshly showered but wearing the same clothes.

He looked down at himself and shrugged. "Sorry, it's all I got."

I laughed. "Have you seen me? Trust me, I'm not judging you."

"You look brave," he said softly. "You look like a woman whose heart has been ripped open and is bleeding out all over the place, but you're so damn concerned about everyone else, you haven't even bothered to take care of your own wounds."

My eyes stung. "My wounds can wait," I said in a shaky voice.

Dr. Wagner came back in the room. He was a huge man, easily as tall as Brody and quite built. His black hair had gray speckles around the temples, and his Polo eyeglasses balanced on the tip of his pointy nose.

"Guess who's coming off her sleepy meds?"

"Really?" I clapped my hands together as my heart pounded wildly.

"Really, really. Her CT looked good, swelling went down. We'll probably keep her one more night just to watch her, but we're going to wean her off her meds in the next hour. Then it's up to her to pull herself out. Her brain function looks great, no permanent damage."

Tears rolled down my face as I lunged forward and hugged Dr. Wagner.

"Thank you, thank you *so* much."

He laughed. "Thank her, she's a tough little girl."

I pulled back and looked at Brody, who was wiping his own eyes.

"Okay, Mom and Dad, just hang tight and we'll get this process started in a few minutes," Dr. Wagner said.

"Oh, we're not—"

Brody gently grabbed my arm. "Thank you, Doctor," he interrupted, reaching out to shake the doctor's hand.

Dr. Wagner narrowed his eyes and studied Brody's face. "You look really familiar. Have you done any acting?"

Brody smirked and shook his head, giving a quick wave as Dr. Wagner turned and left the room.

He looked at me and wiggled his brows up and down. "Except for when I pretend to be the baby daddy."

I grinned and shook my head, elated that this horrible ordeal was going to turn out okay.

38

BRODY

A jolt of pain shot through my neck as I lifted my head to look at my phone and check the time.

Who the hell is banging on my door at seven fifteen in the morning?

I pushed myself off the couch and rubbed my eyes as I slowly walked toward the door.

"Open up, Brody," Andy bellowed from the other side.

I opened the door and almost fell back as he marched past me.

"Since when do you put your dead bolt on? I don't have a key for that," he accused.

"Sorry." I followed him into the living room and lay down on the couch. "My brain is a little fuzzy."

He sat back on the leather chair across from me. His face was tight and I could tell he was anxious. "Where have you been? I called you all day Sunday and yesterday. You never returned my calls."

I'd spent the last two days at the hospital with Kacie and barely even looked at my phone.

"I was up north. I got home late last night, really late." I yawned.

"Oh. I thought you were just dodging my calls." His tone relaxed slightly. "Up north? You two seeing each other again?"

"No, I don't know. It was a crazy weekend."

He frowned and blinked at me, waiting for me to elaborate.

"I went to the charity event with Shae on Saturday, then went up north Sunday to try and talk to Kacie. We barely started talking and there was an accident with one of her daughters."

His eyes grew wide. "What happened?"

"Some asshole in the lake was driving his WaveRunner around like a dick and came in too close, ran her over." My heart raced as I thought about that moment all over again . . . Piper on the ground with blood under her head, the pure fear splayed across Kacie's face as she stared at her daughter. Lucy curled up in my arms, covering her face from the events unfolding around her. I would give anything to be in a room alone with that guy for ten minutes.

"Holy shit."

"Holy shit is right; it was intense. Beyond intense." I rubbed my eyes with my palms, trying to force the images out of my head.

"Is she okay?"

"She has a concussion and she looks pretty beat up, but she will be okay. She woke up yesterday and the first thing she asked for was ice cream." I chuckled. "She's going home this morning."

"You didn't stay up there to take her home?"

My stomach tightened. "I wanted to, but I didn't want to push Kacie. I'd already been there for two days, and she thanked me over and over for it, but I'm trying to give her space, especially now with this stuff with Piper. As bad as I want to force her to talk to me, Piper needs her more."

Andy sighed and locked his hands on top of his head, looking up at the ceiling. "Listen, about all this Kacie stuff . . . I just want you to know I don't blame you for going off on Blaire, or for firing me."

"I'm glad you understand about Blaire; she deserved it." I looked him straight in the eye. "And I'm sorry about the firing thing, but I can't have her interfering with my personal life because *she* thinks I need to concentrate on hockey. I won't let that happen."

"I know. I get it." He sighed. "I'm not worried about the money part, Brody, I just hope that we're okay."

"You and Blaire?"

He laughed. "I couldn't give two shits about how Blaire and I are at the moment. She has some major work to do on herself or I'm taking the kids and I'm gone. I told her that."

I raised my eyebrows in surprise. "You did?"

A sly smile spread across his face as he narrowed his eyes. "Yep, you would've loved the look on her face."

"Hmm, a shocked Blaire? I'd pay a lot of money to see that."

"That face wasn't nearly as good as the one she made when I told her we had to put the Vail house on the market to make up the difference in losing your contract." His head fell back on the chair as another laugh escaped him.

A twinge of guilt rolled around in my stomach. "About that . . . I know a couple young guys just graduating college who are looking for agents. I'll send them your way to make up for it."

"I'm not worried about it, really. I have money stashed that she doesn't know about. We're fine, financially." His eyes darted nervously around the room before settling on mine. "I just hope that *we* are okay."

"Andy, my boy, we've been best friends for almost twenty years. It's going to take something bigger and badder than Blaire to scare me off."

Nodding and smiling contently, he looked at his watch. "Shit, I gotta get to work."

I stood and followed him to the door.

"Please tell Kacie I'm so sorry about what happened. Keep me posted, let me know if you guys need anything."

"I will, buddy. Thanks."

He shook my hand and disappeared down the hall.

I worked out with Viper . . . checked my phone.

I took a shower . . . checked my phone.

I made myself dinner . . . checked my phone.

Kacie brought Piper home from the hospital at some point today, and I was really hoping she'd call or text and let me know how it went. Was she all settled in? What were they doing right now? Did they need anything? Not knowing what was going on and not being there to help out was killing me.

I thought about that morning out on the back deck with Sophia, when she'd told me about Kacie's past and asked me to be patient with her. Patience wasn't my problem; I was in no rush to move on. There were no other women, nor would there ever be now that I knew Kacie was out there. Patience I could do, but how the hell could I win her over if she kept pushing me away?

Everything Sophia said that morning was rattling around in my head.

"Kacie was damaged."

"She blamed herself for her and her dad's failed relationship."

"She fought like hell to keep her family together with Zach, but ultimately it didn't matter."

"To protect herself now, she panics and she runs."

This was it, Kacie's defense mechanism rearing its ugly head. "Get them before they get me," like Sophia said. The feelings were becoming too real for her, and instead of dealing with them head-on, it was easier for her to push me away and pretend they didn't exist. If she admitted that she loved me too, it meant leaving herself vulnerable to the possibility of more pain, and that was something Kacie was clearly willing to go to great lengths to avoid.

What Kacie didn't know was that she may have met the one person on the planet more stubborn than she was. When I set my sights on something, I got it one way or another. I'd never given up easily, and I sure as hell wasn't starting now.

39

KACIE

"I can't believe they're six," I pouted as I plopped myself down at the kitchen table.

Mom handed me a cup of coffee. "I know, where did the time go?"

"Seriously. It feels like I just had them."

"I feel that same way about you." She smiled sadly as she sat across from me. "Now look at you. You went and grew up and had kids of your own when I wasn't looking."

"You know, none of this would have been possible without you."

"Of course it would have, Kacie. You're a strong girl, way stronger than you give yourself credit for."

"I don't know about all that, Mom."

"Well, I do, and Mother knows best, so hush."

I grinned at her as I sipped my coffee.

"It's been one hell of a week, huh?"

"That, my dear, is an understatement." Mom stared outside and her mind went somewhere else. It had been almost a week since that bastard plowed over my baby in the lake, and while Piper was mending, she wasn't completely back to normal yet. Her bruises had faded to a dark yellow, and she wasn't having headaches anymore, but her nightmares were off the charts. Every night since we'd been home from the hospital, she'd woken up with an ear-piercing, bloodcurdling scream that almost made me jump right out of my skin. The only thing that made her feel better was sleeping with me, and that made Lucy feel bad, so she'd been sleeping with me too. Needless to say, I was beyond exhausted.

Mom had suggested pushing their party back a couple of weeks, but that wasn't an option. School was starting in a couple of weeks for all three of us, and it had been such a bad week, I wanted them to have something good to look forward to this weekend. However, I'd thrown it together so quickly, hopefully I hadn't forgotten anything.

"Okay, so today . . . the food has been ordered and should be here by noon. Alexa is bringing the flowers and balloons later, you took care of the cake . . . was there anything else?" I asked.

"Nope, I think you got it all. What time is everyone coming?"

"Two o'clock."

"Good. You should go nap, Kacie." She pushed back from the table and took our mugs to the kitchen sink. "You haven't been sleeping well, and today might be a long day."

"You don't have to tell me twice." I yawned just thinking about how tired I was.

I left the girls snuggled up on the couch watching *Snow White* under Mom's watchful eye as I tiptoed down the hall to my room for a quick snooze.

My body was completely relaxed in that last stage right before you actually fall asleep, where you're still aware of your surroundings but your arms and legs feel heavy and out of control. My mind was starting to drift when I heard my bedroom door open and then close again.

I didn't even open my eyes. "Girls, go back out with Gigi, Mommy needs a nap."

"They're watching *Snow White*, but you look more like Sleeping Beauty."

My eyes snapped open, and I sat up straight at the sound of Brody's voice. He was leaning against my bedroom door with his hands shoved in his jeans pockets, his signature hat on backward, and the killer smile accented by those irresistible dimples cemented on his face.

"What are you doing here?" I scrambled to stand.

"Relax, sit down." He pulled the desk chair next to my bed. "I came to drop off the girls' birthday presents."

"Oh, thanks. I'm sure they're excited about that."

My heart soared at the sight of him and I wondered if that would ever go away. How much time needed to pass before I could be in a room with him and stop worrying that my chest was going to explode?

Leaning forward in the chair, he rested his elbows on his knees as a crooked smile rolled across his face.

"I love you, Kacie."

My heart sputtered to a complete stop as his soulful eyes searched my face.

"I've loved you since that night out on the pier when we looked up at the stars, then I fell in love with you again the next day when you peeked at the sunset from the top of the Ferris wheel, then I fell in love with you again when I saw you in that blue dress, then I fell in love with you again on my kitchen counter, then I fell in love with you again at the cake tasting, then I fell in love with you again at Lauren's wedding, then I fell in love with you again in that hospital room when you stared at your daughter lying unconscious in that bed . . ."

I swallowed, unable to speak.

"I fall in love with you every single time I watch you interact with Lucy and Piper. The love you feel for them is so vast and overwhelming, it absolutely amazes me. I sometimes wonder if there's room in your heart for me too, but then we're alone . . . and it's there. Whatever it is, it hangs in the air between us, so fucking thick I can hardly breathe."

Tears ran down my cheeks. It was almost physically painful to listen to him. "Brody, please . . . ," I pleaded, not wanting to hear any more.

"You're not a summer fling."

My breath caught in my throat as my mouth fell open. How did he know about that?

"I know what Blaire said to you in that bathroom, and she couldn't have been more wrong. You're not a summer fling, a winter fling, or any other fling," he continued. "You're my *choice*, Kacie. I know where the door is and I know how to walk through it if I want, but I *don't* want to. I want to be here with you, with the girls. Every. Single. Day."

I nervously thumbed the cuff of my sweatshirt under the scrutiny of his intense gaze.

"I also know that Kendall was in that bathroom, and I can't even imagine how excruciating that must have been for you. I told them both to go to hell and I fired Andy."

"You did?" I whispered in a shaky voice.

"Kacie, you can't listen to anything Blaire says. She only cares about how I perform on the ice—that's why she wants you out of the way. She thinks you're a distraction."

My brain was moving so fast I couldn't keep up. I lowered my head to my hands, struggling to process the mountain he was laying at my feet.

"I agree with her about that; you are a distraction," he said quietly.

I snapped my head up and locked eyes with him.

"The best damn distraction I've ever had in my life. You and the Twinkies." He scooted over to my bed and cupped either side of my face with his warm hands. "Before you guys, I didn't know life outside of the rink existed. You've made me realize I want more. I want everything, and I want it with you."

"I'm afraid, Brody."

"I know you are. It's a big leap, but I promise it's worth it."

Still holding my face, he leaned forward and softly pressed his lips against mine. There was no hidden intent with that kiss; it was just that, a kiss. Neither of us was in a hurry to break it.

I wanted this; I wanted him, and I needed to tell him. He just laid it all out for me. He needed to know how I felt too.

I pulled back but didn't let go of his hands. "Brody, I'm scarred. Zach did so much damage to my heart, sometimes I feel like he ruined it for anyone else. He mutilated it, and even though I put it back together, it'll always be a little tainted."

"I know, but that's the thing about scars, Kacie, over time they fade and get smaller. It's time for yours to disappear."

The thought of Brody being mine forever forced a small smile to tug at my lips.

"Talk to me . . . what are you thinking?" He rubbed the back of my hand with his thumbs.

I took a deep breath. "I'm thinking that I love you, Brody Murphy. I love you a lot."

A grin slid across his face as he pressed his forehead against mine.

"I've loved you since you first called my girls Twinkies, then I fell in love with you again when you made me jump in puddles with you, then I fell in love with you again when you went fishing with Fred, then I fell in love with you again when you bought twenty kinds of shampoo, then I fell in love with you again in your bed, then I fell in love with you again when you let the girls paint your nails, then I fell in love with you again with a pair of hospital slippers in my hands." I sniffed and looked into his eyes.

He opened his mouth to respond, but I put my finger on his lips, stopping him.

"My heart knew I loved you before my brain did."

That was all he needed to hear. He leaped forward and crashed into me with so much force he knocked me backward on my bed. The weight of his body was heavy on top of me, but there was nowhere else on this planet I'd rather be.

He pulled back just enough to look me in the eye. "I love you, Kacie. I love you so damn hard."

"I love you too, Brody. Completely."

We lay on my bed, lost in each other and completely oblivious to the world happening outside of my room. We kissed and hugged each other so tight, afraid of what would happen when we let go.

"We should probably go out there and see what's going on with everyone," I finally sighed.

"Screw that, we have a couple weeks worth of kissing to make up for."

The laugh that escaped me almost drowned out the sound of the soft knock on my bedroom door.

Brody and I sat up. "Come in," I called out, rubbing my tingling lips.

Lucy and Piper came barreling through the door with the biggest smiles I'd ever seen on their faces.

"Mom, come see our cake!" Lucy squealed.

"Oh, it's here? I didn't know Gigi went to get it," I said as Piper grabbed my arm and pulled me off my bed. Lucy took a hold of Brody's hand and they led us out to the kitchen.

My eyes almost fell out of my head when I saw the cake sitting perfectly in the middle of the island. It was the princess cake that Brody and I saw in the book at the Great Cakery.

"What the . . . how did Mom . . ." I was thoroughly confused.

"I asked your mom to let me handle the cake," Brody said from behind me.

I spun around to face him. "*You* did this?"

He grinned and nodded, wiggling his eyebrows at me. "Cool, huh? I just hope my Twinkies like Oreo cake, because I couldn't resist."

I smiled as Lucy and Piper ran over and wrapped their arms around him.

"This is so awesome, Brody. Thank you." I looked at him with sheer adoration as I walked over to the pantry to make sure we had candles for later, something I'd completely forgotten to check before.

I pulled the pantry door open and gasped when I caught my mom and Fred groping each other like a couple of teenagers against the cereal shelf. The girls started to run toward the pantry to see what I was staring at when I slammed the door.

"What was it?" Piper asked, with Lucy and Brody standing behind her, just as confused.

"Uh . . . a really big spider," I stuttered as my mom walked out of the pantry, smiling like nothing ever happened.

"Gigi, did you kill the spider?" Lucy asked.

"Yes, I got him." She smiled.

"I bet you did." I stared at her incredulously before I turned back to Brody. "Can you take them in the family room for a minute while I clean up after that spider?"

Brody frowned, clearly still confused as he led the girls over to the couch and out of earshot.

I whipped around to Mom, who was grinning at me like a proud teenager. "What's going on?"

"What do you mean, *what's going on*? It was pretty obvious, no?" She beamed and walked over to the pantry door and opened it, letting Fred out.

"How long?" I looked back and forth between them.

"Well, you've been a little preoccupied lately"—she waved her hand toward the couch where Brody was sitting—"and I've been with the girls a lot. Fred was helping me out and . . . you know, it just happened." Her gaze met his and they smiled sweetly at each other.

"Oh my God . . . I need a vacation," I mumbled into my hands in a delirious giggle.

"It's kinda fun, though, right?" she asked.

I pulled my hands away from my face and stared blankly at her.

"Think about it—we can double date." She winked at me as Fred put his arm around her shoulders and kissed her cheek.

"I can't. This is too much." I chuckled as I walked across the kitchen. "I need to hop in the shower. I'll be right back, okay?"

I headed toward our apartment as I looked over at Brody, who was sitting on the couch with the girls watching *Snow White*. He had one arm tucked behind each of their heads as they all focused intently on the TV. I slowed my pace to stare at them for a minute. The sight of my three loves snuggled up on the couch together made my heart warm.

Since my breakup with Zach, I had tried hard to make our life about structure and simplicity. Brody was the opposite of that. He was carefree and unpredictable; no day with him was the same. Hell, no hour with him was ever the same. He crashed into my life and shook it up like a snow globe.

I had no idea my life needed him *so* bad.

Several hours later, Lucy and Piper's friends had left and the family room carpet was sprinkled with enough confetti and glitter to fill a Dumpster. The girls were happily showing Brody and Derek their new toys while Alexa and I cleaned up the kitchen. I had no idea where my mom and Fred were, nor did I think I wanted to know.

"Have you heard from Lauren?" I asked.

"Yeah, they're all settled in their apartment and loving Florence. She said she's gonna call you tonight to wish the girls happy birthday."

I thought about my friend and her new husband living in some adorable, cozy apartment in Italy. "I'm so happy for them." I sighed blissfully.

"Agreed." She peeked at me while she loaded the dishwasher. "I'm happy for you too."

"Me? Why?"

"Well, actually, I'm happy for me."

I stared at her, completely confused.

"You know me—I'm not a super-romantic person," she said.

I laughed. "I know. I always thought that was strange, considering you *own* a flower shop."

"Yeah, yeah . . . whatever. I'm not a romantic person, but boy, do I love to be right."

"What are you talking about?" I finally cut myself a small piece of the castle cake.

"Here, I scooped this out of the garbage a long time ago." She walked over and handed me a small piece of paper that was crinkled and worn. "Once again, I believe that belongs to you."

My mouth fell open when I looked down at the white strip of paper in my hand.

IF YOU NEVER GIVE UP ON LOVE, IT WILL NEVER
GIVE UP ON YOU.

Oh my God, the fortune cookie from the Chinese food that night at her shop.

"I can't believe you saved this." I looked up at her in amazement.

She grinned at me. "I knew then what you've finally been brave enough to admit now. I could see it in your eyes, hear it in the way you talked about him." She hip bumped me as she walked by. "Like I said, I love to be right."

I curled my hand around that fortune, vowing to cherish it forever.

After Alexa rubbed it in my face a dozen more times about how right she was, she tore Derek away from the girls' toys and left.

Brody walked up to me and wrapped his arms around my waist. "I'd say the party was a success; the Twinkies seem pretty happy."

"Absolutely. Look at their little faces." I rested my head against his chest and watched the girls grinning and chattering about their new haul.

"After they go to bed, remind me to hide that big purple case," he sighed.

"Why?"

"It's full of nail polish and makeup—they already asked if they could try it on me later."

Tossing my head back, I laughed heartily. "You started that."

"Started what?" Mom asked, walking into the kitchen with Fred trailing right behind her.

"Well, look what we have here," Brody teased. "The two lovebirds."

Mom blushed as Fred wrapped his arm around her.

"I'm happy for you two, I really am. I didn't mean to sound weird before, I was just taken aback," I said to my mom.

"I know that, honey. It's okay." She walked over, pulling me in for a hug. "I should've told you. That wasn't exactly a good way to find out."

"It was a little shocking." I squeezed her back.

"So, Fred . . . what are you doing in the morning?" Brody asked.

Fred looked at him blankly. "Nothing, why?"

Brody clapped him on the shoulders. "I was just thinking that maybe we should go fishing. There are some things I'd like to talk to you about now that you're dating Sophia."

Fred laughed and shook Brody's hand. "I'll fish with you anytime, Brody."

Standing in the kitchen with my arm around my mom, I watched Brody and Fred devour a chunk of cake while listening to the girls giggling behind me. Overcome with a sense of happiness, I reached in my back pocket and fingered the fortune from Alexa.

Thank God for rainstorms . . . and puddles.

EPILOGUE

KACIE

"Stop obsessing, you look terrific." Brody walked up behind me and wrapped his arms around my waist as I stopped to check my reflection in the mirror for the hundredth time that morning.

"I'm just so nervous, I feel like I'm gonna puke."

"Then kiss me now." He laughed as he spun me around by my hips and planted his lips firmly on mine, causing my stress to evaporate faster with each gentle swipe of his tongue.

"Oh my God," I said against his lips. "I'm gonna be late."

"It'd be worth it," he groaned as he trailed kisses down my neck.

"I'm sure it would." I let my head fall back, enjoying the feel of his lips exploring my skin. "But it's my first day. I can't be late."

I gently pushed him off of me and kissed the tip of his nose. "Save that for later, okay?"

"Deal." He grinned.

I checked my appearance one more time.

New blue scrubs, check.

New shoes, check.

Lucky silver necklace, check.

Today was the first day of my externship and my nerves were a mess. I wanted to make a good first impression, but there was no chance of that happening if I couldn't get my hands to stop shaking long enough to put eyeliner on, let alone insert an IV.

"I think I'm ready," I said a few minutes later as I walked into the kitchen. Brody and the girls were sitting at the island eating waffles; the cozy smell of syrup loomed in the air. A morsel of jealousy sat in my stomach as I packed up my lunch and thought about them hanging out here all day while I was at the hospital. I was also incredibly thankful that Brody was willing to babysit my kids all day. Figures the *one* day my mom had a doctor's appointment and couldn't help me would be the first day of my program.

"Thanks for staying with them today." I wrapped my arms around his neck and planted a kiss on his cheek.

"My pleasure." He grinned at the girls. "We're gonna have fun today, right?"

"Yay!" they cheered.

"I'm thinking we mow the lawn, give Diesel a bath, clean out the gutters, then have a bunch of broccoli for lunch. Sound good?" He wiggled his eyebrows at them.

Lucy and Piper looked at each other with disgusted faces. "Noooo!"

"I think you should make them wash the dishes too. They're six years old now, they can handle it," I teased.

They just shook their heads back and forth, their eyes wide.

"I'm gonna head out. Girls, you go easy on him today, okay?"

"Yes, Mom," Lucy said.

"Piper, you too."

"Mm-hmm," she mumbled, shoving a giant bite of waffle in her mouth. It had only been a few weeks since her accident, and I was so thankful she finally had her appetite back.

I kissed each of their cheeks and grabbed my purse. "If there are any problems, I have my phone with me." I leaned down and kissed Brody's cheek. Both of the girls giggled. They still weren't completely used to our moments of affection toward each other, but we weren't hiding anymore. I loved him, he loved me, and we were going with it.

"We're good." He grinned and wrapped his arm around my waist, pulling me in tight. "Good luck today. I know you're gonna do great."

"Thanks," I sighed, my nerves starting to get the best of me. "I just want this day to be over. I'm anxious to come home and snuggle up with the three of you tonight."

"Sounds like a date," he said.

I smiled at him and turned to head out when he pulled my hand back toward him. I spun around and locked eyes with him: his jet-black pupils swam in a sea of brilliant green and focused right on me. I pulled my brows together and looked at him curiously.

He looked at the girls, then back at me. "Pay the toll." He cupped my rear and drew me in close to him, planting a firm kiss on my lips, while the girls squealed and covered their eyes.

◆ ◆ ◆

The automatic doors of the hospital slid open and the familiar smell hit me. It's unmistakable, that hospital smell, a weird combination of latex and iodine and death. If colors had smells, I think white would smell like the hospital. Pink would be flowers, yellow would be fresh air, blue would be the sea.

White . . . definitely the hospital.

I walked up to the registration desk, where a girl sat chomping on her gum like a cow, looking bored out of her mind.

"Hi, my name is Kacie Jensen. I'm supposed to start my externship today, but this is my first time here and I'm not exactly sure where to go."

She glared up at me from her cell phone, and without saying a word, pointed toward another large set of automatic sliding doors with EMERGENCY ROOM painted above them in bright red. "Thanks," I said as I looked back at her.

She rolled her eyes and turned her attention back to her phone.

Brat.

I slowly crept through the doors like a timid sixth grader who was scared of walking into the wrong classroom. The hallways formed a big square that surrounded the nurses' station, which was decorated with fake plants and cardboard cutouts of apples and rulers for back-to-school time.

"Help me, help me, help me!"

I spun around to a woman walking in my direction, balancing a stack of file folders two feet high that started slipping out of her hands. Dropping my lunch bag and purse where I stood, I lunged forward and caught the manila tower before it spilled all over the floor.

She sighed. "Oh, thanks. That would've really sucked."

"No problem." I smiled at her.

I guessed she was in her early forties, though her face was youthful and could've passed for a twenty-year-old's. She was a little chubby with a bright, contagious smile.

"I'm Darla." She grinned as she set the files on the counter. "You are?"

"Oh, I'm Kacie Jensen."

"You're the new girl, huh?"

"That'd be me. Am I in the right place?"

"Yep, this is it. Fancy, ain't it?" She rolled her eyes.

"Where should I set my stuff?" I looked around.

"Come back here; we call this the Square. Everyone has a shelf to put their crap on."

I followed her into the nurses' station and set my bags down in an empty space.

"Kacie Jensen?" a woman bellowed as she came around the corner.

"Yes." I spun around nervously.

"I'm Maureen, you're with me. Let's go." She waved as she strolled past the Square.

"You're with Maureen?" Darla whispered as I walked past her.

I nodded.

"Good luck," she mouthed.

I quickly stepped in behind Maureen. "Hi, Maureen. It's nice to meet you. I'm very excited to work with you," I said to the back of her tight gray bun as she continued walking.

"No chitchat, we're very busy today. Just follow my lead." She didn't even turn her head when she spoke to me. "Don't expect me to coddle you, this is the real world. If I tell you that you did a good job, it's because you did. If you need someone always telling you how great you are, call your mother."

Whoa, she *was* tough.

My first day was filled with cleaning up puke, changing out bedpans, and perfecting the art of blood pressure taking. What it lacked in excitement, it more than made up for in how fast the day flew by. Before I'd even had a chance to look at the clock once, Maureen was telling me to go sit down for a thirty-minute lunch break. I didn't know exactly where I was supposed to go, so I grabbed my lunch bag and sat at the desk next to Darla while she continued transferring all the files she'd almost dropped into the computer.

"You married?" she asked, staring straight ahead at her computer screen.

"Nope."

"Boyfriend?"

"Yep."

"He got any cute single friends?"

I giggled when I thought of Viper, the only single friend of Brody's who came to mind. And he wasn't exactly single . . . it really just depended on the day and Kat's mood, from what I understood.

"Nah, not any good ones."

"Bummer. By the time I leave here at night, I'm too damn tired to go out, and all these damn doctors are married. Maybe I'll become a lesbian."

I chuckled and chewed on my carrot sticks while I people-watched. A young girl came in needing stitches from a dog bite, a construction worker had shot a nail through his hand with a nail gun, and a little old man was severely constipated. The day was not quite as eventful as I'd hoped it would be.

"Break time's over, Jensen," Maureen called out as she went from room to room. "A woman with chest pains is being brought in by ambulance any minute; can you prep room four and get her vitals for me?"

Hopping up eagerly, I tossed my carrots in the trash. "I'm on it."

I went into room 4, turned on the monitors, and got the blood pressure cuff ready. There wasn't much else to do.

A minute later, the curtain pulled back, startling me as a young man with curly black hair pushed a stretcher into the room. Another EMT, who wore a baseball cap over his blond hair, had his back to me as he pulled the other end of the stretcher and called out stats.

"Female patient in her early sixties complaining of chest pains. BP is 220 over 130, temp is 99.2, pulse is 110."

I awkwardly tried to stay out of the way as they swiftly transferred the patient from the stretcher to the bed. My pulse was probably as high as hers at the moment because I was so damn nervous.

The curly-haired paramedic smiled at me and left the room as quickly as he'd come in.

"Okay, she's all yours," said the blond EMT as he turned around.

I locked eyes with him and stopped breathing, my body grinding to a halt.

Oh. My. God.

Zach.

CONTINUE BRODY AND KACIE'S JOURNEY IN . . .

Room for More
(Cranberry Inn #2)

Room for Just a Little Bit More
(Cranberry Inn #3)

ACKNOWLEDGMENTS

Writing this book was a long, often stressful process for me, and it would not have been possible without help from several people . . .

To my betas, Michelle, Megan W., Megan S., Melissa, Julie, Janna, and Happy: This book wouldn't be what it is without you guys. Your input and suggestions were beyond helpful, and I'll be forever grateful for the time you took to read and give me feedback. Thank you, thank you, thank you.

For all the blogs that participated in my cover reveal and blog tour: You are the heartbeat of the book world. Thank you for all the unanswered hours you put in.

To Pam Carrion from The Book Avenue Review: You are one of the sweetest people I have ever met. Your generosity and selflessness know no bounds. The hours you put in organizing cover reveals and blog tours and doing countless other things to help authors are immeasurable. The world would be a better place if there were more people like you walking around.

A special thank-you to Michelle Kisner Pace, who answered a million questions and helped me make sure certain parts of the book were accurate.

My wonderful CP, Janna Mashburn. You're a little secret weapon when it comes to the brainstorming process. You have this amazing ability to step back and see what direction the story should go in. I so appreciate all the time you put in reading and critiquing everything.

Melissa Brown. I don't even want to write this paragraph because there is no way I'm going to properly give you the thanks you deserve. When you invited me to this little Indie Author event in Chicago a little over a year ago, I had no idea my whole life would change in that weekend, all thanks to you. You were the first person I told about writing this book, and since then you've done it all. You've brainstormed with me. You've read every word of this book, sometimes two or three times. You named it. You put my first chapter at the end of *your* book. Most importantly, you believed in me when I didn't believe in myself. I will thank you and tell you I love you every day for the rest of my life, and it still won't be enough. I might have to buy you a pony. We've already been friends for twenty-five years; I can't wait to see what the next twenty-five have in store.

To Happy Driggs: You are my very best friend on this entire planet. We can have whole conversations with very few words, though I suppose that's what happens when you share a brain. I want to list all of the insanely wonderful things you've done for me, but we both know that's not how we work. The one thing I will always be grateful for is the way you tell me to just shut up and get it done. You get me, completely. You're my favorite asshole. #Namaste.

To my mom: You've been my rock every day of my thirty-five years on this planet. You're more than just my mom, you're my mentor and my best friend. Thank you for believing in me and always sounding interested in my book, even when I'd already talked about it 3,206 times that day. Everything I've always done has been possible because I knew no matter what, you would be in my corner, cheering me on.

To my incredible husband, Chris. You have been my copilot in this journey we call life for the past seventeen years, and I couldn't be happier to have you by my side. When I first told you I needed to do this, you jumped right in and eagerly asked what you could do to help. I don't think you thought it would be so much cooking and cleaning, but you didn't complain, most of the time. Thank you for always having my back, regardless of how insane my ideas can be. I love you a little more every single day.

Lastly, thank you to my four kids, who listened to me say, "I'll be there in a minute," or "Just a second," for months while I was typing away. You guys are the reason I breathe. I love you more than anything in this world.

ABOUT THE AUTHOR

Photo © 2014 Stacey Houston Photography

Bestselling author Beth Ehemann lives in the northern suburbs of Chicago with her husband and four children. A lover of martinis and all things Chicago Cubs, she can be found reading or honing her photography skills when she's not sitting in front of her computer writing—or on Pinterest. *Room for You* is the first installment of her popular Cranberry Inn series, which includes the novel *Room for More* and the novella *Room for Just a Little Bit More*. Contact her at: authorbethehemann@yahoo.com

Or follow her on:
Facebook: www.facebook.com/bethehemann
Twitter: @bethehemann
Instagram: @bethehemann
www.bethehemann.com